A MIDLIFE MARRIAGE

THE MIDLIFE SERIES

CARY J HANSSON

❋ Formatted with Vellum

ABOUT THE AUTHOR

Cary is a fifty something mum of three, an ex-dancer, actress, waitress, cleaner, TV presenter, double-glazing sales rep, fax machine operator ... You name it and she's cleaned it, served it, sent it or sold it.

She writes stories about ordinary people, living lives of extraordinary courage and indestructible humour. She promises only one thing: no knights in shining armour. Her characters save themselves, as in the end we all must do.

She is also a certified practitioner of Writing for Wellness offering digital classes in:
Writing for Self-Care
Writing for Clarity
Writing for Self-Discovery
Writing for Creativity

To learn more visit: https://www.caryjhansson.com/

A NOTE FROM THE AUTHOR

This wasn't a book I expected to write. The Midlife Series was originally intended to be a trilogy. However, as some readers will know, a couple of years ago my own mid-life took a dramatic and unexpected swerve in the form of a divorce I did not see coming. (I write more about this in my blog 5 Minute Reads from a 50Something Woman)

A direct consequence of this new path I am navigating, has been the realisation that there is so much more to say ... about being 50+ and starting over in every aspect of life. Hence, *A Midlife Marriage* (and yes, I hope more). I truly hope that in reading, you will find comfort and inspiration as you tread your own path.

There has however been a slight hiccup and because this extension of the story was not planned, I have had to go back and readjust the back story of a minor character. When I say minor, I mean minor. I'm not talking re-writes on the scale of Bobby Ewing coming out of the shower, (if you don't remember this *Dallas* moment, google it). I doubt few readers will even notice. So, I'm leaving it in as an

'Easter Egg' - that's the term my twenty-two year old daughter tells me is used nowadays.

If you find the egg, write to me at: info@caryjhanson.com

If you're correct I'll send you a little surprise gift!

In the meantime, settle back and enjoy.

PART I

1

Jet-lagged and jowly, Helen stood in front of the mirror in her bathroom. Two hours until she was supposed to be meeting Caro and Kay, and she could barely get moving. By her reckoning it was three am in the morning. If she were to listen to her body, it would tell her to go back to bed. *Come on, Helen,* she said, slapping at her face. If she were to listen to her heart it would tell her to get back on the plane.

In the kitchen she found a packet of teabags, but no milk. In her toilet bag, her toothbrush, but no toothpaste. She used a travel sized all-in-one for her hair and her body, and a squeeze of sunscreen as moisturiser. She found a clean-enough pair of jeans, but not a clean-enough t-shirt. And twenty minutes later, after sorting through a mountain of dirty washing, she settled on what was supposed to be a gift for Jack, her son. *Never mind,* she thought as she pulled the t-shirt over her head. Jack, heading into his last year at university, was finishing a summer jaunt in the states. She'd wear the t-shirt wash it, then fold it back into the packaging and he would never know.

She locked the door of her new flat and headed out into a July morning heavy with latent rain. The sky was grey as socks, the road full of potholes and the station facade weathered and beaten.

'Twenty-four fifty,' the ticket clerk muttered, from behind glass thick enough to contain a serial killer.

'Twenty-four fifty?' She wasn't sure, because he hadn't bothered to look up as he spoke.

Twenty-four fifty.'

'Thank you,' she said pointedly, as without any further attempt at civility, the tickets were slid towards her.

The train was fast but full and for nearly an hour Helen negotiated a personal space marked on one side by a large man with body odour, and on the other by a foul-smelling toilet with a permanently open door.

Kings Cross was even busier, everyone and his dog on their way to London. By the time she found a grubby tube seat and collapsed into it, she was exhausted. Three stops to Oxford Circus. Just about enough time for a micro-nap. Arms crossed over the strap of her handbag, she closed her eyes and let her head drop and the rumble of the track and the black of the tunnel were a lullaby, rocking her back to the summit of Pikes Peak, Colorado. The spruce forests and crisp clean air, the pristine snow-caps of the Rocky Mountains, the space ... so much space.

The train jerked to a halt, a screeching percussion of brakes waking her up. She stood up and on wobbly legs, joined a moving river of human bodies through the open doors of the carriage, along the narrow platform, up a steep escalator and out into a marginally brighter, but no less crowded, Oxford Street.

W*ell,* Kay thought, *this has never happened before.* Twice now, in a little over two years she was looking at beachwear. Like buses, she was thinking, you wait for ages and then they all come at once. Because before that last-minute week in Cyprus a couple of years back, with her two best friends, Helen and Caro, she hadn't bought a swimsuit in over twenty years. Maybe even longer. Cyprus had been her first holiday in who knew how long, and the memory of preparing for it made her smile now. She'd been a fox in a chicken coop! Dashing into Tesco the evening before, picking up frozen dinners, throwing in a cheap scarlet sarong along on the way.

And here she was again, with more time and a lot more choice, literally walled in by bikinis and swimsuits, tankinis and ... monokinis? Kay frowned. Styles had certainly changed since she was last in the market for a two-piece, which she wasn't. Not with her waistline. Leaving the monokinis behind, she moved on to a display of more modest looking one-pieces. But they were prudish-looking things, navy and black, high-cut on the top, low-cut on the bottom. The beach equivalent of a viscose blouse, and more suitable for aqua-fit on a Monday night at the local swimming pool, than white-sand beaches. No. Kay shook her head. If there was one thing she didn't want to be anymore, it was sensible. The sarong was past its best, that much had been obvious on the long weekend she'd taken to Cyprus back in April, supposedly to plan Caro's wedding (although in the end Caro had gone ahead and done what she always did, made an executive decision, so the venue was now a town hall in North London).

She paused. On the other hand, a high cut would cover the scars. Scars that she didn't have when she'd grabbed that sarong. Scars from a successful lymph-node dissection, which had been followed by months of radiotherapy and infusions. All in all, nearly a year of treatment that had proved more successful than anyone had dared hope. So now she was officially a survivor of stage-four skin cancer, standing on the right side of those hopeful fifty percent, the lucky ones praying to live beyond five years. To live! Oh, to live! Yes, she was lucky, and she knew it. Four months since her last scan, another two until the next. And those gaps might only get longer.

Thinking this, she moved on, pausing to stop in front of a leopard-print bikini that had a mercifully large bottom. It was a beautiful thing, tawny colours, gold hoops and much ruching. Beachwear to imagine yourself in, tanned, windswept and carefree. Beachwear that said, 'look at me!' Beachwear that was anything but sensible.

But the price-tag had her moving again. Two hundred and fifty pounds? For something she would probably wear no more than ... As if she had come face to face with a brick wall, she stopped walking, hitched her handbag over her shoulder and looked up. In less than a week she would be retiring. Leaving her role as head of the maths department at the secondary school where she had worked for thirty years and relocating to Cyprus. Flying out on a flight she had yet to book, where – for crying out loud Kay! – she could wear a leopard-print bikini every day of the week. She could wear it until the vivid feline colours had washed out to the pastels of her knickers. And frankly if it lasted as long as her knickers had, most of which had been purchased in the last century, then two hundred and fifty was a bargain.

Without hesitating, she whipped the hanger off the rail and marched herself to the nearest cash-desk, declining a suggestion that she might like to try it on. That, she knew, would break the spell and anyway she was due to meet Helen in less than ten minutes. She watched instead, mesmerized, as with paper as thin as her dreams, the assistant folded the bikini into a small square.

'What a wonderful idea,' her consultant had said. 'All that sunshine and Mediterranean diet.'

'We'll be visiting all the time,' Helen kept saying.

'Once you get used to the travel, you won't even notice,' Caro promised.

'I'll be fine, Mum.' Alex her twenty-four-year-old son had told her. Alex, whose special needs had left him unable to cope with mainstream education, whose career would probably never extend beyond the garden centre in which he worked, who had never left home, who really wasn't like other twenty-four-year-olds and therefore might not be fine.

'It's time you lived your life for yourself,' from her father, a widower of less than twelve months, after her mother had finally succumbed to the dementia that had held her these last years.

'It's gorgeous,' the assistant said, handing Kay the package. 'Are you going anywhere nice to wear it?'

'Cyprus.'

'How wonderful.' The assistant smiled. You'll get plenty of opportunity out there.'

Kay returned the smile. She did, it seemed, have plenty of opportunities, to live, to wear a bikini for the first time in decades. But what would have happened if Caro hadn't invited her on that holiday to Cyprus? And what would have happened if she hadn't got sick? What opportunities would she be facing in that parallel universe?

They were questions she couldn't answer, but as she stepped onto the escalator there was one thing she knew in her bones to be true. If these things hadn't happened, she would have gone through the rest of her life never even thinking about splashing out two-hundred-and-fifty-pounds on a leopard-print bikini.

3

Plushly carpeted and ambiently lit, the bridal department of Selfridges was feminine, pastel, spacious and hushed. Glass cases showed off jewellery, veils and pearl-encrusted bags. Racks of gowns with intricate lacework and luxurious satin, hung from black velvet hangers. It was a space that demanded reverence, a place for believers. It was not, Helen realised as she looked down at her chest, the place to wear Jack's gift: a t-shirt bearing the printed words: *Head-Smashed-in-Buffalo-Jump*.

She glanced across the room. The only other customers she could see were a group of three women, sitting on a rose-coloured sofa. They were sipping wine, and the scene was suddenly so reminiscent of another bridal department, in another time, that it produced an image behind her eyes clearer than anything in front of them: her mother, with her Krystal from *Dynasty* bob, glass in hand, gasping every time Helen had whooshed forth from the changing room. Bursting into tears, every time. Holding her glass out for a refill, every time. What a wonderful day that had been.

They'd had tea and sandwiches after. She remembered the notepad lying on the table between them, her mother picking up the pen and writing. *You're going to want presents for the bridesmaids.* Sadness pressed her chest. *Was* it, *had* it, really been her, neck to toe in statin frills? Whoever it had been, it felt to Helen now like a person she didn't know.

The last couple of years had seen the scaffolding of her life, dismantled. Her marriage had ended, her children had grown and never had been the change in both her and her scenery, been clearer than in the six weeks of her trip across America. She'd climbed a mountain. Several mountains. She'd hiked through a forest, while blowing a whistle to keep bears at bay. What would her mother say about that? What would she have said to see Helen blood-smeared, as she skinned a hide? Yes, she had helped to skin the hide of a deer and eaten the meat, sitting around a campfire with five fellow Frontier-Wildcraft-Co. adventurers. Turning away, from the women on the sofa, she took a deep and measured breath. She didn't know what her mother would say, and the sadness that pierced her now took its strength from under-standing that she would never know. But wasn't that the fate of all mothers? And the sad inheritance of all daughters? It took so long for women. When her mother had died, she had still been fenced in by domesticity. And by the time her own daughter, Libby, was free, really free, would she still be around to see, appreciate and guide, as Libby began again? The thought pushed her back her a step, her hand resting on the desk. 'Oh, Mum,' she murmured. 'I wish you could have seen the view from Pikes Peak.'

4

Like so many before and so many to come, Caro was caught in the spell of a beautiful dress. Lost in a dream of reflected ivory, wrapped in a sheath of satin cut so perfectly it was like a fairy-hand had poured it across her hips. Held like a queen by the weight of material, enriched by embroidered pearl strands that gave an effect of sunlight on water. Ensnared by the moment, she felt herself to be beautiful. A beautiful woman, in a beautiful dress. Everything she had never believed she could be.

She put her hand behind her neck and scooped her hair up. It was longer now, a more relaxed style than the precision bob she had kept when she was in the office every day. With the other hand she traced the seam of the sweetheart neckline that mirrored perfectly the shape of her collarbones, the elegant slope of her shoulders. She would, she thought, as she turned to the side, wear her hair up on the day. She wasn't too old. In fact, longer hair made her look younger, feel more attractive. It made her ... Shaking her head, laughing, she put her hands together and held them at her chin.

Everything made her feel more attractive these days! The sun-kiss of time spent outside, the diamond daisy engagement ring on her left hand, even Tomasz's t-shirts which she'd taken to wearing. At first it was simply that they were so comfortable, now she continued the habit just to see him pick them up from the bed and hold them to his nose, inhaling her scent. Every time it gave her a thrill, all the more exciting for its novelty, more rousing, as the awareness of this new power she possessed, cemented itself. Because if at the beginning anyone had told her, she would not have believed them. If anyone had said, just wait, Caro. Be patient through your twenties, don't fall prey to worry through your thirties, bide your time in your forties, your moment will come ... her younger self would not have been reassured. Could not have imagined it possible to be this age and feel this vibrant, this alive. She turned, angling the mirror to see from the back. Surely then, this was her moment. Why shouldn't she grow her hair to her waist? And why shouldn't she wear this incredible strapless, form-fitting dress? She was engaged to a wonderful man who loved her deeply, and in just over three weeks they would be married.

From behind came a soft whispered hush as the curtain swished open an inch and the assistant leaned in. 'Your friends have arrived,' she said.

'Thank you.' Caro turned back to face the mirror. She had arranged to meet Helen and Kay today because she wanted them to see the dress beforehand. Who else could she ask? She had no sisters, no female cousins, no aunts and the idea that she might have shared this scene with her mother when she had been alive, was inconceivable. All those years, idling away a weekend afternoon on a business trip, passing the bridal department of Macy's in New York, or Robinsons in Singapore, wondering at the women she glimpsed inside, she had never once progressed to imagining a similar scenario for herself. What is unimaginable, cannot be imagined.

And yet here she was.

She ran her hand across her hip and as she did her palm caught on the material, calloused skin against satin, a rough and ugly sound.

'Are you OK?' the assistant said.

'Fine.' She nodded; her hands clasped together now. They were rough as tree bark. Never mind. She had three days before the investor presentation on Wednesday, her last job. More than enough time to splash out on some treatments. She would use her own card and Tomasz needn't know. Having semi-retired nearly a year ago, she was back doing freelance consultation in her role as Investor Relations manager, the flexibility of which she enjoyed. But Wednesday really would be her last job. The smallholding in Cumbria, they had recently moved to, with the intention of becoming self- sufficient, was going to be full-time work.

The assistant leaned in. 'We can always add in a little netting here,' she said indicating the neckline. 'If you feel too exposed.'

But looking at herself in the mirror, Caro shook her head. Exposed was the last thing she felt. She was, finally, a beautiful woman, in a beautiful dress and she wanted the world to see.

5

'It's perfect, Caro. You really did look beautiful.'

Kay nodded. 'There's a glow about you.'

'An aura,' Helen added.

'You look like a woman in love.' Kay smiled.

They were sitting at a corner table in the lower ground floor café. Navy plush velvet on the arms of their chairs, mirrored panels on the wall. A tea of finger sandwiches and fresh scones and champagne laid out before them.

'Thank-you,' Caro said, and her cheeks flushed with pleasure.

'Now!' Kay took a sandwich from the bottom plate of a three-tiered stand and plonked it on Caro's plate. 'I want to hear all about Hollybrook Farm ––'

'It's not a farm, it's a smallholding.'

'Of course.' Kay nodded, mouthing to Helen, as Caro turned her attention to her plate, '*a smallholding.*'

'*A smallholding.*' Helen mouthed back and winked. 'What's the difference?' she said lightly.

'Between a smallholding and a farm?' Caro took a tiny

bite of the tiny sandwich. 'A smallholding doesn't have much more than ten acres. A farm doesn't have less.'

'Oh.' Helen frowned. 'But you have chickens?'

'Yes, and a goat. And tonnes of courgettes. And summer cabbages.' Laughing, Caro held her hands up. 'Look at my hands. I've decided, I'm getting everything done while I'm in London. Pedicure, manicure, facial, the lot.'

'And this is definitely the last job?' Kay said.

Caro nodded. 'Matt asked me to stay on and do it. It's a big one, but it will be the last one.'

Helen picked up a cream horn pastry. 'How do you feel about that?'

'Fine.' Caro smiled as she turned the sandwich over and took another tiny bite. 'I knew that when we made the move. There just isn't time to keep coming down.'

As she spoke, Helen held her hand under her chin, catching cream. 'I just find it hard to picture you in the middle of nowhere,' she said, pastry sticking to her lips.

'Londale is hardly in the middle of nowhere. It has a railway station.' Caro laughed, but it was a lone sound, and it remained one, even as she looked up ready to share the joke. 'The cottage is quite lovely,' she continued. 'Original sash windows, a stone fireplace, the Aga has three ovens, and the high street is so quaint. There's a village store that sells just about everything.'

Kay nodded.

Across the table, Helen wiped cream from her fingertips.

'It seemed like a fair compromise. As soon as we started looking, I knew Poland was too far for me and Tomasz wanted to get out of London.'

'But it is a trial run?' Kay said.

'Three months.' Caro picked up her napkin. 'Of which

we have six weeks left.' Although Tomasz is in his element. He's already decided.'

'And you?' Helen said carefully, 'Have you decided?'

'Almost.' Caro shrugged. Then, 'Yes ... yes, I think so.'

'Are you self-sufficient?' Kay said.

'That's the plan. We're going to have to budget.'

'So, no more botox?' Smiling, Helen picked up her champagne. 'Or is there an allowance for that?'

'Well...' Caro said and smiled. 'As I'm in charge of the budget.'

'I see.' Nodding, Helen held her glass at her lips. *Original sash windows, stone fireplace...* Caro might as well have been describing the family home she herself had so recently left. A house that had started as a home, morphed into an identity and finished as a prison. 'That's marriage I suppose.'

'What is?' Caro said guardedly.

'Compromise.'

Caro didn't speak and as Helen glanced across the table and caught Kay's eye, she knew that if not burst, she had slightly deflated, Caro's balloon. It didn't matter that she wasn't convinced, and it didn't matter that she was a veteran of married life and Caro was a rookie. Today was not the time or place. Abashed, she added quietly, 'I hope it works, Caro ... the smallholding, I mean. Not the wedding.' She smiled. 'Obviously that's going to work, I don't think I've ever seen you looking so well.'

'Me too,' Kay echoed. She squeezed Caro's hand. 'Do you feel different?'

Caro dropped her head to one side. 'Yes,' she said. 'I do feel very different. They say that a change is as good as a rest and this is certainly a change, and after everything that ...' Suddenly she stopped talking, shaking her head as she picked up her napkin, folded it in half and placed it on her plate. For a long moment she looked at it. 'What about you, Helen?' And with a small smile, Caro looked up. 'You must feel different too?'

'Actually,' Kay blurted, but she was speaking through a mouthful of scone. 'Wait a minute.' She swallowed a hasty mouthful of champagne, washed the crumbs away and let out a small polite burp. 'I think,' she managed, 'Helen looks more like herself than she has in years. That's exactly how I remember her in university.'

'You mean the t-shirt?' Helen looked at her chest.

Kay nodded. 'It reminds me of the *For Fox Sake, Stop the Hunting!* you wore all through the second year of university. Remember?'

'I do.' Helen laughed. 'This is supposed to be for Jack, but I haven't unpacked, and I couldn't find anything else.'

'Is it really called that?' Kay said, titling her head to read.

'Yes, it is!' Helen pulled the t-shirt taught. 'Native Americans use such figurative language. You know, White Feather? Raging Bull? And when you see this place, it makes total sense.'

'So, what would they call you?' Caro smiled. 'She Who Is Born Again?'

'I don't know about that.' Helen laughed. But Caro was closer than she knew. She was almost born again, and she did feel very different. From the inside out, she had grown confidence, like Kay had grown her hair back. Six weeks on the road, had shown her what she was capable of. Just imagine six months. She had. She'd only been back forty-eight hours. Only had a brief couple of hours with her daughter Libby, and her grandson Ben and already she couldn't stop thinking about moving on. It felt like a betrayal. Libby had been overjoyed to see her, voicing a desire to be gone again would be a dagger to her heart.

'I do feel different,' she settled on, leaving out *torn,* leaving out *conflicted,* leaving out *guilty.* She took a sip of champagne and looked across to a table by the window, where two women of a similar age to herself sat. They wore matching floral blouses and had matching honey-highlights. One was even picking away at what looked like a piece of lemon-drizzle. Her favourite. 'Places like this,' she said turning back to Caro and Kay, 'used to be my happy place. The day Jack started school, the first day I'd been child-free in seven years, I took myself off to the garden centre cafe, ordered a latte and sat and read the paper for two hours. I think it was the first coffee I'd managed to finish while it was still hot for years.'

Caro smiled. 'I remember you telling me that.'

'And I can't count how many wet Saturday afternoons I spent there, trawling through the gossip pages, stuffing myself with cake while everyone else was off doing something ...'

'Exciting?' Kay finished.

Helen paused, her mouth curling into a rueful smile. 'More exciting than eating cake,' she said. 'I was even there before we went to Cyprus. I'd just seen the doctor to go on HRT, and I was so miserable, I was thinking I wouldn't go, but imagine ...' As she stopped talking, her eyes fixed on a point halfway across the room. 'Imagine if Cyprus hadn't happened?'

For a moment no-one spoke.

'Do you think you wouldn't be divorced?' Caro said.

Helen looked at her. 'I don't like to think about that. The idea that I would have just kept on doing the same thing.' She sighed. 'As it is, I'm not looking forward to going back to work.'

'When do you start back?' Kay said.

'Next Wednesday.'

'Oh, how funny.'

'What is?' Helen turned.

'School finishes on Wednesday,' Kay said. 'That's my last day.'

Helen put her mouth to her hand. 'I haven't even asked! How ironic. My first day back, is your last.'

'Do you have anything planned?' Caro said, turning to Kay. 'A leaving party?'

'Nothing.'

'Nothing?'

'I'm just having a quiet night.' And the pocket of silence that followed was unnaturally deep. 'So,' picking up her glass, Kay nodded at Helen's t-shirt. 'I presume you'll have to unpack for work?'

'Yes.' Helen said quietly. 'I suppose I will.'

6

'Wait! Eyebrows is coming! I have to hide.'

'Who is eyebrows?'

'Sophia. You don't know her. She's the area manager. She has a degree in tourism and the eyebrows of my grandfather.'

Kay picked up her cup and peered at her screen. Marianne had her phone positioned under her chin, so mostly all she could see were nostrils. She smiled. Marianne worked as a receptionist at the Hotel Adagio in Cyprus, where Caro, Helen and herself had stayed. They had kept in touch, had in fact become such good friends, Marianne had joined their trip to Vegas last year and been part of the wedding planning party in April. Thinking this, she shivered, and it was such a violent movement the tea in her cup wobbled. The trip to Vegas had ended with her waking up under a sheet in her airline seat, after a doctor on the flight had declared her dead. Never mind that Helen had panicked, or that the 'doctor' being a Doctor of Podiatry, was good at feet and obviously not much else. Never mind that, utterly exhausted by the highs and lows of Vegas and overwhelmed with relief to be on her way back to Alex, Kay had simply fallen into the deepest, calmest sleep she'd experienced since she'd first heard the word cancer. She might have been buried alive! This time the tea jumped the cup. It was a time and a moment she didn't like to dwell on.

'She draws them on,' Marianne said, 'very thick.' And leaning even closer to the screen, she drew her finger across her eyebrow to mimic the action.

Relieved to be distracted, Kay laughed. Over numerous FaceTime calls since they had become friends, she had seen parts of Marianne she wasn't sure anyone else had. The insides of her nostrils, like now, the pink-caved walls of her inner ear, even her belly button, as Marianne had sunbathed, blissfully unaware of the direction in which her camera pointed. Suddenly the view changed again, and she found herself looking at Marianne's bosom, heaving like the Southern Ocean as Marianne began an awkward half-jog, half-walk.

'I'm going out the gates,' Marianne panted. 'She won't find me there. Ouch!' The bosom disappeared, so now Kay was looking at blue sky. '*Oi mana mou!* I dropped it...'

'Is it cracked?'

More panting, more sky and a smudge of dust. 'Leonard Cohen,' Marianne breathed as her face came back into view, 'says there is a crack in everything. I told you the story of how my mother gave me my name?'

Kay laughed. 'Yes, you told me.'

'Let me ca ... catch my breath.'

'Why don't you ring me back,' she said. 'Find a seat, catch your breath and ring me back. I'm not in any hurry.'

A weak wave from Marianne signalled her agreement and propping her phone on her kitchen windowsill, Kay turned to look at her own sky, which was steel grey not blue.

Soon, she really wouldn't be in any hurry, ever again. Today was the last day of her working life. The last day she could legitimately call herself a teacher and it had come around so fast that from her toes upward, she felt the surge of a worry that left her weak as a kitten.

Her phone rang. She jumped, stared at the screen and realised it was Marianne calling back. How lost she'd been, swamped with an apprehension that was sudden and blinding. Taking a breath, she swiped the screen and Marianne's face came into view.

'Ok. I'm ready, Marianne gasped, 'Just a mo ...'

'Catch your breath.' Kay waited. Behind from where Marianne sat, she could see tendrils of fuchsia pink bougainvillea scrawled across a white wall. Everything else in the picture was a soft blurry ochre, from the scrubbed slopes of the Kyrenia mountains, to the rocks beyond. It was a view she remembered well, a view that offered a beautifully simple contrast: a strike of colour from the bougainvillea, a muted, quiet background behind. Just as her decision to take early retirement and move to Cyprus had once been beautifully simple. Those days felt far away now, days when watching the ceiling during radiotherapy sessions, her prayers had been the prayers of a woman with few options. *If I get a second chance, I will do this ... If I'm lucky ...* Now she watched the ceiling and tortured herself in other ways and the more she did, the more Cyprus was beginning to feel difficult. The weekend in April had brought home just how far from home she would be, had her thinking that it was all just a morphine-induced pipe dream she had perhaps smoked too much of. She picked up her mug and blowing air to cool her tea down, glanced across at the package on the kitchen bench. It had been there since Saturday. Her leopard-print bikini still unwrapped.

Looking at it, Kay felt her shoulders drop. It was astonishing to her now, the small amount of consideration she had given to how hard this was going to be. No, she wasn't selling the house. No lampshades to stuff into her luggage. No tables and chairs strapped to a wagon, pulled by a weary donkey, a fiddler on the roof playing a mournful lament. *I'm looking at it as extended holiday, rather than anything permanent,* she'd begun explaining to everyone who had never asked. Including her father, who had asked. But how on earth could she have contemplated leaving him for months at a time so soon after her mother had died? He'd been like a ghost lately, every time she saw him, he seemed to have diminished in height, in energy, in sheer physical presence, as if one by one, all the ties that tethered a being to this life were being snipped away. She had hoped that after the last few years of caring for her mother, the opposite would have happened. That he would have started living again. She'd even gone so far as sign him up to a seniors' social club, but without her mother by his side, in sickness and in health, he seemed directionless: a boat without a rudder.

Hands wrapped around her cup, she took a long contemplative slurp. And then, of course, there was Alex. Although since he had gone out and got a girlfriend – something she had never even tried imagining he would do, she'd hardly seen him. Her awkward, painfully shy, often monosyllabic son had a girlfriend. Emmy-Lou. Or was it Emmeline? She wasn't sure, having met the girl only once, and then for not more than a few brief seconds as they had crossed paths on the doorstep. Alex seemed determined to keep her under wraps.

'I'm ready now!' Marianne sat upright. 'I wanted to ring and wish you all the best for today.'

'Oh.' Tears smarted. Kay put her cup down and covered her mouth.

'I hope you have a wonderful day, Kay. You deserve it.'

'Thank you,' she whispered.

'Don't cry now,' Marianne scolded. 'Chin up. It's the start of something new. I'm wishing all good things for you.'

Unable to speak, Kay nodded. If she had a pound for every good wish she'd received ... So many texts, so many students popping into her classroom all week long, bringing her gifts, shyly handing over cards. The mantle in her living room overflowed. It was overwhelming. Thank goodness there really was no party planned, all she wanted to do was make a quiet exit before her cold feet turned to ice, dropped off and she changed her mind.

'Well then. I don't have long I'm afraid, eyebrows, wants to go through our new customer satisfaction forms.' Marianne's face pinched in disgust. 'If they're satisfied,' she snorted, 'they come back. It's simple. No forms, no stupid smiley face, no, *what could we have done better?* Why do they make it so complicated? Nothing is simple anymore.'

Kay smiled. If Marianne could read her mind.

'She must justify her degree I suppose. They all have to justify their expensive educations. So,' brushing dust from her skirt, Marianne leaned forward. 'Do you have a date for your flight yet? I know it will be after the wedding.'

'I've bought a bikini!'

'But no flight?'

'Not yet and speaking of which, the wedding I mean, I saw Caro and Helen on Saturday. Helen's back from America.' Her voice was bright, the swerve of direction deliberate. The last few times she had spoken with Marianne she'd managed to avoid talk of dates altogether, falling back on the fact that with the end of term and retirement approaching, she simply had too much to concentrate on. Which was true. But the excuse was reaching its expiry date. 'They look so well,' she added, before Marianne could speak. 'They have great tans. Helen from hiking and Caro, I suppose from all the work on the farm ... smallholding, I mean. She has chickens. Can you imagine?' She was garbling and she knew it, but at least it was steering the conversation away from where she didn't want it to go.

And it worked, because now Marianne laughed. 'No,' she said, 'I can't imagine it. Caro a farmer? With chickens!'

'I find it hard too,' Kay murmured.

'So how is she in her farm, that is not a farm?'

Kay opened her mouth ready to speak.

'Having second thoughts?' Marianne said, filling the gap.

'No.' She glanced to the window. She was searching for the right word. It was hard, almost impossible to imagine Caro with chickens, but there hadn't been any second-thought vibes at the weekend. If anything, Caro looked ... 'Content,' she said, as she turned back to her screen.

'Are you sure?'

'Yes, I think that's the right word.'

'It's the sex.' Marianne nodded.

'Sex!'

'Yes. She will be having lots of sex. It makes anyone content.'

'Oh, well I didn't ask —'

'It's the best skincare a woman can use.' And suddenly Marianne leaned to her screen and turned it left to right, showing her profile as if she were posing for a stamp. 'Haven't you noticed my face?'

Frowning, Kay tilted her head. She wasn't sure where this conversation was going, but now she'd been asked, Marianne did look well. Very well. And yes, she did have a glow, maybe even similar to the glow she'd had back in Vegas, during a brief fling with her old flame, Tony. 'Are you seeing someone?' she asked, a small smile forming.

'Not *someone.*'

The stress on the *one* had been unmistakeable, still the conclusion was slow to arrive. Did Marianne mean more than one?

'Friends with benefits, Kay.' Marianne smiled. 'That is what the young people call it.'

'How many friends?' she gasped, the question flying out of her mouth like a missile. Why on earth had she asked that? And what was an acceptable number anyway? Two? Three? Fifteen?

Marianne's face darkened. 'You and I talked about this, Kay.'

'Did we?' Her jaw fell slack. There had been many conversations with Marianne over the last twelve months, for which Kay was, and always would be deeply grateful. In a way, because their friendship had been new, it had been easier to open to her than to Helen or Caro and together they had trawled the depths of the deepest subjects. But friends with benefits? Sex, with more than one man? No, she couldn't recall touching on that.

Marianne turned away from the sun, bringing her hand up to shield her eyes. 'We agreed that we needed to get out more. Make new friends.'

'We did,' Kay blustered. 'But...that's not... I ––'

'So, I joined Tinder.'

'You joined Tinder?'

'And you should too.'

Kay opened her mouth, nothing came out.

'It's very easy,' Kay. Look.' And before she could respond, Marianne had swiped her phone and opened her Tinder account, so now Kay was looking at the profile of a handsomely proud, and confident middle-aged woman.

'Oh,' she whispered, as Marianne swiped through the photos. There she was, her friend, in all her glory. One of the pictures had been taken in Vegas. It showed Marianne leaning against a ranch fence, horses grazing in the background, looking for all the world as if she were about to saddle up and ride off. Kay threw her head back and laughed. She'd taken this picture herself; Marianne never made it anywhere near the saddle!

'Did you ...' she started, and then paused, remembering the afternoon and the way she had tried to frame the photograph. 'Did you cut Tony out of that last picture?'

'Of course I did!' Marianne said. 'Magic eraser, Kay. It's brilliant. Imagine having it in real life? You can just rub out anything you don't want around anymore.'

'I thought you said you weren't good with tech stuff.'

'If I have to, I have to.' Marianne shrugged. 'And I know I don't look quite like that in real life, but if I put a picture of myself without any filter, do you think they would come? Anyway, by the time they've made the journey, they don't want to go back empty-handed, if you know what I mean.'

Kay didn't speak. She did know what Marianne meant, but she had no idea how to respond.

'Are you shocked?' Marianne broke the silence. 'It's not so many friends like this, Kay.' Her voice was quiet. 'But you remember Tony and Vegas?'

'Of course I do,' she whispered.

'It didn't matter that it didn't last.' And even though there were only mountains to hear, and flowers to tell, Marianne too, whispered. 'It was enough that it happened, Kay. He awakened something in me. And it's nice. It's so nice to have a cuddle.'

The sting of truth was so sharp it pricked Kay's heart, and her heart pricked her eyes and tears smarted. A cuddle? She put her hand to her mouth. When was the last time she had had a cuddle from anyone other than her parents? Years? A decade?

'It's even nicer to wave them goodbye and not be left washing their socks for the rest of your life.' Marianne stood up. 'I thought, why not? I'm only fifty-five. I have, I hope, many years left. Why not?'

But again, Kay had no answer, and Marianne had no response and the distance between them was fragile with miscomprehension.

'I have offended you, Kay. I didn't mean ––'

'No.' She put her finger to her lips. 'No,' she said again.

'Then I have upset you?'

'No.'

'Then what?'

But she didn't know what. First Helen in Cyprus with her holiday fling, then Marianne in Vegas and now Caro, content with that most vital thing, sex, companionship ...a cuddle. Even Alex whose life was lived within in a five-mile radius of home had found himself someone to hold. 'I'm not upset,' she managed, 'and I'm not offended. I suppose,' she said quietly, 'I'd like a cuddle too.'

7

S tanding in front of her three colleagues at Rosehill Heath Centre, Helen felt removed from reality. Firstly, Tina, Daisy and Anne had formed a welcome line-up more suitable for a royal visit, than a co-worker returning from a six-week break. Secondly, absolutely nothing had changed. The poster on the door with 'new' opening hours still peeled back from the top-left corner, the same lone *Measles Aware!* leaflet, still spilled from a plastic holder on the table in reception. And thirdly, Tina had just handed her a Tupperware box containing a huge slab of lemon drizzle cake.

Smiling, Helen looked at the box, the dense round contained within. She was thinking about the women with honey-coloured highlights and matching blouses on Saturday. She was thinking about her Instagram feed. The constant stream of adverts for special diets and special training methods and special coaches, all designed to get rid of that specially problematic midlife belly. Which she did have once but now didn't. Oh yes, this time last year and the linen trousers she wore would have been slicing her belly in half. By coffee time she'd have given up and undone the button, all the better to enjoy a slab of cake which she would have eaten to stave off boredom. The thing was, she wasn't bored anymore.

'I know it's your favourite!' Tina giggled.

Helen's smile faltered.

'I'll put the kettle on,' Anne said. 'We can have a piece now.'

'I'll get some plates.' Daisy grinned.

Hadn't they noticed? Caro and Kay had. Didn't her colleagues also see the difference? Dazed, she watched them scuttle off, full of all the anticipated excitement a tea-break still mustered. The problem was she didn't feel the same. The problem was, while Daisy and Tina and Anne had been drinking tea and eating cake, she had sat under canopies of stars and lain under skins of canvas, listening to the scratching and snuffling of creatures to whom the darkness belonged. And when the light had come back, she had woken to azure skies, sipping coffee from a tin mug as she watched the sun lay a rosy mantle over mountains that straddled countries. She hadn't been afraid, and she hadn't been bored. Not once. She'd trekked empty crevices gouged by glaciers that had melted in her own lifetime, filled with wonder and sadness for the world her children's children would live in and she hadn't – not once, not even in her deepest dreams – given a single thought to cake. Couldn't they see this?

IN THE BACK KITCHEN, she took off her jacket and hung it on the rack. 'It's still here then,' she said, lifting the sleeve of a pale green cardigan.

'What is?' Anne didn't turn from the sink where she was filling the kettle.

'This.' Helen held the sleeve high. 'I think it's been here as long as I have. So that would be ten years?'

Daisy bustled past, a cup in each hand. 'I hadn't noticed.'

'Really?' she said, letting the sleeve drop.

'She doesn't say anything now.'

'Who?'

'Dr Ross.' Tina peeled the lid from the Tupperware box. 'We were a bit worried she might start again, what with you not being here to organise us, like last time.'

'Sorry?'

'You know.' Anne grinned.

'No.' Helen shook her head. She had no idea what they were talking about.

'That time she tried to stop us drinking coffee at the desk?' Tina said. 'I do it all the time now, and she doesn't say a word.'

'Me too,' Daisy added.

'Oh.' And as Helen looked at the expectant faces in front of her, her jaw dropped. Coffee-gate? The rebellion she had led – and won – against Dr Ross's rule that coffee cups were not to be bought to the front desk was something she had forgotten ever happened. What did they want her to say? It had been a tiny event, in a long-ago day of what now felt like someone else's life, but her colleagues were looking at her now as if they expected a speech.

She laughed, turning away to busy herself opening her handbag. She'd been back at work for less than fifteen minutes and she had another three hundred to get through, but already the ground beneath her feet felt unstable in a way it never had fourteen thousand feet up the Rocky Mountains.

She knew why. Up there, where the sky was close enough to touch, she had felt anchored to a world that was tangibly real. Here, it was going to be a battle to stay standing, to stop herself getting dragged down by the undertow of banality.

'She's started something else now.' Anne groaned.

Helen turned.

'She wants us all to do something called, *Excellence- in-Service* training.'

'At least it's in working hours,' Tina muttered.

Helen looked from one to the other. 'It doesn't sound that bad.' She was playing for time. *Excellent in Service* training didn't sound like a barrel of laughs to her either, but if Dr Ross, had suggested they all take a course in *Modern Nail Art,* or *How to Go Viral on TikTok,* it would, she suspected, have resulted in the same wash of indifference.

'Actually, I don't mind doing it,' Daisy said.

Helen smiled. 'It might be interesting?'

'Oh, I don't know about that,' Daisy said pulling her mouth down as she handed Helen a cup. 'But there's a free lunch. You're on phones, by the way.'

IN THE SMALL, windowless phone room Helen logged into the computer, then the phone system, her work email, the filing system, clinic access, patient records and appointments system. As she took a headset from the top drawer of the filing cabinet she glanced at the clock.

07:56.

She had four minutes. At 08:00 the telephone lines would open, and she would spend the next two and a half hours answering non-stop calls from people trying to get an appointment, only a few of whom she would actually be able to help. Her coffee break was at ten-thirty. After that she would swap one windowless room, for another, larger, windowless room, where she would work on the front desk, talking to people trying to get an appointment, or people complaining about the appointment they had just had ... only a few of whom she would actually be able to help. She finished at one o'clock, ready to repeat until the end of the week ... the end of the month ... the end of the year. She took a pen, a notepad and a block of yellow Post-it notes from the drawer, sat down and twirling the pen between her fingers, stared through the open door to the corridor beyond.

Was this someone else's life? The moment felt surreal enough for her to believe that it was. Someone who would have been delighted by Tina's thoughtful gift, whose mornings *had* been consumed by the thought of eating cake, when all the time just outside the door, the world had waited.

The clock was noisy, she could hear the seconds pass ... tick, tick, tick ... She had years yet. At the very least a decade before retirement, and suddenly she was thinking about Kay and the irony of the fact that Kay was retiring, just as she was just returning. And Caro, with her chipped nails and her new life. It wasn't jealousy. She didn't begrudge them the changes they were making, and she didn't want them for herself. So, what did she want? Looking down, she drew a circle on the top sticky note, and then another and another, smaller and harder until the circle was nothing more than a dot. Caro and Kay had both had fulfilling and demanding careers, while she had simply passed the time waiting for Libby and Jack to grow up. Ten years she'd been at the surgery. A decade in a job she'd never intended to do longer than twelve months. What was that, if not passing time?

07:59.

Slipping the headset over her ears, she clicked a window open on the computer, staring without seeing the grids of typeset. Now Libby and Jack had grown up, and what a shock! What an outrageous, painful shock to lift her head and find that while she had been treading water, they had learned to swim. The minute-hand shifted; she heard it as a crypt door closing, heavy, solid, final. She reached for the mouse and clicked. 'Rosehill Health Centre,' she said. 'How can I help?'

8

Five hundred and fifty feet above one of the wealthiest square miles in the world, Caro stood, seven centimetres of reinforced glass separating her from fresh air. Hands by her temples she pressed closer, all the better to see a thousand years of London: the Gherkin and St Pauls, the neo-classical facade of the Bank of England, the great wheel of the turning Eye and if you knew where to look, which she did, small but stubborn chunks of Roman wall, left behind like the broken teeth of a giant.

How had she not remembered this? How had she not made the connection when Helen had tried to explain just a couple of days ago. She smiled, so close now her nose was almost pressed to the glass. What Helen had been talking about as she'd described the view from high in the Rocky Mountains, how powerful it had made her feel, was exactly this. The feeling she had – had always had – every time she had stood and looked out over London, or Singapore, or New York. Stepping back, she let her hands drop. It hadn't clicked, her head had been too full of wedding dresses, and it simply hadn't clicked.

'It's quite some view, isn't it?'

She turned.

'I can never decide if I prefer this, or the view from the Observatory.' The man who had spoken was tall. Half an inch of snow-white shirt peeped from the precisely cut cuffs of his suit, his grey hair held the sheen of top-end products, and his face was clean shaven, carrying the kind of healthy glow that spoke of time in the sun. Every inch of him whispered wealth.

'Ah, but there are no Roman ruins in New York,' she said, and the expression of surprise that crossed his face was exactly what she'd been aiming for.

'There are none here ...' He leaned to the window. 'Are there?'

'If you know where to look.'

'And I presume you do?' There was a challenge in his voice, that she didn't hesitate to accept.

'Here.' She held a finger against the glass. 'Can you see? You have to know what you're looking for, but along the base of that building you can just about make out a tiny grey line. See how it juts out? That's a roman wall.'

The man leaned closer and suddenly she was light-headed, an exquisite note of cedarwood in his cologne sending all sorts of signals through her head.

As if he sensed this, he took a step back and stretched out his hand. 'Spencer Cooper.'

'Caro Hardcastle,' she said regaining her composure.

'Caro? As in Caroline? You're giving the presentation?'

'I am.' And as she shook his hand a maelstrom surged. Relief that she had had a manicure, anxiety that he would still feel the coarseness of her weeks in the garden, confusion that she should be feeling anything, and a deep, deep desire to press her nose to his neck and breathe in.

'Well,' he murmured, an amused expression lighting his eyes. 'Thank you for showing me something new. That doesn't happen very often.' He was still holding her hand.

She could feel the heat in her face.

'I'm looking forward to hearing this. I've heard you're an impressive woman.' And finally, Spencer Cooper let her go.

'Well ...' Caro laughed, her hand at her side now like a fallen puppet.

'Well,' he returned and smiled. It was a smile that managed to combine shyness with confidence, a smile worth thousands in dental work, a smile that made her a rabbit in headlights.

She made a half turn to the window, as if she would walk out into thin air, turned back, blushed again and pointing toward a raised platform on the other side of the room said, 'I'd better make my way over.'

Hands in pockets, Spencer stepped back to let her pass, and as she walked across the room Caro knew she was being watched.

So, she performed. Quite possibly the best performance of her career. Her suit was Max Mara, her belt Hermes, her pumps Manolo Blahnik, her confidence sky-high. Light poured in through the glass walls. Lush foliage created a sense of serenity. 'Good morning,' she started. 'My name is Caro Hardcastle and I'm the investor relations manager at Eco-Innovate.'

All eyes turned to her.

'We have invited you here today because we see an incredible opportunity in the energy management system market, and we would like to share how Eco-Innovate is poised to capitalise on this.' She was at the beating heart of an enclave in the sky, an exclusive space for the very rich and the very powerful. Click. With the projector remote in her hand and Matt her CEO, proud as a parent stage right, she powered on. 'The EMS market is currently valued at forty billion. Conservative growth rates stand around thirteen percent.'

IT WAS all over in thirty minutes. Months of research, weeks of revising, writing, editing and testing.

'Thank you for your time.' And to the sound of polite but enthusiastic applause, Caro unclipped her microphone, handed it to a waiting junior and stepped off the stage: an empress having delivered a victory speech.

'Superb!' Matt offered her a glass of Champagne. He tilted his head. 'Listen to that.'

Indulging him, Caro too tilted her head.

'Kerching!' He grinned. 'I hear the sound of fifty million.'

Fifty million? The goal had been thirty. She turned to look at the crowd behind her. She had done enough equity offerings to be able to gauge the PH level afterwards and this time it was clear. The room buzzed, so much so that there could be no doubt that the atmosphere was energetically acidic, rather than insipidly alkaline. Matt, she was thinking, could be right. Dipping her head she took a sip of champagne, eyes scanning the room. There was much that could still fail. A slick presentation was just a slick presentation and what was really needed to get the high-end guys to open their wallets, was the same as what was needed to get the low-end guys to open their wallets: an old-fashioned charm offensive. 'Let's get mingling?' she said.

IT WASN'T until ninety minutes later, that she felt the first twinge of fatigue, the slight droop in her otherwise upright back. It was a slackening that she sensed mirrored in the room, with the drift toward the buffet tables, the tonal dip of background chatter. Good, because now she'd paused, she was hungry. Over the course of the morning, she had spoken to every portfolio manager and analyst that needed to be spoken to. She had charmed and impressed, challenged and blindsided with facts and statistics, counterarguments and persuasions. She had done her homework. But then Caroline Hardcastle of Artillery Terrace had always done her homework. *Diligent and conscientious,* those were the most consistent comments on every school report. And it wasn't that the thin-haired, bespectacled child who had shut herself in her room, had understood that one day this was where it would all lead to: a stage in the sky, where she was a queen. It was simply that doing her homework was what her mother had expected of her, and if she did what her mother expected of her, then her mother would love her … would, one day, show her that she loved her. All this passed through her mind in an instant, a snatch of fragmented words and briefly glimpsed scenes that vanished before they were tangible. So much the mind held, an ambush around every corner.

Closing the door on a past that brought no comfort, Caro moved across to the windows, put her hand to her eyes and looked up. The sun was directly above, and she found herself thinking of the smallholding, of Tomasz and what he might be doing. If he had broken for lunch yet, and if so, what he would be eating. Thinking this, she smiled. If she knew him well, and she did, his lunch would be a sandwich piled with slabs of ham and mayonnaise. A server brushed past, catching her elbow, whispering an apology. Waving it aside Caro turned just in time to see a tray piled high with crab legs. As she followed the server across the room, her stomach twisted in hunger.

THE SPREAD WAS PHENOMENAL. Salads of peach and prosciutto, lobster and avocado. Oysters and tuna tartare, caviar, noodle bowls, baby potatoes tossed in rosemary and sea-salt, wild rice, artisan bread. As she looked along the table, she held her plate close to her chest. Even if she and Tomasz worked every day for a year, they could never even come close to achieving this: the kind of bounty cold-hard cash could buy.

'Now this could be a problem.'

At the sound of the voice, so close behind, Caro felt a twinge of excitement. Spencer Cooper had found her again. 'Quite,' she said, as she turned. 'I don't know where to start.'

'That's not what I meant.' He smiled.

'It wasn't?'

'I was going to ask you if would like to join me for dinner later?' He raised his hand to the table. 'But if you eat too much now ...'

'Oh.' Heart racing, she too looked at the table.

'Or...' He put his hands in his pockets and tipped his head to the side. 'We could skip dinner, and go straight for cocktails?'

'I have a train to catch.' The words came out so fast, so blunt, she might as well have lifted her plate and cracked it over his head and, judging by the way he seemed to recoil, she felt as if she had. 'Otherwise,' she blurted, 'I would have loved too.'

He smiled, slow as a lizard. 'Another time then? I'm over for a week.' And opening his jacket he pulled a card from the breast pocket. 'This is me.'

'Thank you,' she said, as she took the card. When what she should have said was, *Thank you, but I have a train to catch because I'm going back to my fiancé. Who I'm planning to buy a smallholding with, who I'm marrying in three weeks.* Those were the words that should have come out of her mouth to cut it off, stop it before it started, whatever *it* was.

9

The man who stood on the other side of the reception desk was young and angry. Having kept his sunglasses on thus far during the conversation, he had now pushed them to the back of his head. In order, Helen supposed as she watched him, to demonstrate just how angry he was. She didn't care. He wasn't having a cardiac arrest, he was here to get a certificate for travel insurance signed, for which he would have to wait.

'This is an emergency!' he shouted.

It was almost as if she'd spoken out loud. She raised an eyebrow. *Avoid intense eye contact which could be seen as provocative.* Straightening up she pulled her shoulders back. *Put a little more physical distance between yourself and the patient.* 'I'm sorry,' she said, 'but an insurance form is not an emergency.' *Speak softly and abstain from being judgemental.* She'd been doing the job so long, it was almost impossible not to stay calm, not to put her training into place.

He took the sunglasses off and flung them on the counter. Helen watched as they flipped over. What next? Would he snap them in half?

'I'm leaving tomorrow,' he snarled.

'And if you leave it with us, the doctor will sign it this afternoon. You can pick it up first thing.' *Show your intention to rectify the situation rather than reprimanding the patient for their behaviour ...* For being an arsehole, more like ...

'And what time is that?'

'We open at eight. Thank you,' she called to his back, as he slapped the form on the desk, picked up his glasses and stalked off.

'Next.'

A young girl sidled up to the counter, her friend lingering behind. 'I've come for the morning-after pill,' she said, a little too boldly for Helen's liking.

Show your intention to rectify the situation rather than reprimanding the patient for their behaviour ... 'When was the last time you had unprotected sex?' And as Helen looked up, her face softened. Closer now she could see, the girl was close to still being a child. Sixteen, maybe. Seventeen, at most. A baby was the last thing she needed. She turned to her computer. The window for effective use of the morning-after pill was only seventy-two hours; she needed to get this girl in front of a doctor as soon as possible. The way someone should have got her own daughter in front of a doctor. At least this girl was being proactive, trying to help herself. Away from home, in her last year at university, and the father, an American exchange student, long since back across the Atlantic, Libby had stuck her head in the sand for nearly seven months. The result of which ostrich-like action had been Ben. Who nobody could regret ... Even so ...

'I haven't,' the girl said.

Helen blinked. 'You haven't what?'

'Had unprotected sex.'

'Then why are you here?'

The girl shrugged. 'I'm going out tonight.'

'Try the pharmacy,' she snapped, and using her pen as an arrow held it up. 'Out the door on the right. *Next.*'

A middle-aged man shuffled up. 'I'm telling you it's a migraine. I need to see someone now.'

'Are you dizzy'?'

'No.'

'And you can look at the lights?'

'Those lights?' He tipped his chin and looked directly at the glare of the fluorescent ceiling lights.

'Please go and wait in the waiting room, sir,' she said tightly. 'The doctor will see you at your appointed time. It's not a migraine.' Sir? He'd hadn't even bothered to change from the joggers and stained t-shirt, it looked like he had slept in. '*Next.*'

'But it feels like I'm on fire, love.' Grey skin, orange-rimmed teeth and the rancid breath of a heavy smoker.

'And, as we just agreed, it sounds like a urinary tract infection. The pharmacist will be able to prescribe something directly.'

'I don't want a bloody chemist. I want a doctor!'

'You can ring tomorrow,' she said keeping her mouth just about shut. The woman's breath was foul. 'Or as I said, try the pharmacy.'

'If I die it will be your fault!'

'*Next.*'

'I want them out now.'

'You were told yesterday, the doctor won't remove hospital stitches. You can wait all afternoon to hear that for yourself, or you can listen to me and go back to ... Ouch.' She ducked as a pen flew past her ear.

'It's my daughter, she has this rash ...'

'I've had this cough for three weeks now ...'

'I think it's piles, I'm walking like I've shit my pants. Excuse my language ...'

'*Next.*' As the morning wore on, so did Helen's voice, and by the time she looked up to see a small, neatly dressed woman, it was barely more than a bleat. 'How can I help you?' she croaked.

'I really don't want to bother you ...'

It wasn't just the polite tone, that sent a shiver down her spine. Plenty of patients were polite *and* timewasters. No, it was the terror in the woman's eyes, the panic that Helen could see had made a rag doll of her. She watched as the woman put her hand out to the desk, gripping it like it was the last solid thing in the world. 'It's my husband,' she whispered. 'I'm really concerned. Could you ...' Her arm wavered as she raised it to point toward the waiting room. 'I did ask if we could be seen earlier.'

'You have an appointment?'

'At twelve forty.'

Helen glanced at the clock. 'That's another twenty minutes.' Turning back, her eyes narrowed. 'How long have you been here?'

'An hour and a half. I didn't want to wait at home. I thought if we came in there'd be a chance to get seen earlier, but the girl said no and he's only getting worse.'

'OK.' And hurrying out from behind the reception desk, she followed the woman into a waiting room that was noisy and full. As it always was. A waiting room where, despite the huge sign on the wall that read, *Please your phone considerately,* she counted at least three people, using their phones inconsiderately: talking blithely, talking loudly, talking as if they were in the privacy of their own homes. Scowling, stepping over a pile of Lego bricks that no-one had bothered to return, she headed straight for what was obviously the sickest patient in the room. A heavily built man who despite the heat of the afternoon, shivered uncontrollably. He had fallen into a hunched position, his skin white as satin, shiny with sweat, his breathing shallow and ragged. 'Was he like this when you arrived?' She bent low, her hand on the man's shoulder. He was freezing.

The woman nodded.

Helen pressed her lips together. Having spent the first part of the morning answering the phones, she hadn't seen this patient arrive. If she had, she wouldn't have dismissed him to the waiting room, she'd have called one of the doctors. It was clear he was very sick. Who, and she was thinking fast, had been on the desk this morning? 'Are you in pain?' she said.

He managed a nod. 'Where am I?'

'OK.' Helen straightened up, no doubt now about the urgency of the situation. 'I'll be right back.'

THE FIRST DOOR she knocked at was Dr Ross's. She didn't wait for an answer, before opening it and sticking her head in. 'We have an emergency,' she said. And then Dr Ross was on her feet and a minute later she was eye to eye with the patient, removing her glasses, examining him, standing again and moving Helen just far enough away, so Helen felt she could whisper, 'Sepsis?' without the either the man or his wife overhearing.

Dr Ross nodded. 'I'm going to call an ambulance. Can you print off an encounter report?'

'Of course.'

'An ambulance?' the woman said, her face draining of colour.

'Try not to worry,' Helen hurried back across the waiting

room. As she reached the door she turned back. 'Can I have your attention please?' she called to the dozen or so heads that had looked up. 'There is a phones policy in here. Please observe it!' And she raised an arm stiff with anger to point at the sign.

10

The bin in the corner of Kay's classroom overflowed with photocopies, and the walls were bare. She'd taken down her maths jokes poster (Why was the equal sign so humble? Because it knew it wasn't greater than anyone else), and her Shakuntala Devi quote: "Without mathematics, there's nothing you can do." Whoever came in next would replace them with their own jokes and quotes (she hoped). In a classroom fast becoming unfamiliar, only the whiteboard still showed the evidence of who she had been. There it was, her very last equation, written in patchy marker, lingering on now like hieroglyphics in a buried tomb.

$3 (2) + 4 2 = c^2$
$9 + 16 = c \ square$
$25 = c \ square$
$c = 5$

. . .

$$9 + 16 = c^2$$
$$25 = c^2$$
$$c = 5$$

IN A BURST OF ENERGY, she took the eraser and wiped the equation clean, then she popped the lid off the marker-pen and wrote out more numbers, the ink squeaking its resistance as she scribbled.

52 + 8
  23
  3
  - 5% (estimate)
  50% average < 5
  =

WHEN SHE HAD FINISHED, she stood back, the pen pressed against her lip, the familiar acrid smell of marker ink, filling her nose. She didn't have the answer to this problem. How could she, when she wasn't able to write the last part. *How many years left?* That's what she was reaching for. A definitive answer, that would enable her to calculate how and where she should spend the rest of her life. It would be easy then. Ten or more, and the joke corner would be back up. Five or less, then of course it was time to go and sit in the sun. The sound of laughter filtered through the open window. It was young and easy, and it scattered her thoughts, like wind scatters leaves. She turned to look. Three girls, hair swinging, walked across the school forecourt. They had clustered together like cells on a slide, their shoulders tipped forward in laughter, conjoined by the sheer enjoyment of the moment. She recognised the girls as students she had taught the previous year. Still children then, they were teenagers now, would-be adults stepping into the first summer they would remember for the rest of their lives, the one that might include a first kiss. Who wouldn't be laughing?

Turning back to the rows of empty chairs, her throat went hard. How had she got through the day? Right up until the last bell of her last lesson, she had kept her composure. Even as they'd had barrelled past … *Bye Miss Burrell! We'll miss you, Miss Burrell!* … *Enjoy your retirement, Miss Burrell!* Even when little Paul Emberson, for whom she'd always had a soft spot on account of his body's evident refusal to embrace puberty, had stood in the doorway and called out in his fluting, unbroken voice, *See you in September, Miss Burrell,* she had only nodded and whispered a hoarse, *No you won't.*

Her fingers were slack as she looked at the clock. The class had ended quarter of an hour ago, after which she'd spent at least ten minutes folded over her desk in a weeping, sodden heap. Thank goodness no-one had come in. Nick, her headteacher, she guessed was giving her space before the 'small reception' he'd organised in the staffroom.

Thinking this, Kay turned to her handbag, took out her phone, opened the camera and flipped the lens so she could see her own face. What a mess. What a bloated, splotched mess she was. If it had been left to her, she would have just exited stage right. No fanfare, no fuss. But Nick had insisted, and she knew he was right. There would be people waiting in that staffroom now who had shown her nothing but kindness and support throughout what had been a tough year. Some she would always stay in touch with. It was right to take the time to say goodbye. She put her hand on her chest and took a deep and difficult breath. The teaching of her last lesson, the good wishes, the waving goodbyes had taken the wind out of her. Doing it all over again with grown-ups suddenly felt too much.

She was still thinking this when a small tentative rap tripped through the empty room. Startled, Kay turned. 'Come in,' she called and watched as the door inched open.

'Miss Burrell?'

As she blinked the boy in the doorway blinked back: Zachary Woods.

'Come in, Zach,' she said quietly, watching as he stepped in, his body tense with nerves. He had grown, but then again, she was thinking, she hadn't seen him much recently. It had been two years since his mother had filed an official complaint against Kay, accusing her of unconscious bias towards him. A swiftly taken decision on the part of Mrs Woods, which had led to a permanent stain on Kay's otherwise unblemished career, a mandatory unconscious-bias training session (in her free time), and worst of all, Zach separated from his friends and moved to a different maths class. Where, she had heard, he had struggled. But she'd been sick, had had a lot of time away and, in the meantime - her hand went to her mouth – the boy that he was, had grown into this nearly-man, someone she might pass on the street in another few years and never even know. This young soul, who at one time had kept her awake at night, as she'd tried to understand if she really was guilty of what she had been accused. 'Come in,' she said again, because he was still standing in the doorway. And then she was asking herself, how often had this already happened? How many of her former pupils had she unknowingly brushed shoulders with? Men and women, who were once boys and girls in over-sized blazers, with over-sized teeth. She bit down on her lip. How fleeting life was. How brutally fleeting.

'I wanted to give you this,' Zach said, holding up a package. And even from where he stood, because he had only managed two steps, Kay could see the care that had been taken with the wrapping, the neat bow on top. 'Someone said you were moving to Cyprus.'

As she took the present, she smiled. 'I'm certainly thinking about it.' And for a moment they both stood looking at the package in her hands.

'I thought it might be useful,' Zach murmured.

'Shall I open it?'

He nodded.

She slid her thumb underneath the join and pulled the paper apart, her hand settling on the smooth gloss of a book. '*Undiscovered Cyprus*,' she read as she held it up. 'What a thoughtful present. Zach, thank you.'

'I just wanted ...' His voice trailed off, his chin dropping as he knitted his hands together. He was, Kay saw, already inching back, a battlefield of emotion raging across his face. 'You were the best teacher I ever had Miss Burrell,' he said his voice thick with tears, 'And I hope you have a nice retirement.' And he was gone, the door swinging shut behind him.

Tears in her own eyes, Kay stood watching the door. For all his height, Zach was still a boy, and she didn't, not for a moment, underestimate the courage that it had taken him to come. Nor the thoughtfulness of the gift, which she was sure his mother would have been unaware of. *Undiscovered Cyprus*. She flicked the book open to a page with a photograph of turquoise water and creamy white cliffs. A place of perpetual summer, where someone in a leopard-print bikini might start their day with a swim and a fresh orange juice, and as she thought this, peals of laughter rang through the window again. The girls on the forecourt had lingered. *Go.* Kay looked up. She wanted to lean out of the window and shout at them. *Go! Run to your summer, it won't ever come again!* She closed the book and turning back to the white-board, stood looking at the numbers of her life.

52 years and 8 months old.

23 months since diagnosis

3 months since the last scan

NSD (NO SIGN OF DISEASE) Five percent reduction (overall) in size and number of tumours.

50 percent average chance of living longer than five years.

It didn't matter how many times she wrote it out, it didn't matter what order the equation, she would never have the answer. No-one did and no-one ever would and the only thing to do in life was to show the kind of courage Zach had. She picked up the eraser. When it was all over, when the good wishes and the speeches were finished, she would go home to her quiet house and try on that bikini. She went to wipe the board clean and as she did, the door swung open again, whoever it was this time not bothering to knock. Kay turned. 'Craig?'

'Sorry I'm late, Ms Burrell.' Grinning, Craig slipped into the room and sat down at a desk near the front. He was a former pupil from years back whom she'd met again when he came to work as a carer for her mother. Thank goodness, he'd stayed on to help with her father. He was, by far, the best carer they had had: hopeless with numbers, brilliant with compassion.

'What are you doing here?'

'I've come to learn some maths.' He nodded at the whiteboard.

'Well, you're ten years too late.' She frowned. 'What's going on? Where's Dad?'

'Don't panic.' Craig smiled. 'Your dad's fine. He's gone ahead to the staffroom. We thought we'd surprise you and stop by. You can have a drink then, can't you? And I can drive back.'

'It's just a quick goodbye thing,' she said. 'Nothing to get excited about.'

'Well personally I can't wait.' Craig tapped out a drum-roll on the desk. 'I've never been in the *staffroom* before.'

And despite herself, despite the waves of doubt and sadness that had threatened all day, Kay laughed. 'You've never been in the staffroom? All the years you were here?'

'Nope.'

'It's nothing special,' she said as she turned to clean the board. 'A cross between an Ikea showroom and a doctor's waiting room. And besides,' she added, looking over her shoulder, 'you're in the wrong seat. You always sat at the back, it's probably why you never learned anything.'

11

By the time Helen had printed the encounter report, handed it to Dr Ross and watched the ambulance doors close, her shift was over. She went into the kitchen to rinse her cup and collect her jacket. She was thinking about the way panic had undone the very fabric of the man's wife, like wool unravelled. It was a feeling she understood. She knew how it felt to dissolve under the force of extreme fear, the cold acidic wash of it. The last few weeks of her mother's life she had been no more stable than a loose thread and it was (always) a miracle to Helen how, in time, everything had knitted together again, how she had, slowly, been incorporated back into her life. Her mind had re-learned how to rest, her body to sleep. Even her sense of humour had come back. Remembering all this, she felt suddenly very tired and very sad. She popped the cup in the dishwasher, took her jacket from the peg and stood looking at the green cardigan. She hadn't been joking when she said it had been here longer than she had. Daisy hadn't been joking either, when she'd said she hadn't noticed. Daisy, who spent her breaks staring at TikTok, whose manicured nails and perfect eyebrows and contoured nose, gave away a personal care regime that required discipline and attention to detail, the same kind of attention she'd failed to bother with this morning. Because it had been Daisy, she remembered now, who had been on the desk earlier. Helen's mouth turned down. It had been Daisy who had sent that man through to wait for over an hour, Daisy who was only interested in a free lunch. That man could have died, might still die. She yanked the cardigan free from the peg and dropped it into the bin and just as she did, the door opened, and Dr Ross came in. 'It's been there years,' she said, as she looked at the cardigan.

But Dr Ross didn't speak.

And neither did Helen. The expression on the doctor's face, she could see now, was a mix of shock and fatigue. She was obviously still processing what had happened, as well she might. Dr Ross was a partner; claims of neglect against the health centre, accusations of professional ineptitude, stopped with her. 'Has the ambulance left?' she said quietly.

'Yes,' she said, still distracted. She took her glasses off and rubbed her eye. 'That was well spotted, Helen' she said, as she put them back on. 'He shouldn't have been left like that.'

'No.' Helen bit down on her lip. Dr Ross had turned to look at the cardigan now, the heap of it lying at the top of the bin. 'I hope it wasn't yours?' she said. 'I didn't think it belonged to anyone ... It really has been here years.'

'As long as the copy of *Good Housekeeping*, outside my room?' Dr Ross smiled.

'Oh, I don't know. How long has that been there?'

'It's dated March 2017.'

'Then the cardigan wins.'

Dr Ross nodded. 'Are you heading straight off?' she said. 'I'm going to make a coffee. Would you like to join me?'

THEY CARRIED their cups out to the inner courtyard of the surgery to sit under the wide-spoked branches of a plane tree. From here, Helen could see all four sides of the surgery. The waiting room, the doctors' consultancy rooms, the corridor that joined them and behind, if she turned, the front reception desk. She didn't turn. She sat under the umbrella of green, her face tilted to the sun, her eyes closed. Beside her, Dr Ross was silent and understanding the shape of the moment, Helen too stayed quiet. Close up, serious illness is frightening, a mangled, ugly tear in the fabric of an otherwise smooth world and the only way to allow the fissure to close again, was to do was exactly as they were. Sit in the sun and wait it out.

Minutes passed, above her head, hidden amongst thousands of leaves, she could hear the rhythmic chirrup of sparrows, from the open windows the muted but constant sound of a phone ringing. She opened her eyes.

'So,' Dr Ross said. 'How was your trip, Helen?'

Helen nodded. She drew in a deep breath, her shoulders rising. In the five hours she had been back at work, this was the first time anyone had asked. And it wasn't just the girls. A couple of the doctors had stalked past her with nothing more than a curt nod, as if she had simply walked out the door for five minutes and come back again. Which, she thought bleakly, she might as well have done. 'Transformational,' she said, looking across the courtyard. 'Quite transformational.'

Dr Ross smiled. 'You'll have to tell me all about it.'

Helen shook her head. 'Honestly? I wouldn't know where to start.'

'Did you do much trekking?'

'Lots.'

'In the Rockies?'

She nodded. 'And Yosemite, Canyonlands, Redwood National Park, Glacier Park.' Pushing her hair back, she turned. 'Did you know that two-thirds of the glaciers in Glacier Park have melted? Fifty years ago, there were over eighty, it's about twenty-five now. It's so sad.'

'It is, yes.'

'Actually, it's more than sad.' Helen shook her head. 'It's outrageous, and no-one seems to care. You know, you're the first person since I got back, who has even asked how my trip was. Cake apparently is far more interesting than global warming! Cake ––' As abruptly as she had started, she stopped. 'I'm sorry,' she murmured. 'I shouldn't have said that I ...' But her voice drifted off and her hands were clumsy as she put her cup down and bought them together under her chin. She felt oddly exposed in front of this young woman, who was also her senior. She shouldn't have spoken like that. She should have politely refused the offer of coffee and just gone home, put it all behind her, Daisy's callous incompetence, the man's terrified eyes, that leaden lump of cake.

'Helen?' Dr Ross put her hand on Helen's arm. 'Are you OK?'

No. Lips pressed tight together, hand at her mouth, Helen shook her head. She did not feel OK. The strangeness of earlier, that feeling of having stepped into someone else's life had not diminished. What was she doing here? Where else should she be? Caro and Kay were taking huge steps forward, while she – it couldn't be denied – was taking a giant step back.

'Is it difficult?' Dr Ross said. 'Coming back?'

'More than I imagined.' Helen gave a short harsh laugh. 'Ironically, just as I'm returning, one of my best friends is retiring.'

'I see.' Dr Ross nodded. 'Are you thinking you'd like to?'

'God no!' she said. The question was like a poker, prodding her upright. 'If anything, I'm feeling the exact opposite. I feel like I haven't even started.' And as she looked at Dr Ross, Helen's smile was small, almost apologetic. 'I never meant to be here longer than twelve months.'

Dr Ross smiled back. 'I understand. Perhaps it's time to move on?'

'I'd like to.' Helen sighed. 'But at my age? Who's going to take a fifty-two-year-old woman with an unfinished PhD in Medieval History and limited technology skills?' As she finished talking, she looked up and across the courtyard. She'd never said that before, never nailed down what had been a jelly-like worry for years. She would, very much, like to move on; she just didn't know how. She hadn't known how when Libby had started sixth form and then left for university, and she was none the wiser now Jack too was gone. And, judging by the silence, Dr Ross couldn't point her in the right direction either. She lifted her chin to the sun and closed her eyes again. She felt wholly lost. The world had changed, and the window of time in which she might have had a career, might have put to good use her education and hard-earned knowledge, had long since closed. Heading towards her mid-fifties, and without the financial cushion now to re-train, it was a supermarket till, or the health-centre.

'You're asking the wrong question, Helen.'

Helen opened her eyes.

'You should,' Dr Ross said, 'be asking who is going to snap up a smart woman with no familial responsibilities and a decade's worth of experience in primary healthcare – which, by the way, shows itself clearly in emergency situations, as we have both just witnessed. *And* ...' Dr Ross raised a hand. 'Before you give your response, it's a question I think I can answer. I have a friend working in primary health care. In Bolivia.'

'Bolivia!' Helen laughed. 'Bolivia?'

Dr Ross nodded. 'The NGO he works for has just been awarded a grant to open two more clinics. They're actively looking for admin staff.'

Helen shook her head. 'It's nice of you,' she started. 'But ... well ... I mean, first off, I don't speak Spanish.'

Now it was Dr Ross's turn to laugh. 'You wouldn't need to,' she said. 'Right now, Christian just needs someone experienced and capable to get things up and running. Local staff would take over later.'

'No.' And again Helen shook her head. 'I couldn't. I couldn't do that.'

'I think you could.' Dr Ross held her eye. 'I didn't need to see what I've just seen to know how capable you are.'

'I'm too o ...' She pressed her lips together, before the sound could escape *old. I'm too old.*

'It would involve much of the same work you do here, Helen.'

'It would?'

Dr Ross nodded. 'Record-keeping. Helping prioritise patients. Running clinics, vaccination programmes. Doctors really depend on good admin staff and you, Helen, are very good at what you do.'

Helen didn't speak.

'I think you would find it very rewarding.'

Still, she didn't speak.

'Would you like me to make an introduction?' Dr Ross smiled. 'I know Christian very well, we were at medical school together.

Stretching her legs out, Helen looked down at her cup. 'My son still has a year left at university,' she said. 'And my daughter, Libby, well you know she has a young child.'

'It would just be an introduction, Helen. It might give you an idea of what your options are.'

Helen nodded. A minute ago, her options had seemed bleak. Not that she could take a job in Bolivia. Jack was still at university. Ben was …

'So that's a yes then.'

'Yes,' she said quietly. 'That's a yes.'

12

As the train began to slow, Caro stood and reached to take her wedding dress down from the luggage rack. She placed the bag on the empty table and laid a hand over the smooth white packaging, watching as the platform of Londale station slid into view and the dark peaks of the Lake District rose up like walls. *I would have loved to.* Why did she say that? *I'm getting married in three weeks.* Why didn't she say that?

Off the train, she trundled her suitcase through the bricked archway of the station, parked it against the wall and opened her handbag. She'd had two percent left on her phone when she'd boarded in London which hadn't concerned her until she realised there wasn't a charging point to be found. Feeling the cool smoothness of glass, she eased the phone out, relief rising as she glanced at the same two percent. She tapped in her code, swiped to open and the screen went black. Exasperated, she squeezed the on/off button, put it back in her handbag, took it out ... and it was still black.

In the pit of her stomach, panic unfolded. Which was

ridiculous. She was a middle-aged woman, at a Cumbrian railway station, in the broad daylight of a July afternoon. This wasn't the wilds of Siberia. She wasn't stuck in the Amazon. And anyway, hadn't she spent the best part of the last thirty years getting herself halfway across the globe and back? Albeit in a lot more style than the scruffy, unconnected train carriage she'd just spent the last three and a half hours in. Still, a taxi would be handy. Pulling at her bottom lip she scanned the rectangle of cracked tarmac that passed as a carpark. Bar a transit van with a flat tyre and a sprinkling of decaying petals across the windshield, there wasn't a vehicle in sight and the few passengers who had disembarked with her, had already vanished. So that left her alone with no taxis, no bus stop and no way of getting home ... except. She lifted her sunglasses, frowning as she squinted across to the other side of the station. A phone box! Caro smiled. A good old-fashioned phone box. She hadn't used one in years, but it was like riding a bike, wasn't it? Once upon a time her wallet had been stuffed with phone cards: Singapore dollars, American dollars, Japanese Yen. She'd been a traveller of the world, prepared and resourceful and, she was sure, she had a few coins in her purse still. Light with relief, she trundled her case across, yanked the door open and went to pick up the phone. But there was no phone. The gap where it should have been had been covered instead by a crocheted teddy bear, with dangling pom-poms. Alongside sat a pile of mouldy paperbacks, an empty box and a hand-written sign: *Donations welcome.*

Donations welcome, Caro mouthed. What was she supposed to do? What was anyone supposed to do in an emergency? Drop a pound into the box and read themselves home? Fuming she let the door swing shut, the idiocy of decorating what should have been an emergency resource with pom-poms fuelling her as she bumped her case across the carpark and started an angry stalk up the rise towards the high street.

But it was hot. So hot she could feel it on her scalp, and her suitcase rattled, and the plastic of her dress bag kept sticking to the bare flesh of her arm. Sweat trickled down her spine and on the back of her right ankle she could feel raw skin, as her Manolo Blahniks scraped a blister. She reached the chemist and paused. The windows were dark, a yellow *Closed* sign in the doorway ending any thoughts she had about popping in to buy a packet of plasters. Head down, she pushed on until a few minutes later flashes of orange swung into view, and she looked up to see the hanging baskets of the pub. Another five minutes then and she would be at the top of the hill, on the road out of Londale, to Hollybrook, and home. As she passed, she nodded at the three men sitting outside. It felt like the polite thing to do. There was no one else around and she was pretty conspicuous.

One of the men nodded back. 'Did some shopping in the big smoke?' He was looking at her dress bag.

Caro stopped, glanced over her shoulder and then looked back. Was he talking to her?

The man grinned. He raised his pint, and the other two did the same.

'Umm, yes, thank you,' she managed. Obviously, he was talking to her. Even though she'd never seen him before in her life and it was none of his business what she'd done ... in the big smoke.

'Hard on the wheels,' he said, looking at her suitcase.

'I'll manage.' Her smile was razor thin. Was this what passed as entertainment? It must be, because besides herself, the high-street was deserted. She gave them another curt nod, tightened her grip on her case and rattled past, her dress bag, flapping at her side like a broken wing.

TEN MINUTES LATER, turning her key in the door, she was still sweating and still smarting about a telephone box covered in pom-poms, a chemist shop that kept archaic opening hours, and a stranger asking if she'd been shopping. She turned the handle, stepped inside and was instantly hit by the sweet and pungent punch of roasting meat. Thirty-degree heat, and Tomasz was cooking a roast dinner? She kicked off her pumps and turned to the mirror, the first time she had looked at herself since she'd left London. Her face was tomato red and her hair lank, semi-circles of sweat staining the arms of her blouse. It was hard to believe she was the same woman. The woman at the centre of a stage in the sky, the one who had said, *I would have loved to.*

'Why didn't you call?' At the end of the hallway, Tomasz appeared. He was barefoot, his toes pale and hairy against the quarry tiling.

Caro stared. It hadn't escaped her that here, at Holly-brook, Tomasz was always barefoot, whereas at her London flat (as if his clothing had been asked to reflect his status as a visitor), he'd keep both his socks and his work sweatshirt on. How quickly, by comparison, he had made himself at home. She smiled, remembering how after his last shift, he'd thrown all three of those horrible sweatshirts in the bin, which although it had been amusing, wasn't something she intended doing with her Max Mara suits or her Manolo Blahnik pumps. It wasn't the same of course. Tomasz had hated his job. Besides, he had no occasion any more for a

FarmFresh sweatshirt, whereas a Max Mara suit? There would always be a place and time. Or there should be.

'If you'd rung, I would have collected you,' he said.

She looked up. 'My phone went dead, and there were no chargers on the train.' She dumped her handbag on the table. 'And pom-poms instead of a phone.'

'Pom-poms?'

'Don't ask,'

'I'll get you a gin and tonic.' Spatula in hand, Tomasz kissed her cheek. 'How did it go? Come and tell me all about it.'

'It went really —' But she didn't get to the end of her sentence because turning into the low beamed kitchen, she was knocked back by a wave of heat so solid she felt her earlobes tingle. A huge pan stood on the Aga, steam rising. 'What are you making?' she gasped. The kitchen table was covered with empty jars and in front of the sink, the compost bin overflowed with peelings.

'Courgette and tomato sauce.'

'More?' Caro wiped her brow. She'd spent two days last week harvesting courgettes, chopping, sterilising, bottling.

Tomasz grinned. 'They grow quickly, Caro. I'm using some for dinner, with pork.'

'OK.' She took a glass and filled it with water. She could barely look at a courgette, let alone eat one. 'Can we turn it off?' she said, nodding at the Aga. The heat was palpable, even from where she stood, six feet away she could feel it on her legs.

Tomasz shook his head. 'If we turn it off, we'll have to get it serviced to turn it back on again. That will cost hundreds, you know this.'

Hundreds. Caro gulped the water back. The skincare she had bought at the spa had cost three hundred pounds and a few hours ago she was mingling to the tune of millions. She held the glass against her cheek, its coolness stinging. 'That would be OK, wouldn't it?' she said. 'It's just getting so hot in here and I don't think the weather's going to break anytime soon.'

Tomasz looked at her and as he did, they both felt the gulf. The difference between the person who would say what she just had, and the person who would never have said it.

'We can't. This needs to be done now. Nothing will keep, you know.'

'I know.' There was a ripple of irritation in her voice. Tomasz had grown up on a farm and all through this process, she had ceded to his superior knowledge. It was just that, sometimes his superior knowledge was irritating. She knew vegetables didn't keep, of course she did.

'Dinner at six?' he said as he wiped his hands on a tea towel. 'And I'll see if I can turn the Aga down, OK?'

'Perfect. I'll get changed.' But she wasn't even slightly hungry, and grabbing her bag from the hall, she hurried up the stairs, aiming for the coolness of the bedroom, as far away as she could get from the heat of the kitchen.

13

As Kay walked along the narrow corridor that led to the school staffroom, a walk she had done thousands of times, the eyes of hundreds of children watched her. From the fresh faces of year sixes, all shiny hair and rounded cheeks, to the long limbs and awkward smiles of year elevens, all of them forever young behind the functional glass photo frames that held them. Because to walk from the potted fern that marked the beginning of the corridor, to the faded notice stuck to the staffroom door: *Staff only,* was to pass through a permanent exhibition in the fleeting nature of time.

It wasn't that she'd failed to notice, more that it hadn't always had the effect it had now. As a newly qualified teacher, rushing in for a swift coffee break, arms full of papers, she'd looked at the photos without seeing them. She'd been so young herself and was yet to experience the swift cycle of the school years once, let alone twice, let alone thirty years' worth. But it didn't take long. Five years in and the air would stick in her throat, as she realised the laughing face of an eleven-year-old she was looking at, had morphed into the sullen, scowl of a fifteen-year-old. And then there were the years that the walk had been almost impassable - the year she'd had to take Alex out of mainstream education, the lonely years after her marriage broke down, the first weeks of her cancer diagnosis, episodes when what she had thought was the solid reality of her life, had proven to be glass after all, shattering as easy as a bauble. Those times, she had kept her head down. What else could she do?

As she stopped in front of the year-eight photograph, her own class, her last class, she put her hand to her mouth.

'You haven't aged a bit,' Craig said kindly. 'I've got one of these at home and you look exactly the same.'

'Don't ...' she started and waved her hand. This was ridiculous! If she could no longer walk this corridor without crumbling under the weight of nostalgia, it was time to move on. The thought was as unexpected as it was welcome, like a door opened to let in a cool breeze. She blinked her eyes dry and turned to Craig. 'Are you ready?' Yes, maybe it really was time.

'It's very quiet,' Craig whispered as he looked at the closed door ahead. 'Doesn't sound much like a party.'

'It'll be a few paper cups of warm white wine and some Pringles,' Kay whispered back. 'Don't say I didn't warn you.'

'I don't care.' He grinned. 'I just want to see the staffroom'.

'OK,' she said. 'Let's do it!' And she pushed the door open.

The wall of noise that hit her was physical. It had her gripping the door handle, as her jaw went slack and her mind, for a brief extraordinary moment, was wiped clean with astonishment. Never, she thought (when sense returned), had she seen so many people, packed into such a small space. From the entrance to the wall opposite, the staffroom was a sea of smiling faces. All of whom she recognised. Nick, her headmaster, a head taller than anyone else, stood right at the front, his arm raised high in a welcome salute, a paper cup in his hand. There was Emma the school secretary, and Michael and Suzanne from the board of governors who had been such a support to her through the difficult months of Zach's mother's complaint. And Wendy and Marion from the canteen, and, Oh! Kay covered her mouth. Not just Wendy and Marion, *all* the girls from the canteen were here. And over to the side, Joanna the scattiest funniest drama teacher, who'd moved schools years ago, and Dan, who she had mentored in his very first term, who had also left years ago. The room was a montage of her teaching career, from the very beginning to the very end. Colleagues who had retired themselves, colleagues who had only started at the school this last year. All of them gathered here, for her. Just for her? With her hand still at her mouth, she shook her head, only a tangible force of goodwill and good wishes keeping her upright. 'I don't believe it,' she whispered and because she couldn't say anything else, 'I don't believe it. I just don't believe it.' She felt her cheeks warm. This party, *her* party, had been planned, had been discussed and organised. People had gone out of their way, used up their own precious time, contacting and arranging and discussing. For *her*.

Nick stepped forward. He had a second paper cup in his hand now, which he handed to her.

'How did you find ...' But again, words failed. She took the cup. Nick had only been at the school for five years. How did he know about Joanna? Dan too had left before he'd even started.

'Someone helped me with the names,' he said, as if he had read her mind. 'Would you like to meet her?'

'Her?'

'The person who helped me find everyone.'

'Yes ...I ...' Kay frowned. She felt utterly confused, reeling with a shock that was softening to delight.

'Here she is.'

And suddenly the crowd parted like a biblical sea to reveal a tiny woman, leaning on a walking frame. She was dressed in a smart blue cardigan and tweed trousers, her hands splattered with dark liver spots. Her back was rounded as a question mark and, when she lifted her chin, her head shook, but her eyes were stars of intelligence. Exactly as Kay had remembered them. 'Lizzie!' she gasped.

Elizabeth Parsons, her first (and best) headmaster, stretched a hand forward. 'Kay.'

The tears started again, swifter than ever, unstoppable. 'I can't believe you're here,' she gasped.

Lizzie laughed. 'I wouldn't have missed this for the world, Kay. You were always my favourite teacher.'

'And you were always my favourite head.' Looking at Nick, she mouthed, 'No offence.'

He held his hand up. 'None taken.'

'And to think you were just going to sneak off, love.'

At the sound of her father's voice, Kay turned. There he was, with his own paper cup, dressed in his navy suit, wearing a white shirt and a patterned tie. And the sight of him, so smart, cracked open a vault in her mind shining light upon the only words of poetry she'd ever managed to commit to her mathematical mind: *Joy and woe are woven fine.* Because the last time she'd seen her father in his suit was at her mother's funeral, nearly a year ago now. Blake's words rolled past, the truth of them echoing on. Life was varied, its light and shade as unpredictable as it was unavoidable.

'I'm glad I didn't,' she said as she turned and beamed at all the faces in the room, beaming back at her. 'I'm so glad I didn't.'

14

———

Back home, Helen dumped her handbag in the hall and her Tesco shopping bag on the kitchen table. In the bedroom, she pulled off her work blouse, threw it on the bed and picked up a t-shirt from the floor. As she pulled it over her head she laughed. She was turning into her son. *Jack,* she yelled, ready to share the joke. But the name echoed off the walls. *Jack,* she whispered. *Libby?* No-one answered. Jack was still in Florida, and Libby was in her own home, with her own baby.

She wandered back into the kitchen and stood looking at the glossy white cabinets and quartz worktops, the mirrored surface of the induction hob, the gleaming stainless-steel hood. All those years of piled dishes and sticky surfaces, how often had she wished for a kitchen as clean as this. Now she had it, she wasn't remotely interested in using it. She went to the fridge, opened it and stood staring at the contents. With no Jack and his abhorrence of anything fish related, and no Lawrence with his high protein/ low carb demands she could have whatever she wanted for dinner. She didn't, she found, want anything. She shut the door and as she turned once again to face her empty flat, it felt to Helen like she was waiting for something. It felt like the flat was waiting too.

I could run a vaccination programme standing on my head, she said. Was that it? Was that what this unspoken air of anticipation was about?

Silence grew, snaking up her legs, tingling at her fingertips, brushing the back of her neck. Her fingers played at her lip. The flat looked different. Before her trip it had been full of exciting things like visa forms and hiking clothing, a stack of camping utensils she'd invested so much time researching and buying. Now it was blank walls, and unpacked boxes full of all the things she had walked out of her marriage with. Things that it turned out she hadn't missed, wasn't sure where she would put, and was beginning to wonder if she even wanted. The trip, it was clear, hadn't so much as given her a focus, as bestowed her with tunnel vision. So much so that moving into this flat hadn't even felt like a move. It had felt like a pit-stop. *Helen.* She dropped her hand to the table, tapping out a tiny gallop with her fingertips. Could she really run a vaccination programme? *Helen, Helen, Helen.*

She went back to the fridge, opened it, stared again at the contents and closed it. She had no idea what to do next, because (and the shock was extraordinary as the realisation dawned), she had never done this before. No, that was ridiculous! Wasn't it? Arms crossed, she went to stand by the window, her brow creased with concentration.

Had she done this before? At eighteen, she'd gone from her parents' home, to university halls of residence, to a shared flat, to another shared flat in London, to living with Lawrence, to living with Lawrence and their children and, at various times, three dogs, one cat and an indestructible rabbit. So astonishing as it was, it was looking like she really hadn't done this before: never completed an ordinary day, at an ordinary job before coming back to an empty home, with nothing more to look forward to other than repetition. The weeks leading up to her trip didn't count, then she had a destination, then she knew where she was going. Now, she didn't have a clue. She tipped her head back and stared at the ceiling. How had she not anticipated this? All those months battling for a divorce, looking for her escape, how had she not seen, or at least prepared for this? How (and the thought was a hammer), had Caro done this for so long?

Caro led to Kay, and Kay she remembered anew, was retiring today. Immediately, Helen went to her bag, took out her phone and called. But the number rang out. She cut the call. It would have been a tough day for Kay, and the last thing she would want, or need, was to listen to Helen regurgitate how awful her own day had been. Tapping the phone on her chin, she looked at the clock. It wasn't too late to try Caro. She could test out the Bolivia idea. But Caro's phone rang out as well, and sighing Helen cut that call too. Caro would be out digging carrots or something. Her children were off living their lives, and she could hardly call Lawrence. Who could she talk to? A lump caught in her throat. Where had everyone gone? Standing in the middle of her sunny living-room, it felt to Helen as if she had turned her back for five minutes and everyone had vanished. *I could do it,* she whispered, went back to the kitchen, uncorked a bottle of wine, poured herself a giant bowl of crisps and, ice-cubes sloshing in the glass, went out to the balcony.

Across the road in the park, she watched as a woman laid out a blanket. Nearby a man played football with a tiny boy. They were obviously a young family, making the most of this glorious evening. She kicked her shoes off and stretched her feet out to the empty chair opposite, her toes waggling in the warm air. A year ago, during the dark days of trying to decide if she should stay in her marriage, or leave, this was the image that she had clung to. The view from this balcony across to the park. Picturing herself, with a coffee on a Sunday morning, a few pots of begonias and tomatoes, a stylish patio set and Radio Four burbling away in the background. Those had been the first baby steps to a new life. The images that had kept her floating when storms of guilt had threatened to capsize. But she'd learned to walk now. More, she'd flown across a continent, putting thousands of miles between herself and Radio Four, and images she couldn't have imagined then, were opening now because she *could* run a vaccination programme, she just knew she could.

15

'Congratulations, Kay!'

'You can go to the toilet whenever you like now. Don't have to wait for the bell.'

'You know what happened to me? I got my coffee table back. No more piles of exercise books. Ever.'

EVERYONE WANTED to talk to her, and she wanted to talk to everyone, of course she did. But her face was beginning to feel tight from smiling.

'AT LEAST YOU won't have to deal with a husband. You know what mine did? First day of his retirement he came into the kitchen and told me I was loading the washing machine wrong.'

'MINE STARTED RE-ARRANGING the kitchen cupboards. I couldn't reach anything. He didn't think of that of course.'

.   .   .

'So, what will you do? I heard Cyprus was on the cards?'

With every new conversation Kay found herself repeating the same lines: 'Well I have a friend there. I'm going out in a few weeks; it's just a reconnaissance.' And every time the words sounded less real, as if she was reading a part in a play. If only she had kept them in her head, secret and safe from this universal enthusiasm she didn't quite share. It made her feel like a fraud. It was making her face ache even more.

'I'm just going to get a quick top-up,' she said to a tall man with flushed cheeks and a single tuft of surprisingly long grey hair. Patrick, a retired history teacher who she'd always liked, but who she suspected was on the verge of launching into a long and extremely detailed explanation of the history of Cyprus.

'I'll get it.' Patrick stretched his hand out for her paper cup. 'Can't have you serving yourself. It's your party.'

'It's OK.' In an awkward but swift movement, Kay drew her arm tight to her chest. 'I have to check up on my dad,' she said, turning way before Partick could insist.

But making her way across the room, was to battle through an onslaught of congratulations and hugs, so by the time she reached the drinks table, she really did need a top-up.

'Over here,' Craig mouthed, waving from where he stood at the far end of the table.

Kay smiled. He was pouring wine for a couple of the canteen ladies, chatting away as if he'd known them all his life. At the other end of the table, seated next to each other were her father and Lizzie, chatting away – Kay smiled – as if they too, were old friends.

'So,' she said as she reached Craig, and handed him her cup. 'What do you think of the staffroom?'

'Noisy, aren't they?' Craig said. 'Teachers, I mean.'

Kay picked up a sausage roll, cupping her hand at her chin as she looked the nodding heads and waving arms of what, she had to agree, was an increasingly rowdy bunch of teachers.

'I've been talking to your old headmistress. Lizzie.' Craig handed her a full cup of wine. 'She's hilarious. She was telling me how she used to end parents' evening.'

'By getting the janitor to turn out the lights?' Kay laughed. 'That was last century, Craig.'

'Can you imagine that nowadays?'

'No.' She took a sip of lukewarm wine. 'Unfortunately, I can't.'

'And I heard about how you used to celebrate the end of term.'

'Well teachers like to party too, Craig.' Kay smiled.

'I even showed her how to use this.' He held his phone up. It was open at Spotify. 'She was really interested. She likes Queen.'

Kay nodded. 'I remember, and I must go over and chat. I haven't seen her in years.'

'QUITE A MARK OF RESPECT,' her father said, as she approached. He nodded at the table. 'I hope you're proud.'

'Oh, Dad.' But as Kay turned to look, she had to admit it was a good spread. A lot more than the Pringles and warm white wine she had been expecting. Nick hadn't just pushed the boat out; he'd launched a whole flotilla for her party.

And, if it was possible to count respect in sausage rolls and mini quiches (in her world it was), then yes, she was brimming over with pride.

'Your father's right,' Lizzie said. 'You're very well thought of, and rightly so.'

Kay smiled. The noise level in the room was loud so she bent to lower herself to speak nearer Lizzie's ears. As she did, her knee clicked louder than a castanet and she had to jerk upright again.

'Get a chair,' her father said.

'That,' Kay muttered as she pulled a chair into place, 'is the first thing I'm going to do. Yoga lessons.'

Lizzie chuckled. 'That's what I said.'

'And did you?'

'Noooo.' Holding her cup at her lips, Lizzie shook her head. 'I did lots of other things, but I never did get round to yoga.'

'That's what I wanted to ask you.' She didn't pause. 'What's it been like, Lizzie? I don't think I ever met anyone as dedicated to their career as you. What did you do? How did you fill your time? Did you miss it?' Question after question tumbled out, her voice rising with each one. The quizzical look in Lizzie's face, made the colour rise in her own. Kay stopped talking and looked down. She felt silly, like a child scared of a trip to the dentist, *Will it be all right? Tell me I'll be all right.*

'Kay?'

'I'm OK,' she managed, as she lifted her chin to look at her father. 'I'm OK.' But he wasn't fooled, and neither she could see, was Lizzie. And why would they be? She watched as without a word Lizzie stretched her cup towards her father, and he leaned forward to take it.

'I'm OK,' she said, uselessly.

But Lizzie had her hands now, grasping them with the strength of feathers. 'There will always be things you'll miss,' she said, her head wobbling. 'Those moments when you saw the spark in their eyes and you realised, you'd got it right. I never stopped missing that, Kay and neither will you. Working with children is special. We've been lucky to have had that.'

'I'm scared,' she whispered. 'I didn't think I would be, but I really am.'

'And that's natural, Kay.' As Lizzie spoke, Kay felt the feeble squeeze of her hands. 'Will you take a little advice from someone who's been there?'

Kay nodded.

'Start saying yes. No matter how scared you are – say, yes. You can't spend all your life in this school.'

As the heavy truth of Lizzie's words pressed down, Kay's head dipped. It didn't matter how much time was left, how much was still in the bank. What mattered, what she needed to concentrate on, was how much had been spent. How much it had cost her. Enough, that's how much. When she'd started this job, she'd been twenty- two years old, she could do a full day in the classroom, go out in the evening, come back and mark books until midnight. She could wake up, leave the house in half an hour, be at her desk within the hour, and not forget a single thing along the way. She could still fit into size twelve jeans. Lizzie was right. She had to stop being scared.

'You always knew me as a spinster,' Lizzie said as she released Kay's hands.

Surprised, Kay looked up. 'I've never liked that word.'

'Neither do I.' Lizzie agreed. 'But it's the label I was given. I didn't intend it that way. I was engaged once.'

'You were?'

Lizzie nodded. 'We had the church booked. I had ordered my bouquet and chosen my dress.'

'What happened?'

'He got kidney disease.' The arrow of memory was blinding. It had Lizzie blinking and her eyes so bright before, misted over. 'This,' she said, 'was 1957.' 'There was no dialysis back then, no transplants. It was only a month from being diagnosed that he died.'

From the corner of her eye, Kay saw her father lower his chin. 'I never knew,' she whispered.

'I still have his letters. The last one he wrote was just two days before.'

She didn't speak. A decade of working alongside this formidable woman, and she had never known.

'Please go and live your life.' Lizzie smiled. 'That's what he wrote, Kay. That's what he ended the letter with. So, I did. I decided I needed to try as many things as possible, visit places, do things, have all the experiences he didn't.'

'I see.' Her throat was sore as she tried to swallow.

'And you know something, Kay?'

Kay shook her head. What did she know? Compared to Lizzie, what did she know?

'I've been retired nearly thirty years now. That's almost as long as I was working for. How about that?'

'How about that,' she echoed.

'So go, Kay. Go and live your life. I haven't been far in the last few years, but I've travelled the world since I retired. So, I haven't just lived one life, I've lived two. One for me and one for Gerry. That was his name.'

And as Lizzie finished speaking, her father leaned forward and silently handed the cup of wine back to her, and she silently received it. Like telepathy, Kay thought as she watched. She sat back in her chair, fenced off from the noise and the movement by her own thoughts. Thirty years? Did she also have that long? Because if she did, Lizzie was right. It was another lifetime.

'IF I MAY ... If I may just have a moment's silence!' Nick's voice boomed across the room like a sonic wave, loud and strong. But not loud and not strong enough, to cut through the chatter of what was now a crowd of very merry teachers.

'They're not very good at listening,' Craig mouthed from the other end of the table

Kay laughed.

'If I may just have a moment's silence!' He was standing on a chair now. *'If I may just say a few words.'*

The reluctance was tangible, but eventually the chatter receded.

'Everyone in this room,' Nick began, 'knows the dedication that Kay has shown to her work over the last thirty years.'

Murmured approval rippled through.

'Never more so,' Nick continued, 'than when she faced the difficulties of last year.'

As Kay's smile stuck, the ache in her jaw came back. She didn't want any public acknowledgement of her cancer. She didn't want to hear words like *battle* or *overcome.* It wasn't that she thought by not mentioning it, it ceased to exist. It was more that like a wound healed, the best course of action she had intuitively felt, was to leave well alone. It was better for everyone. She didn't mention it, they didn't ask. Her presence was enough. Back in the classroom, still here, still alive. Not much need, if any, for more. She wrapped both hands around her paper cup and looked down at her feet, deeply uncomfortable that after so many months of getting on quietly and privately, her health should now be made such a public thing.

Next to her, Lizzie reached across and patted her hand. Kay smiled. Lizzie understood. Lizzie who had also kept her heartache private.

'We've watched her battling through,' Nick boomed on.

'Can you get me over to that young man?' Lizzie said.

'What young man?' Confused Kay looked up. But Lizzie, she realised, wasn't talking to her. She was talking to Kay's father.

'Her cheerful determination ...'

Distracted, Kay drew her feet in to let the wheels of Lizzie's chair pass.

'Her absolute determination to continue ...'

She shifted her weight, smiling back at every eye she met. No matter that these were her friends and colleagues, the speech was making an object of her. She wished he would stop, she really wanted him to just ...

'And cue the music!' Someone called.

'...personal journey ...' Nick's voice tailed off.

Kay turned; it was Lizzie who had cued the music. She'd been wheeled across to Craig, who stood winking back at Kay as she stared. He lifted his phone, still winking, still grinning and pointing to a speaker on the table.

'...personal journey ...' As Nick tried again, he was drowned out by a chorus of voices rising in tight harmony, with soaring energy.

It was cue that everyone seemed to recognise and bemused, Kay watched as Wendy and the other canteen ladies pushed chairs back, as Patrick piled them into stacks, as Daniel threw open windows ... So, by the time the drum and base of Queen's *Fat Bottomed Girls* began, the room had been cleared.

Standing up, she laughed. There was no doubt who was behind this interruption. Lizzie. When she had been head-mistress, this was how she had ended every term: with an impromptu party in the staffroom. With Abba and Queen on the stereo and a couple of bottles of warm Lambrusco. Lizzie, grabbing every opportunity for a bit of fun, every chance to dance, living her life for herself and her lost love.

Patrick emerged from the throng, his lone lock of grey hair flying like a victory flag.

'Care to dance?' he said.

'Of course!' she answered, twirling under his arm until she was in the middle of the room with Lizzie, in her wheel-chair, on one side, a bent and tiny arm raised as she fist-pumped to the music, and her father on the other, elbows wide, bobbing along.

16

W ith a slight but steady breeze drifting in through the open window, Caro lay on the bed stripped to her bra and knickers. She had her hands stretched above her head as she held her phone high and scrolled through. To her surprise she only had one text from Matt.

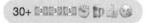

FOR A SMART MAN, he was useless with words.

Excellent,

SHE TEXTED BACK.

. . .

SHE KNEW WHAT HE MEANT. They had surpassed the goal, and the offering had already passed thirty million. She dropped her phone and rolled onto her side. As she did, another message pinged through. This time a photo of Matt and a few of the crowd from the office. They were obviously finishing the day at the pub. Eyebrows knitted, she tapped the screen and zoomed in. Even Mel, her former secretary was there, and looking at the familiar faces a strange feeling came over Caro, a feeling that if she hadn't known better, she might have mistaken for envy.

But she had nothing to be envious of. Two years ago, still recovering from a traumatic miscarriage, and numb with shock at her mother's catastrophic stroke, she had walked out of the office into a nightmare. This was when she had met Tomasz, on what was probably the worst day of her life. The evening she had taken Libby's baby and walked too long, and too far with him. The evening the police had been called, the evening she had put Libby and Helen through so much pain. Tomasz had come to find her. Sat down next to her and asked if she knew where she was. *Let me take you back,* he had said, and from the ashes, wings of hope had stirred. The hope of a different life. The hope of being loved.

Matt had been magnanimous when she had explained she would not be coming back. Empathy embodied, until the share price in Eco-Innovate had taken what looked like an irreversible decline.

'Consultancy only,' he'd offered. 'No pressure. No deadlines. No stress and no high-net arseholes ringing you up at midnight.' He'd even sent a photo of a pair of Gucci loafers, the suggestion being that he could find no-one to fill her shoes. Remembering this, Caro smiled. Sometimes words were superfluous and picking up the phone to him had been like picking up the phone to a still-beloved ex. They had, after all, had the perfect work marriage, and if today hadn't proved the truth of that image of the loafers, nothing would. It had been clear that she'd known more about the current market than anyone else in the room.

Rolling onto her back again, she stared at the ceiling. The stress in the office these last few days had been off the scale, and she had thoroughly enjoyed it. What she had said to Helen was true, a change was as good as a rest and now, having spent the last year doing not much more than growing tomatoes and visiting potential smallholdings, she felt thoroughly rested and raring to go.

She picked up her phone and opened Matt's message again, smiling back at all the faces in the photo. The problem was there was nowhere for her to go. That was it. This had been her last job and without a deadline she didn't know where to start, without pressure she could feel her edges slackening like a balloon deflating.

The bedroom door swung open.

Sitting up, she swiped her phone behind her back.

'Are you OK?' Tomasz stood in the doorway, a tea-towel over his shoulder.

'I'm fine,' she said. 'Just tired. The train was hot.'

'Do you want to rest? I can do the poo-pick.'

'The poo-pick?' Caro rubbed her eyes. In the five days she had been away she hadn't thought once about the chicken-coop poo-pick, a daily chore that was her responsibility. Along with feeding the goats their pellets and checking their hooves and raking away their manure. Or, if she was completely honest, any of regular jobs required to keep the smallholding going.

'I'll do it.' The door was closing. 'You rest.'

'I'm OK,' she said. 'I'll do it.'

Tomasz looked at her. 'You need food,' he said. 'I can keep it warm. Just say when you're ready to eat.'

'I'm not sure I can face it.' How could she tell him? How could she begin to describe that table of champagne and oysters, the lobster, the caviar. How could she explain what fifty million sounds like? Or how it feels, as a woman in a roomful of men, to stand as a queen on a stage in the sky. How could she confess that she had said, *I would have loved to.*

'Do you feel unwell?' He frowned.

'Yes,' she said. Then, 'No. I don't know ...It's just hot.'

'Caro.' She watched as he came over and sat on the edge of the bed, shifting her weight to accommodate the space he took up. The sofa, the bed. He wasn't even a big man, but everything shifted when he joined her.

'What's the matter?'

Looking back at him, Caro shrugged. She loved his eyes. They had been the first thing she had noticed about him, and the thought that she was causing the trouble so clearly reflected now, hurt her. But she couldn't take it away. She couldn't give him the answer he wanted, say, *Nothing! Nothing is the matter!* bounce off the bed, go downstairs and eat roast pork. Let alone roast pork with tomato and courgette sauce, not after bottling gallons of the stuff last week. She sat up and looked at her hands, at the shimmering lilac gel of her manicure winking back at her now, tenfold.

'Forget dinner,' he said. 'You're tired. Come down when you're ready.' And lifting her damp hair from her neck, he pressed his lips against her skin, a soft pressure, like a pillow she wanted to lean into. She watched him stand, the bow to his legs and the very slight stoop of his shoulders as familiar to her now as her own imperfect body.

Exhausted by the day, she rolled onto her side, watching

the sun sink lower. Her eyelids drooped and her cheek pressed her hand and by the time the sun had taken its leave, Caro too had fallen asleep.

SHE WAS WOKEN by the twit-twoo of owls calling through an inky twilight. Like they were lost. Like one was calling, *are you there, are you there*? And another was answering, *I'm here, I'm here*. Apart from that, the cottage was quiet. Downstairs, she found Tomasz in the kitchen, drying what looked like the last of the dishes. Aside from a neat pile of jars by the sink, the room was spotless.

'Tomasz.' She put her arms around his neck. 'You must be exhausted.'

'I could do with sitting down,' he whispered, his hand in her hair.

'Me too.' And taking the tea-towel from his hands, she led him through to the front room, poured them both a glass of wine and handed him the remote control. Within another minute, her feet rested in his lap and his hand rested on her thigh, a quiz show played harmless on the TV, and outside the owls had fallen silent.

'Sydney,' Thomaz said, nodding at the TV.

Caro frowned.

'Summer Olympics, year 2000.' He took a sip of wine.

She put her head to one side. 'Wasn't it Athens that year?'

'No. I was in Gdansk, and I remember getting up at six to watch before work.'

'I must have been closer,' she murmured. 'I vaguely remember it being on in the evenings. Singapore?' She looked at him.

'You don't remember?' How about if I do this ...' He squeezed her big toe. 'Does that help?'

Caro sneezed.

Laughing, Tomasz squeezed again.

'Stop it!' She managed, but she was still sneezing and laughing herself now.

'What this? Stop this?' He kept squeezing and now she was rolling from side to side, helpless with laughter. 'You like it,' he said as he let her foot go and leaned forward to kiss her.

Smiling, Caro fell back against the cushion. Yes, she liked it. She liked all of it. The ease, the gentle companionship, these spontaneous explorations they undertook together, excavating fragments of their past lives as carefully as if they were pottery pieces from a lost civilisation. It was only last week that he'd told her about the raised fist of the Communist Salute, he'd been expected to perform at school. And she had told him about her dungaree-wearing drama teacher who'd run off with the deputy head. And they had laughed, and she had thought how it was true. How love is wasted on the young.

'Sidney, Australia,' the TV host said.

'Told you.' Tomasz patted her leg. 'Let's see how many more we get.'

But she didn't get any more, because she didn't hear any more questions. She didn't hear the theme music that marked the end of the show, and she didn't feel him ease the glass from her hand. Her feet still in his lap, her head on the cushion, she fell into an easy but dreamless sleep.

17

The next day.

Caro: I missed your call last night. Everything ok?

Helen: 🍵 Just something I wanted to run by you.

Caro: Want to talk now?

Helen: Can't. No time. But also, I was thinking, let's do something for Kay? Yesterday was the big day.

Caro: I know.

Helen: I wonder what she did.

Caro: I expect she spent it in her pyjamas watching Real Housewives. She said she wanted a quiet night. ₂ᶻᶻ😴

Helen: 😄 Sounds wonderful. I still think we should do something. And you! You need to have a hen night!

Caro: What are you thinking?

Helen: Not sure yet. Dinner at my new place? You haven't seen it yet.

Caro: I have.

Helen: Not properly. Not with everything in it.

Caro: 👍

Helen: We can make it a joint retirement/hen party. 😊🥂

Caro: 😄 Sounds great, although I think we'll have a problem getting themed party ware!

Helen: You'll be able to get down so soon again?

Caro: Overnight, yes. No problem.

week later

THE BUILDING that Google maps had directed Helen to was a celebration of modern design. Asymmetrical and glass-fronted, it was a world away from the Victorian frontage of the health centre with its red brick and gabled roof. A little like herself, she thought, as she stood by the entrance, watching sleek young people hurrying past. She felt out of time and out of place, a relic from another age, and heart beating, hands sweaty, she couldn't decide if she should go in or turn and run.

The indecision was a natural result of a week in which she had seized every opportunity that had presented itself, to talk herself out of a job she hadn't even been offered. Chastising herself in the mirror as she brushed her teeth, muttering as she schlepped around the supermarket, sitting on her balcony, sipping wine and playing on repeat, excuse after excuse as to why she wouldn't get the job, why she couldn't do it and why she was a fool to have even considered it in the first place.

Christian's email had been to blame. Phrases he had used like 'crisis response,' 'community engagement,' 'field activities,' had been to blame. She'd read through with a rising sense of dismay. The 'crisis responses' she had experience of, were black socks mixed in with a white wash. And field activities? Football? Cricket? She didn't even know what the term meant. She was (as she kept reminding herself), an under-qualified, middle-aged woman whose CV could probably be summarised with one sentence: *Good at matching socks, keeping the milk stocked, catching spiders.*

It might have helped to talk to someone other than herself about it, but not knowing what she would have said, or what exactly the opportunity was, she had chosen not to. 'Just go and have a chat,' Dr Ross had said. 'He's very nice.' So, here she was.

Craning her neck, she looked up. Caro, she was thinking, would have spent her entire career in buildings like this. Smiling at the thought, Helen opened her phone and took a photograph. She'd be seeing both Caro and Kay at dinner tonight and whatever the outcome of this 'chat' there would be a lot to talk about. *Guess Where I am?* she typed. *Feels like we're swapping places!* As she sent the picture to Caro, Helen ran the words again, *swapping places.* Once upon a time they had been equal. Then Caro's world had expanded, and her world had shrunk, and it was nothing more complicated than that. And, for heaven's sake, it was just a chat. She could do that, if there was one thing she could do, it was chat.

But one step inside, and she lost her nerve all over again. The space she had entered was not a place of work so much as a lifestyle. Stretching out in front of her a vast and open-plan ground floor had been designed to mimic a town square. Along each side neat eating places sold fresh juices, and raw sushi, poke bowls and grain bowls. Tables and chairs had been set in front of the restaurants and a huge domed ceiling rose above. Trees in Titanic-sized pots grew in obedient shapes and people walked past, with heads tall and clothes that fitted extremely well. The scene was a fantasy, a dream realised of what a world full of health-conscious, wealthy people might look like. Her mouth turned up in a rueful smile. No Tupperware boxes of lemon drizzle here then.

At the far end of the square, security gates marked the boundary of make-believe and business. Behind the gates, she could see the swirl of the rising storeys, the glass balconies that delineated every floor. It was a dazzling building, clean, modern, and impressive. Everything, she thought as she looked down at her Marks and Spencer blouse and her comfortable shoes, that she wasn't.

She gave her name to the uniformed man, guarding what looked more like a wooden island than a desk, took a seat on a blue sofa and concentrated on counting how many people were choosing poke bowls over sushi. A short time later a young man came hurtling through the security gates, he had plenty of hair, a rope bracelet on his wrist and his arm was raised in the kind of greeting you might give evacuated children retuning home after war.

'Helen!' he called. 'I'm Christian!'

She didn't yell back. Opting for a more reserved style, she smiled politely and went to stand and as she did, she yelped with surprise. The sofa was lower than her knees had anticipated. It was only by throwing a hand out to claw the cushion, that she managed to haul herself upright. 'And there was I thinking I'd get beamed up.' She joked.

'Sorry?' Christian's face was a blank.

'*Star Trek*?' she said, digging herself in further. 'It's so modern!' And she did an embarrassed little turn to indicate that she meant the building, and not him. *Stop talking, Helen. Just. Stop. Talking.*

'Ah.' Christian titled his head to the gates. 'Would you like to follow me?'

'Of course!' Head bowed, she gathered her bag and her jacket. *Great start, Helen. Great bloody start.*

TROTTING TO KEEP UP, Helen followed as Christian led her through the offices of Stronger Together.

'This is our collaborative area,' he said as they passed an area filled with high tables, spaced in front of a whiteboard.

Good height for tapas, she almost quipped, and remembering her last joke, settled on, 'Very nice.'

'Our tech space.'

She turned to see a closed office, with individual desks and screens.

'It's booked through an app.'

'I see.'

'The hydration station.' Christian had stopped next to a strip of kitchen. White gloss cupboards, under a granite bench, a sink with two taps. Two taps?

'Would you like some water?' he said.

'Yes please.'

'Fizzy or still?' He picked up a glass and turned to the taps.

'Still is fine.'

'Mint or lemon?'

Helen blinked, glancing across at two huge glass dispensers on the bench, one topped with lemon wedges, one with sprigs of mint. 'Plain is fine,' she said. 'Plain, still water.' She was thinking of the tea-stained sink in the kitchen at the health centre. The white crust of limescale around the lip of the kettle. Clutching her glass, she followed on. Past a 'creative breakout space' which, with its stack of board games, box of Lego (Lego!) and chess set, looked to Helen more like a sixth-form common room. At least they put their toys away here. Past a 'game-zone' with a screen and handsets and past the 'quiet zone' with cocoon-like pods and noticeably softer lighting. And she couldn't help it. 'So, where's the naughty step?' she quipped, not noticing that Christian had stopped. Not noticing and walking right into him. 'Oh gosh!' She stepped back. 'Sorry.'

Christian winced. She'd trodden on his toe.

'This is my office,' he said, his smile noticeably less bright than the one he had greeted her with.

19

S tiff as hell from hunching over a sink that had been built a hundred and fifty years earlier, for people several inches shorter, Caro walked on the spot. 'Ouch! God, it hurts.' She jigged her weight from foot to foot, hands burning with cold as she lifted them from the freezing water. 'How many more?' she gasped.

At the Aga, Tomasz turned. Pushing his glasses back on his head, he raised his hand to count the huddle of cabbages on the kitchen table, one, two, three ... the knife in his hands a sheath of silver.

'Nine,' she said, a tinge of impatience in her voice.

'Nine.' He agreed. He nodded at the sink. 'Use the sieve. You don't have to put your hands in then.'

'If I use the sieve,' Caro groaned, 'we'll be here till Christmas. At least this way I can get a good load done at once.' And turning back to the sink she plunged her hands in again, gathering the flow of shredded cabbage together, lifting, squeezing and finally dropping it onto a tea-towel. She folded the tea-towel in half and then half again, pressed and rolled and shook it open, spreading the pieces onto a baking tray that had been lined with paper. She put the tray in the freezer and leaned against the sink, looking out of the window. High above, the torch of a July sun had risen steadily, Helios driving his chariot halfway across the world, while she had been chained to the sink, blanching cabbage. 'Can we take a break?' she said.

Tomasz looked up from the skull-sized cabbage he was busy quartering, and Caro looked down at her hands. Her knuckles were as creamy white as the cabbage heads, her nails already splitting, the varnish, so recently applied, flaking and chipped. 'There's an awful lot in the freezer already.' She shrugged. 'I mean, how much cabbage does anyone need?'

Smiling, he put the knife down. 'I could always make Sauerkraut,' he said. 'We don't have to do all this then.' And he waved a hand at the tea-towels laid the length of the kitchen bench, the paper-lined trays stacked next to the sink. 'Sauerkraut is more of a one-person job.'

'If we do that, we'll have time for coffee in the garden before I go. I can make it,' she added. Because *if we do that*, meant *if he does that*. If Tomasz carried on fulfilling the obligations of this trial run they were in the middle of, while she escaped again. Escape wasn't the right word of course, she just couldn't think of another one right now. It was Thomas who had insisted she go in the first place. When she'd told him about Helen's idea for a joint retirement/hen evening he had waved aside any reasons she had made not to and booked her ticket, presenting it with her over break-fast. And of course she was looking forward to the evening, it's just that the one excuse she hadn't voiced, was the one he wouldn't have waved aside: that while Spencer Cooper was still in town, it was better that she wasn't. She hadn't exam-ined this idea, she had in fact done the opposite, shut it away, and covered it up with other thoughts, such as arranging delivery of her bouquet, double-checking that the car company had all her instructions. But it was stubborn, and every time her guard fell, it was there, this persistent notion that if he was in town, it was better that she wasn't. She watched as Tomasz took a huge pan of boiling water and poured it down the sink.

'I don't even like cabbage,' he said.

Smiling she put her hand on his cheek. It was OK. Helen's place wasn't even in town. Close, but not London. Not really. 'Neither do I,' she said and kissed him.

'Let's not tell the Sullivans then.'

'I won't if you won't.' Caro smiled. Laura and Neil Sullivan were the couple who owned Hollybrook Farm – the people they were leasing from. The husband-and-wife team who had handed them a file containing A to Z instructions of everything they would need to know about running a smallholding. A: assess your soil quality regularly. D: Ditch management. It was the size of a brick and equally dull, and frankly she'd seen merger proposals between companies worth billions use fewer trees. She hadn't made it beyond F: (fertilise the soil regularly), although Tomasz read it regularly. Sitting by the stone fireplace, night after night leafing through the pages with the devotion of a true believer.

'I was thinking we should invite them to dinner next week.'

'Why?' Turning away, Caro pulled the plug from the sink. She hadn't meant to sound so abrupt, but she didn't want to invite Laura and Neil for dinner. So far, they had managed to contain any necessary socialising to coffee. Dinner was a different matter. Dinner could spill over for hours, way past F: (fertilise the soil regularly) ...

'Well.' Tomasz wiped his hands on a tea-towel. 'We have

the solicitor next week. I thought it would be good to go through some stuff before —'

'Before what?' This time the abruptness was intended. The trial run wasn't over. They hadn't decided anything, they had discussed many things, but there was a difference between discussing and deciding, and going by the language he was using, Caro wasn't sure Tomasz appreciated that. The solicitor's appointment was merely to go through the legal implications of some of the changes they were thinking of making *if* they went ahead. *If.*

'Before we make a decision,' he said, and looked at her. 'That's what I was going to say.' He folded the tea-towel back on the drainer and went to the door. 'I'm going to check on the chickens.'

'OK.' She watched him walk out the door and along the garden path. This last week he'd spent so much time with the chickens, she'd started teasing him. *Your babies,* she'd said, but he was always there. Fixing a runway that didn't need fixing or mending a fence where she couldn't see a break. Almost as if he needed space. As if he too was having doubts. Thinking this she made a steeple of her hands and covered her face. The feeling that had started small as a stitch only a week into this trial, was growing. Laura and Neil, the photo Matt had sent her of the after-work celebration, that view of London, tomato, after courgette, after tomato .... She could hear the quiet whispers, growing louder every day. *I'm not sure, I don't know. I'm having second thoughts.*

She turned to the table, and in a movement born of frustration, scooped up a handful of cabbages and dropped them in the compost bin. Nobody needed too much sauerkraut either, and this she could personally vouch for! Around the time she was trying to get pregnant, she had eaten it with every meal only to suffer constant wind. Those months when she was doing everything she could to make her body as healthy as possible, and then her body had betrayed her anyway. Looking back out to the garden, Caro breathed deeply, holding onto the air as if she were deep underwater. *Our babies,* Tomasz had answered, when she'd teased him about the chickens. But she didn't think of the chickens as her babies, and the unborn soul who really had been her baby was a memory that no longer hurt. Motherhood had been such a fleeting experience, a few precious weeks for which she would always be grateful, but what she had said to Helen only a few months ago was true. She had accepted the fact that she would never be anyone's mother and set about concentrating on the fact that she would be someone's wife. It was eleven am on a sunny July morning so there was no reflection from the window to reveal the frown on her face, and the movement had been so subtle, she hadn't felt it.

20

'Helen.' Christian raised his palm and as he did his rope bracelet slid across his wrist. 'I'm sorry to stop you,' he said, 'but I have to tell you, you're not doing a very good job of selling yourself.'

Helen blinked. 'Selling myself?'

He smiled. 'I'm hearing a lot of negatives. Not too many strengths.'

'Oh.' Stunned, her mouth stayed in a round, while her mind began a furious re-wind. What had she said that was so negative? He'd asked her to tell him a little about herself, so she had. Actually, he hadn't said that at all, he'd said: 'What's your story, Helen? What's brought you to this point in your professional life? I'd like to hear what you think your strengths and weaknesses are?' And resisting the urge to slap out a few hard truths such as, Boredom? Divorce? Cake, she had remained on track. She'd explained that she wasn't brilliant with the smart scheduling system recently introduced at the health centre and, until five minutes ago she'd never heard of POCT kits, although the idea of point-of-care testing, the ability to detect diabetes or heart disease, in the field, sounded wonderful. *In the field,* she'd had really said that.

'I'm sorry, it's not ...' Christian raised his hands. 'You're not quite what I was expecting.'

'No?' Her blood pooled at her feet. She felt humiliated and furious. Embarrassed and astonished.

'How about you?'

'Me?'

'Are we what you were expecting?'

Helen looked at him. This young man with his rope bracelet and his over-the-top bonhomie and his vacuous, *what's your story?* He wasn't as young as Libby, but he wasn't far from it. He was in fact ... Her breath caught in her throat and swallowing was suddenly painful. Christian was about the same age Daniel, her first son, would have been, had he lived. 'I didn't know what to expect,' she said tightly.

Christian looked down at his hands, then smiling, looked up again. 'Can I ask why you're here?'

Helen blinked. 'I'm here because you invited me,' she said. What a stupid question!

'Yes, of course. What I'm trying to say is ...' And leaning back, he looped his hands behind his head in a movement of such casual indifference he might as well have been settling down to watch a movie. 'What do *you* want, Helen?'

It was petrol on the fire, and she was a bear grievously poked, and he was all the complacent men who had ever asked her a version of this question and then not waited to hear her answer (which in any case had always been pre-empted to suit what she knew they wanted to hear). Well, not anymore! 'I'm glad you asked,' she said, 'because I'm beginning to wonder myself. You invited me to a 'casual chat' in offices that look like my son's bedroom, and all you've done so far is ask me what my story is! You want to hear what my strengths are?' She stood up. 'What if I told you that I'm the only one in my family who can get the lid off a new jar of pickled onions? Would that be strong enough? Or if I said that every year on the twentieth of April, I cry for at least an hour because that's the day I gave birth to a dead baby. Would that be just another negative?'

Now Christian stood up.

'I don't know what you want from me,' Helen cried. 'I don't know why I'm here and I have no idea if this is an interview or if you're just passing half an hour before it's your turn in the gaming room.' So that was that then. If she hadn't blown this by treading on his foot, she most certainly had now.

'I ...'

'Oh, never mind!' she interrupted. And with hot tears forming, she turned to grab her handbag. There was no way she was going to let this young man see her cry; besides she had a dinner to cook. One thing at least she knew she could do.

'We're looking for an administrator to run the centre,' Christian said helplessly.

'I know that!' Helen threw her hands up in the air. 'I knew that before I left home this morning! Are you interviewing me for that role, or not?'

'Yes ...' he stammered. 'Yes, I am. Please.' And he indicated that she should sit again.

'OK.' Helen sat, heavy as a sack of potatoes. 'I'll make it easy,' she said, because now she felt sorry for him. He looked as if he'd seen a ghost. Was she that scary? 'Front line medical admin is what I do and have done for years. I mail chemists and pharmacists and hospital secretaries. I type clinical letters and test reports, arrange all referrals and patient files. I scan, code and action clinical requests, translator requests. I source translators. I arrange the loaning out of medical equipment. If there's a wheelchair to be found south of the Watford Gap, I can find it. I help implement community health drives and organise transport when needed. I'm in charge of implementing emergency test runs and keeping policy updated. I'm even in charge of the office coffee budget and I organise the Christmas lucky dip. I have two living children and one grandson; I've cleaned bottoms and mopped-up sick. I've fed my family as healthily as I could for twenty years. I've stitched, painted and dug a home for them, held my dead baby in my arms and sat up all night nursing my daughter through a fever that barely stayed below forty.' And ... suddenly she stopped talking. 'There's really nothing more to tell,' she said, 'either I'm what you're looking for or I'm not.'

Speechless, Christian nodded.

'So.' Again, she stood. 'If you'll excuse me, I must get going. I have a joint retirement and hen party to prepare for, and I'm sure you'll agree that kind of celebration doesn't come along very often.' She didn't see his face as she turned to go, she only heard him say quietly *'push'*, because she was at the door, pulling on a door handle that wouldn't give.

21

The train was already thirty minutes behind schedule, and now it had ground to a halt somewhere in Lincolnshire. Leaning back, Caro put down the seed catalogue she'd been trying to read and stared out across fields of what she recognised as cabbages. Perhaps now that she was so acquainted with the species, she would never stop seeing them. From behind she could hear the loud and tinny soundtrack of someone's phone. Distracted, she picked up her own phone, opened Helen's photo again and smiled, then scrolling through she re-read the message that had arrived twenty minutes after she had boarded the train, and which she had read at least six times.

This is me. If you're in town. Spencer.

A screech pealed out, so loud and so close she jumped. Turning to the seat behind, she saw a young girl, one hand in a crisp packet, one hand holding her phone up. The screech came again, followed by raucous laughter. Someone, locked away in the infinity of this girl's phone was either very amused or very frightened. 'Excuse me,' Caro said wearily. Tomasz had booked a standard-class ticket, something she never did exactly to avoid this kind of thing, but the noise had been going on for the last fifteen minutes, yelping and squealing and screeching, piercing her thoughts and rattling her nerves. 'Excuse me,' she said again.

The girl did not look up.

'Excuse me.'

No response.

Now she hissed: 'Excuse me!'

Still the girl ignored her.

Caro made a fist of her hand and tapped on the chair back, and finally the girl looked up.

'Do you have headphones?'

'What?'

'Do you have headphones?' She smiled. 'Because if you do, I'd appreciate it if you put them on and listened to whatever it is you're listening to, through them.'

'TikTok,' the girl said, a slow rise of hostility filling her eyes.

'TikTok.' Caro nodded. 'Can you listen to it through headphones?'

The girl glared at her. 'This is *public* transport.'

The stupidity of the response was like a punch; momentarily, it stunned her. 'Exactly,' she said as she came to her senses. 'You're on *public* transport, in a *public* space, subjecting everyone else to your *private* entertainment.'

Scowling, the girl pulled her shoulders back. 'And you're knocking on the seat like I'm your servant.'

For a nano-second, not more, Caro closed her eyes. The intensity of the hostility, the suddenness of it had pushed her to a precipice. She could feel it, the currents of air rising from the drop in front, caution behind tugging at her sleeve, urging her to back away ... Making a coward of her. She hadn't been unreasonable; she hadn't been nasty. To back down would be cowardly. Would make her a wholly different person from the woman who had owned that stage in the sky. 'An impressive woman,' Spencer Cooper had said. What would he say now? She opened her eyes to see the girl staring, the scent of victory turning her lips up. 'I tapped,' Caro said. 'I didn't knock, and I did it to get your attention. I had already asked three times.'

The girl dropped her head to one side, raised her phone and began filming. 'This *Karen,*' she drawled, 'is knocking on my seat, yeah, to get me to turn my phone down, yeah. Like she's the train police.'

'What are you doing?' She was so angry, so astonished, her voice shook.

The girl laughed. 'This is gonna go viral.' And holding her phone higher, she whispered, *'Karen.'*

'Switch it off.' The command, spoken by a man, came from above.

The girl looked up.

Caro turned. He wore designer sunglasses and an obviously expensive suit, and she recognised him immediately. 'Emir!' She hadn't seen him in months. He had been an early investor in Eco-Innovate, and her persuasive skills had made him substantially richer.

Returning Caro's smile, Emir leaned to the girl. 'I said, switch it off.'

'What's it to you, bro?' The girl sneered. 'She's just another *Karen.'*

Emir didn't speak. He leaned in closer, so close his nose was inches from the girl's nose. 'Number one,' he said, 'I am not your bro. Number two, learn some manners, and number three, my mother's name is Karen, and I don't like to hear it disrespected. Now, turn your camera off, put your headphones on, and leave this lady in peace.'

Slowly, Caro eased back in her seat. She was aware that behind, Emir hadn't moved. She heard a rustling sound, a retrieval of headphones? And then Emir had straightened up and was leaning toward her. 'Why don't you come and join me in first class?'

'With pleasure,' she said, gathering her bag and following him along the aisle without a second glance back.

'IF THE CONDUCTOR COMES ALONG, I'll pay the difference.' Emir indicated the empty seat across the table from his own. 'Please, there's been no-one there the whole journey.'

'Thank you, but if an inspector comes along, *I'll* pay the difference,' Caro said. The seat she took was a third wider than the one she had come from, and the carriage was blissfully quiet, still the setting was nowhere near as salubrious as the last time she had sat across a table from Emir. Then, he had also offered to pay, and she had had no problem accepting. She had been with Matt, in a Michelin-starred restaurant, with a W1 postcode, celebrating the fact that Emir's investment had quadrupled. The wine had cost more than her train ticket; but it had been appropriate and expected, that they accept his hospitality. This was different. It was bad enough that he'd stumbled across her like this, in a standard carriage. He might actually be thinking that she couldn't afford anything else. 'That will teach me to book my own tickets.' She waved her hand, attempting to laugh off her embarrassment. She was lucky there wasn't a third class. So committed was Tomasz to their budget she had no doubt he would have booked that.

Emir nodded. Whatever he thought, he was keeping it to himself. 'You look well,' he said. 'Sun-kissed.'

Caro smiled.

'I heard the offering was a resounding success. Forty million and counting? Outstanding, Caro.' He shook his head. 'Matt's going to be lost without you. Oh, and congratulations by the way. He said you were getting married.'

'I am. And thank you.'

'He also said you were buying a farm?'

'Smallholding,' she corrected. 'And we're doing a trial run first.'

'Very sensible. Do you have chickens?'

'Lots.'

'Pigs?'

'No, but goats and cabbages and loads of courgettes!'

Tipping his head back, Emir laughed. 'I don't know an awful lot about growing my own vegetables.'

'Neither did I!' she said, and leaning forward clasped her hands together, bringing them to rest on the table.

'Sounds like a lot of work.' He was looking at her hands.

Mortified, Caro dropped them to her lap. 'Have you seen Matt lately?' she said. The way Emir had spoken made it sound as if he had.

Emir nodded. 'I had a drink with him and a guy called Spencer Cooper a couple of days ago.' He scratched his chin. 'If Matt hadn't told us about you leaving, I think you would have been hearing from Mr Cooper.'

'Really?' Caro dropped her head to the side. Her expression was neutral but inside, her heart pounded.

'He would have tried to poach you, I'm sure of it. As it is, Matt is panicking, about replacing you.'

'But Matt told him?'

Emir frowned. 'Told him what?'

'That I'm getting married ... So, I wouldn't be interested anyway ... If he was serious. I mean ... about poaching me.' Under the table she pressed her hands together.

'I think he did. It's not confidential, is it?'

'No! Goodness no!' Caro waved her hand. Blood rushing to her cheeks, she turned to the window. Spencer Cooper had heard this news, and he had still sent that text. Watching field after field blur past, her thoughts kept pace. It was presumptuous of him. And confident. And arrogant. And sexy. And, after all, she had said: 'I would have loved to.'

'So, no chance of a change of mind?'

'No.' Turning back to Emir, her laugh was too quick. 'The smallholding is a trial but it's going well.'

'That's good.'

'I'm really enjoying it actually.'

'I'm sure.'

'It's such a refreshing change.'

Emir nodded.

'And we make a good team.'

He smiled.

'Yes, we're pretty much decided,' Caro said. 'Pretty much decided.' Her voice rang with falsehood, and she knew it. As an escape she turned to the window again, aware that Emir had taken out his phone. 'By the way,' she said, a few minutes later. 'Is your mother's name really Karen?'

'No.' Emir laughed. 'Her name is Sharon.'

'I see.' Caro nodded. 'And how is she doing? I remember you retired her to a flat in Malaga. Richly deserved I should think. A lady of leisure, lying in the sun all day.'

'She never lies in the sun.'

'No?'

'No. She got herself a job as a cleaner again. She's up at

six, cleaning toilets. Loves it!' As he spoke, Emir turned his palms upward, they were Caro noticed, a soft pink, like the inside of an earlobe. He clearly didn't know anything about growing vegetables. 'What can I say?' He smiled. 'It makes her happy. Like you and your courgettes. We must do what makes us happy.'

'Yes,' she said managing a smile. 'We must.'

22

'Sorry about the boxes. I meant to make a start but ...' As Helen turned to look at the wall of boxes in her living room, her voice drifted away. She hadn't even tried to unpack. It defeated her, just to look at them. Four of the boxes were labelled *dining room* and were full of her best plates, her best cutlery, her best glasses. Three more were labelled *living room* and were full of books, CDs, photo albums, ornaments. Four more contained bedding: single feathered duvets, dozens of pillowcases. Another two had gardening stuff. What was she supposed to do with it all? Her flat only had two bedrooms, no dining room, and no garden.

Kay nodded.

'I wanted it to look nice, but I had this thing today and ―'

'It's fine.'

'I was going to do salmon, but I can't find my non-stick pan.' Face flushed, hands on hips, Helen waved a limp hand towards her kitchen. 'I might have left it with Lawrence,' she said, looking at the boxes. 'Believe it or not, I haven't taken everything yet. I didn't realise I had so much stuff. I honestly don't know ––'

'Helen!'

'Sorry.' Helen slumped. 'I'm a little out of sorts.'

'I can see.' Kay smiled. 'Is this a good idea? We could take a raincheck?'

'No!' Moving across the room, she flung the balcony doors wide open and tipped her head back. 'I just need some air. That's all.'

'Helen? Are you OK?'

'I'm fine.' But Helen didn't turn. She couldn't turn. Couldn't bring herself to look once more at the boxes she hadn't unpacked, the flatpack shelving unit still in its delivery carton. The flat was a mess. Her long-dreamed about, much-cherished place of her own, was chaos and she couldn't, for the life of her, summon up the slightest desire to sort it out. 'I suppose,' she said as she turned back, 'I've run out of steam.'

Kay sighed. 'Well, I know that feeling.'

'No.' Helen shook her head. If anyone had the right to have run out of steam, it was Kay, not her. She hadn't run out of steam; she just wasn't inclined to start the engine up in the first place. 'The truth is,' she said. 'I think I've lost my domestic gene, Kay. If I didn't ever have to cook again, I don't think I'd care.' Framed by the balcony doors, Helen ran her hands through her hair. 'This thing I said I had? It's a chance to work in Bolivia.'

'Bolivia?' Kay's eyes widened.

Helen nodded. 'It's not much of a chance. In fact, after today I'm pretty sure it's no chance at all but ...'And shrugging she added, 'I just can't seem to be bothered with all this now.'

'Bolivia?' Kay opened her mouth to speak, but the loud

buzz of the intercom interrupted whatever it was she might have said.

'That'll be Caro.' They both spoke together.

'We should have gone out,' Helen said.

'It doesn't matter.'

'I wanted this to be special. I told Caro I would organise it.'

'Helen it really ...' Kay put her hand to her cheek and stopped talking. Helen was already in the kitchen. For a moment she stood listening to the sound of cupboard doors opening and slamming, of Helen muttering. 'Shall I buzz Caro up?' she called, and when Helen didn't answer she lifted the intercom and let Caro in.

A MINUTE later flushed and breathless, Caro fell through the door. 'I used the stairs,' she panted as she thrust a bottle-shaped package at Kay.

'Why didn't you take the lift?'

In response, Caro lifted her nose to the stream of fresh air coming from the open doors of the balcony. 'I need to cool down,' she gasped and in two strides she was across the room, gripping the ironwork with both hands, as she breathed deeply.

'It's no good.' Helen came back into the room. 'I can't find it.'

'Caro's here.' Kay nodded at the balcony. 'She took the stairs.'

Helen turned. 'Caro, I'm sorry. I'm a bit behind. I was going to do salmon, but I can't find my bloody pan.'

'Fish?' Caro groaned.

'Don't you fancy it?'

'And why did you take the stairs?' Kay added.

'Because I need to lose some weight!' Caro threw her hands up. 'There's no wiggle-room at all in that dress, and Thomaz cooks all the time. There are three ovens on the Aga, and I swear he uses all of them, every night.'

'Can't you say something?' Helen said, her lips twitching with amusement. She knew how many ovens there were on an Aga. Hadn't she had one for twenty years?

'I've tried. I was telling him about intermittent fasting the other week.'

'And how did that go down?' Kay said mildly.

'Well, he seemed interested, but then the next day I sat down to a casserole with dumplings.'

Now Helen laughed.

'I think you're going to need to be clearer than that, Caro.' Kay held up the package. 'Can we open this? Do you have glasses?' She turned to Helen.

'Umm ... there's a box somewhere. But ––'

'Don't worry.' Kay raised her hand. 'I'll use cups if I have to. Someone has to get this party started.' And clutching the package she went into the kitchen.

'KAY'S RIGHT,' Helen said as she joined Caro on the balcony. 'You are going to have to be clearer with Tomasz. I lost count of how many times I said, *divorce,* before Lawrence actually heard me. It was getting to the point where I was thinking of painting it on the front door. Like they did in the plague,' she added grimly.

'Oh, Tomasz isn't like ...' Caro's voice dried. 'I didn't mean ...' She stopped again.

'It's fine, Caro.'

'I wasn't ...'

'I know you weren't.' Helen smiled. 'Let's not go there. As

far as I'm concerned, it's all in the past. I just want to concentrate on the future now.' She meant it. The decades long rivalry between them, the secret torch Caro had carried for Lawrence, the awful rows they had had in Cyprus and Vegas. It felt like village gossip now. Gossip about people she didn't know and wasn't interested in.

'Me too,' Caro said. Her face brightened. 'Talking of the future, where were you?'

'When?'

'The photo you sent this morning. I presume it was the city?'

'Oh.' Helen frowned. She'd forgotten all about the photo. 'I'll explain later,' she said.

Caro arched her brows. 'Promise?'

'I think so.' It was as far as she could go. To tell Caro how she had thrown away the most exciting opportunity to pass her way in years, to explain how she had stalked out of the office like a stroppy teenager, wasn't something she could commit to. Maybe in time, but certainly not now. Now, regret and disappointment lashed her, and if she didn't get a grip and put the day's events to the back of her mind, it would ruin what was supposed to be a special evening. Squeezing Caro's arm, she went back inside and dropped into the nearest armchair. 'Let's just enjoy ourselves,' she called back, and to her immense relief, Caro came in, collapsed onto the sofa opposite and said: 'I'm up for that.'

Kay came back in, bearing a tray with three glasses of champagne.

Stunned, Helen stared. 'Where did you find those?'

'In a box, labelled glasses,' Kay said. 'Under your kitchen table.'

'Oh.' Helen smiled. 'It's been such a long day,' she said as she took the glass Kay offered. 'And I know I invited you both to dinner, but now you're here I really really don't want to cook. Is that awful?'

'Terrible,' Caro said, as she too took a glass.

'What about takeaway?'

'Takeaway?' Helen's face lit up. 'I could hug you, Kay.'

'I can't think of anything better.' Caro eased off her shoes. 'Just a poppadom for me and a bottle more of this, and I'll be fine.'

'Oh, my goodness!' From her head to her toe, Kay shivered. A whole-body movement that had the champagne in her glass wobbling. 'I just had the most amazing flash of Deja vu,' she gasped. 'Do you remember our first night in the Sydney Road flat?'

Helen and Caro looked at each other.

'We had Indian then, didn't we?' Helen said.

Caro nodded. 'It was my first time. I'd never had it before.'

'That's right.' Kay laughed. 'Me neither.'

Helen put her hand to her mouth. 'I remember! I had to persuade you both, and you both loved it.'

'Well, it's just like old times then.' Caro raised her glass to the wall of boxes. 'We hadn't unpacked then either had we?'

'No, we hadn't.' Kay laughed. She looked at the boxes. 'Although I suspect we had a lot less to unpack.'

'That's true.' And Helen too turned to look. Oh, the baggage those boxes contained. Books she'd once read and never would again, eight different coats and jackets, for what would only ever be four seasons, strappy heels, that, fifty-two years of gravity hammering her feet wide, she would never fit again, photographs of Cornish coastlines, photographs of Welsh coastlines, of dogs, once beloved and now deceased, vegetables planted, grown, long since eaten.

Why was she keeping all this? 'I don't need half this stuff.' She put her glass down. 'I haven't had anything to drink, so I'll drive. I've got a menu somewhere.'

Caro reached for her handbag. 'You're so last century, Helen.' She laughed. 'If you use a delivery service, they'll bring it to the door.'

'Alex does it all the time.' Kay nodded. 'They send a text when it's here.' She took a sip of champagne and shrugged. 'Your chips have arrived.'

'Chips?' Helen said incredulously. 'You can get chips delivered?'

Kay burped. 'That's what they text,' she added and burped again and put her hand to her mouth and giggled. 'Your chips have arrived.'

'I COULDN'T HAVE ASKED for a better retirement dinner,' Kay said.

The table was spread with her favourite food; the room filled with her favourite people. Along with the wonderful surprise party at school, she was riding a wave of contentment. The bikini fitted, (just about). And she had finally taken her suitcase down from the loft. It was just a reconnaissance trip after all. A month to start, she'd decided that much. 'Caro?' she said, stretching a chicken dish across the table.

'No thank you.'

'Sure?

Caro waved her arm.

'Is that a yes, or a, no?'

'Oh, just a bit then.' And as Kay ladled a large spoonful of creamy korma onto her plate, she groaned. 'It's not going to fit.'

Standing up, Helen took the empty bottle of champagne. 'We need another one.'

'You still have time, don't you?' Kay said. 'To lose an inch?'

'Sex!' Helen called as she went to the fridge. 'Sex is good exercise!'

'Sex?' Kay smiled. 'What's that?'

'Ask Caro!'

'I'm not sure why you'd say that, Helen,' Caro said.

'Ignore her.' Kay leaned across the table, her hand cupped at her mouth as she stage-whispered, 'She's just jealous.' And leaning back she put a fist to her chest and burped again. 'These bubbles,' she gasped.

'We're both jealous!' Back at the table, Helen opened the bottle and filled every glass she could find. 'Seriously though,' she said as she sat down, 'It's such an important part of a woman's life.' She picked up a poppadum and snapped it in half, lumping chutney on as she looked sideways at Kay. 'When was the last time?'

'I'm not answering that!' A fountain of bubbles erupted from Kay's mouth. 'No.' She raised her palm. 'Stop looking at me.' But they didn't, and eventually she lowered her glass and said quietly, 'I honestly don't know.' But she did.

'Kay?'

Kay shrugged.

'Kay.' Now it was Caro's turn.

'What did you expect?' she said defensively. 'Alex was only eight when Martin left. I wasn't going to be bringing anyone into the house.'

'Of course.' Helen nodded. 'But you know what they say?'

'No, I don't.'

'Use it, or lose it,' Caro finished.

'Use it or lose it?' Crossing her arms, Kay leaned back. 'How can I lose it, Caro? It's an integral part of my biology.'

'We mean,' Helen said, 'that women of our age need help. It dries up.' And mimicking the action of a zip closing, Helen drew her hand across her lips.

'Shrinks,' Caro added.

'Well, if that's the case,' Kay said, 'mine will be vacuum-packed.'

'Like my hands.' Helen raised her hands and looked at them. 'They always say if you want to know a woman's age look at the back of her hands.'

'Or the inside of her vagina?' Kay said lightly.

'We're serious,' Caro scolded. 'You're only fifty-two.'

'I know how old I am!'

'And starting a whole new life,' Helen said.

'Am I?'

'I had a few problems with Tomasz.' Caro nodded. 'But it's lovely now.' She reached across, took one of Kay's hands and shook it. 'I want you to think about something. When was Viagra invented?'

Helen frowned. 'I don't know.'

'Me neither,' Kay said.

'1999.'

Helen turned. 'Really?'

'Yes.' Caro waved her arm. 'And hello! Why do you think it was invented?'

'Well, that's easy.' Kay smiled. 'So, men could keep an erection.'

'Ta dah! And who is making a fortune from it?'

'Men with erections?' Helen picked up her glass.

'Men with erections, making money from men keeping erections?' Kay said, and the three of them looked at each other and burst out laughing.

'It's true though,' Helen shook her head. 'Viagra has been around for ages. Everyone knows about it. But topical HRT.' She turned to Kay. 'Have you even heard of that? It's a cream you can get for ... and it sort of ... well, rejuvenates it.'

'Rejuvenates?' Kay frowned. She could recite maths equations that were two pages long, do complicated long-division in her head, but there were parts of her body, she was beginning to realise, she had simply come to accept she would never see again. The back of her knees for example, her vagina, definitely. It was a sealed vault, an abandoned mineshaft that hadn't seen the light of day, or human contact, for many years. But she was the same age as Caro and Helen, and a year younger than Marianne. And the idea of a secret key that might open a part of her she thought had been permanently sealed was all sorts of things: intriguing, scary, exciting. 'Topical HRT?' she murmured, her glass at her lips.

'Vibrators too.' Caro tipped her glass.

'What!'

'I bought one in America,' Helen said.

'I've used one too,' Caro added.

'Oh ...' Kay shifted her weight. 'Oh,' she said again, feeling the heat of embarrassment spread up her neck and across her cheeks. This conversation was a rollercoaster and with anyone other than Helen and Caro, she would have stopped the ride and stepped off. Then again, with anyone else she wouldn't have got on in the first place. 'Marianne,' she said quietly, 'is on Tinder. '

Helen laughed. 'Now that doesn't surprise me.'

'She has what she calls "friends with benefits".'

Caro nodded.

'Really?' Kay looked from one to the other. 'You're not shocked?'

Helen shook her head. 'Are you?'

'No ... and yes.' Kay looked at them. 'I don't know!' She was thinking of the photograph Marianne had shown her. The image of a woman in her prime, a handsome, confident, experienced woman. A woman who had cropped an ex-lover out of the frame. What did she think? She still didn't know, in fact the only thing she did know was that she could never be that woman. And never could have been. She was the kind of woman who had worn dungarees all through university. CND t-shirts and Doc Martens. All of which was OK, because at twenty you can wear anything and still have sex. But now? Who was going to look at a grey-haired woman in size eighteen jeans now? She was shaking her head, because when she thought about it, she found she wasn't shocked. And she was shaking her head because when she thought about it, she found it was a shame. But somewhere along the line she had mislaid her sexuality and hadn't noticed, and now that she had, it was simply too late. Like neglecting to water a pot-plant for a decade.

'Why not though?' Helen's voice broke her chain of thought. 'She's not looking for a hero, or a sperm donor. Just some fun. I understand what she's doing.'

'Some intimacy.' Caro nodded.

Kay pressed her lips together. 'A cuddle would be nice,' she said wistfully.

No-one spoke. Helen looked at Caro and Caro looked back at Helen and across the table, Kay looked at both of them. 'No,' she said and shook her head. 'Oh no. I couldn't ... I mean I *really* couldn't.'

'You really could, Kay,' Helen said.

'Are you on it?'

Helen smiled.

'You are!' Caro cried.

'I downloaded it in the States, but I haven't had time to do more than just chat with a couple of people.'

'You've chatted?' Kay said. 'You can chat to people?'

Helen nodded. She leaned her elbows on the table. 'I think it's marvellous, getting to talk to all sorts of people you'd never have had the chance to otherwise. I mean, what did we have before dating apps? We had to stay home and grow our hair long enough to swing it down, while we waited for the next knight to come along and rescue us.'

'And we didn't get to check if he was crushingly boring,' Caro said.

'Or self-obsessed.'

'Or had bad breath.'

'We had the pub!' Kay interrupted. 'It wasn't all bad.'

'It was pretty random though.' Caro laughed. 'I may as well have thrown a dart at a dartboard, blindfolded, for all the forethought that went into some of my relationships. At least there's a little stab at compatibility on these things.'

'You've been on it too?'

'Not Tinder.' Glass at her lips, Caro turned her mouth down in distaste.

'Elite-singles?' Helen said.

'Of course.'

And across the table, Kay smiled.

'Let's do it!' Caro stood up and pushed her chair back. 'Phone.' She stretched her hand to Kay.

'It's on the kitchen bench,' Helen said.

Kay laughed. 'You won't guess the code.'

'Alex's birthday?'

Now she paled.

'140999' And looking at Kay, Helen winked. 'Six months before Libby.'

Kay covered her eyes. 'I can't look.'

Caro was back in the room. 'Right, what do want your username to be?'

'Nothing! I don't want a username.'

'KB.' Caro said. 'That's fairly anonymous.'

'KB?' She turned to Helen who was also on her feet. 'Where are you going? Don't leave me now.'

Helen leaned over and squeezed her shoulder. 'I'm getting the last bottle, KB. Who's even going to know it's you?'

'Every student I've ever taught?'

'And then we'll take some pictures.'

'I'll do wardrobe,' Caro said.

'Wardrobe? We're nowhere near my wardrobe.'

'Exactly!' Caro picked her glass up and drained it. 'That's why we should get it done now. As far away as possible from your actual wardrobe. OK, Helen, what have you got?' she said, already on her way to the bedroom.

'I've no idea.' At the fridge again, Helen waved the bottle in her hand. 'It's all still in boxes.'

'I'll find something!' And within another minute, Caro had found something. She came back in, a V-neck blouse in one hand, a t-shirt in the other.

'Not that,' Helen said, as Caro held up her *Head-Smashed-In-Buffalo-Jump* t-shirt.

'I like it,' Kay said.

'I agree. It's a better design than the *For Fox Sake, Stop the Hunting ...*' Caro laughed.

'But they did, in the end, didn't they?' Kay said. 'They did stop the hunting.'

'I was never in any doubt.' Helen nodded.

Kay smiled. 'We were pretty sure of ourselves back then, weren't we?'

'It's easy to be sure,' Caro said, 'when you haven't been tested.'

No-one spoke. No-one needed to. They knew each other's sadnesses as well as their own, the ways in which life had failed them, the ways in which they had failed themselves. And they knew now, what they could never have then. How life was a book that started easy but only became more difficult. Each chapter more challenging than the one before, as all that was once solid, family, beliefs, opportunity, thinned to air.

'This,' Helen said quietly, 'is supposed to be a party.'

'Two, actually,' Caro said.

'That's three parties in a week.' Kay smiled. 'More than I've been to in a decade.'

'Music?' Helen put her glass down.

'Music,' Caro agreed.

'Music,' Kay echoed.

So, the music went on.

And on ...

And on ...

And hours later, with the sofa drowned in clothing, a mascara wand in the chicken korma, Helen crashed out in her bed and Caro in the spare room, Kay answered the intercom to the taxi she had called. 'Not bad,' she said as settled herself in the backseat and opened her newly installed Tinder app. There she was. With a profile picture that showed a handsome, confident woman, skin flushed with the warmth of a July evening, features softened by humour and champagne.

23

I n the end it was easy.
    In the end all she had to do, was open her phone and send the text.

> This is me and I'm in town for today only.

AND THEN ANOTHER TO TOMASZ.

> Matt called. Crisis with the offering. He's asked if I can come in. It's lucky I was here. I should make it back, but I'll be late. I'll order a taxi. Don't wait up.

SHE DIDN'T STOP to ask why she was doing what she was doing. And even if she had, she wouldn't have been able to say. Wouldn't have been able to explain how it didn't matter that she wasn't in competition with Helen anymore, because she was, and always would be, in competition with herself. Perhaps she had thought it was over? Felt the distance was run? 'Beautiful,' the bridal assistant had said and for the first time in her life, Caro had looked in the mirror and believed that too. And surely it was then that peace could have been made? A truce between the awkward child she had been, and the woman she was now. 'There's a glow about you,' Kay had said. 'An aura.' The glow of a woman loved. The aura of a woman who – at last – was comfortable in her skin, confidence and pheromones oozing because she was, finally, beautiful.

Like Helen had been when they first met. Helen, who had blown Caro away with her easy confidence and natural beauty. Who had turned every head when she walked into a room. Who could and did have her pick, had her fun, in this one and only life.

All this, unexamined and unthought, stoked the engine that had Caro taking a taxi from Helen's flat to her own, where she showered and changed and was, within another hour, walking onto the terrace of the Langmere Riverside Hotel where shiny beautiful people, with good skin and deep pockets were enjoying the sunshine. A world in which for the first time in her life she truly felt she belonged.

And who would not want to test that? Who would not, just once, want to turn heads? Bask in the sunny uplands they had long coveted? Which was all she was doing. That's why she was here, to do a little sunbathing, to test the water after all, dip a toe and nothing more. Drinks with a handsome man, on a sun-dappled terrace, by a river that had seen so much worse.

·   ·   ·

SPENCER WAS WAITING by the bar wearing that enigmatic smile and an exquisitely cut shirt. Watching every step she took.

'Can I get you a drink?' he said and looked at a watch worth upwards of thirty thousand pounds. 'Although it is a little early.'

'It's five o'clock somewhere,' she joked. And a few minutes later as he handed her a glass of champagne, deliberately letting the back of his hand brush the back of her hand, she felt the explosion of desire in her stomach. 'Cheers.' She lifted her glass to her lips. One drink. That's all.

'Cheers.' He had raised his own glass, and was looking at her over the rim, his eyes drilling through flesh, easy as a knife through butter. 'You look beautiful,' he said.

As she struggled to hold his eye, her hands tightened around the stem of her glass. No-one had ever said that to her before. Not once.

'I'm hoping.' He smiled. 'That you don't have a train this time.'

Returning the smile, she leaned back in her chair and crossed her legs. She had changed into a sleek summer wrap-over, a dress that showed her legs, that, sitting like this, rose high above her knees. She sipped her champagne and watched his eyes travel up her thighs, her stomach squeezing as she imagined his hands doing the same. Her whole body tingled with excitement, with the awareness of a power that was as extraordinary as it was novel. Often, standing upright, suited and buttoned, she'd been aware of the power she held over men. But that was cold, hard-earned and hard-edged; a power that came from being better prepared, and confident of the win. A power that

stayed tame, confined as it was to the office or the boardroom. Nothing like this, nothing at all.

She felt as if she had stepped through the looking glass.
A newly discovered land in which she was queen indeed,
with knights like Spencer Cooper in the palm of her hand.
And with his Rolex watch and his tailored shirt, Spencer
Cooper was a knight of such calibre that Caroline Hardcastle of Artillery Terrace, would never have dared throw
her handkerchief at. The decision was hers. She held all the
cards.

Ah, but I'm afraid I do have a train to catch, she could say,
allowing his disappointment to pool at her feet.

'Not this time,' was what she said. 'No train this time.'

THE SECOND DRINK they took up in Spencer's room.

THE THIRD DRINK Spencer poured wearing a white towel
around his waist, his hair wet from the shower. His waistline
held the shape of a rubber-ring, his back was covered with
moles and, as Caro put her glass down on the bedside table
and poured herself a tumbler of water instead, her arms
were molten lead. What had she done? Underneath his
amour, Spencer Cooper was a pale and heavy man. A
phrase, she was thinking as she pulled the sheets around
her knees, that could have described the sex. Pale, heavy
and disappointing.

'Shall I order typical something else?' Spencer said,
nodding at her untouched champagne.

'No.' She shook her head, watching as he took clean
underwear from a drawer and went into the bathroom.
Above her head an air-conditioning unit hummed, and

across the room she could see herself in the large wall mirror, naked and small, adrift in an ocean of white sheets. She wanted to grab her clothing and run away, but she couldn't move. She felt dull to the point of inertia. And where would she run to anyway? Where could she go that would rid her of the sight of his pale and hairy bottom, take away the weight of guilt filling every pore.

Besides, Spencer was acting as if there was nothing to run from. He was up, opening another bottle from the fridge, showering, as if this was something he was wholly accustomed to. As if he were only tidying up before the cleaners came. The water in her mouth doubled in volume, became such a lump she had to put her hand to her throat to help it down. Spencer, she understood, wasn't acting. This *was* something he was wholly accustomed to, and there had been no pretence. A rush of selfish desire had taken them from the bar to his room, to bed, where two middle-aged people had had pale and heavy sex. He hadn't put his arms around her and pulled her close. He hadn't stroked the small of her back, he hadn't pushed her hair behind her ear or looked into her eyes or kissed her neck. They had fucked. And after, he had got up and asked her if he should order something else, because he was the type of man who had the means to be able to order something else.

The bathroom door opened. 'Are you going to shower?' he said, pulling a shirt on.

Tumbler in hand, Caro looked up. He wasn't a knight, and she had never been a queen.

'It's just ...' That smile came back, the manipulative self-awareness of a man, pulling a woman's strings. 'It's just that I have an appointment at six.'

In other words, it's time for you to leave. In other words, I hold the cards now. In other words, ... in other words ....

She didn't get to the end of the thought. Scooping the sheet around her body she stood up and took the first step into fifteen blurred minutes of excruciation. A brief episode in which parts of her mind were utterly scrambled and other parts ordered with precision.

'WE COULD SHARE A TAXI?' he said, as she stood dressed by the door.

This was all she would ever be able to remember, whenever she tried to touch upon a scar of time that never managed to heal, one kaleidoscopic moment.

Numb, she shook her head. 'I really have to get going.'

Spencer put his hand on her shoulder and gave her a chaste kiss on the cheek. 'That was fun,' he said. 'Look me up if you change your mind? I'll take you for cocktails at One World. Show you the view of my town.'

'Change my mind?' Confusion swept through Caro like a flood. Had she mis-read the situation?

'Matt told me you were leaving the city?' He smiled.

'Of course,' she managed. And turning to go, she stopped. 'Did he also tell you why I was leaving?'

'Yes.' Spencer nodded. 'Yes, he did.'

'And you still sent me that text?'

'Which you answered,' he said.

PART II

24

*I*f you wait long enough.

Kay smiled. She was standing on the pavement outside her parents' house, looking at the front border of their garden, at the triumphant crowd of blood-red lilies that filled it. They were vibrant blooms, that nevertheless disappeared every autumn for so long it was possible to forget they had ever existed. But they did, and every summer they came back, and with them memories of the spring her mother had planted them and yes, *if you wait long enough the answer will come.*

Where had she read that? It didn't matter. What mattered was that it was true, because the answer to a question Alex had asked when he was no more than four years old, had finally arrived.

Where do people go when they die?

It had been the kind of fact-seeking missile of question only a small child can ask. She could still see his face, the way his tiny eyebrows had knitted together as she had tried and failed to provide an answer he might understand. But back in those days she had been learning too, how difficult it was going to be for him to negotiate a world that was not black and white. Perhaps, she was thinking now, instead of the muddled response about spirits and heaven she remembered giving, she should have just said, 'let's wait, shall we? Let's wait and see where they go?' Because twenty years later, here surely was the answer. They don't go anywhere. As long as those lilies bloomed and she was here to remember the planting of them, how could the answer be anything else? Her mother was present: in spirit and in love. As long the wooden egg Alex had given to his grandmother still sat in the front room window (she could see it now), and Alex remembered the gifting of it, her mother hadn't gone anywhere.

She walked up the short drive, stopping at the porch door to look back at the lilies, and as she looked it felt to Kay that this was the first time she had really noticed them. She couldn't understand why. They were such a vivid colour. Shaking her head, she opened the door to the empty space where her mother's wheelchair had been kept, the shelf where her mother's coat had hung, the rack where her shoes had sat. And suddenly, her head felt too light, her legs loose as straw. Grief was an animal she was only just beginning to learn to live with. It could not be managed, or tamed. If, one day she thought she had it under control, another day it would jump out and claw her legs from under her. Like now. She reached for the handle of the front door, composing herself and, when she was ready pushed it open and stepped into a darkened hallway. 'I'm here,' she called. There was no answer; her shoulders slumped. Her father, she guessed, would be in his usual chair by the window, hands locked together, thumbs rubbing away, that bit smaller, that bit more withdrawn. 'I'm here,' she said, a little quieter and leaned around the door to the living room. He was in his usual chair, but his hands weren't locked together. He had his phone at his ear, listening, smiling.

'Just popping some shopping in.' She held up a carrier bag.

Glancing over, he raised a hand in greeting and turned back.

Kay frowned. 'I'll put it in the kitchen?'

'Did you really? What an extraordinary woman you are.'

'I said,' she repeated. 'I'll put it in the kitchen.' Who was he talking to?

As he turned again, he placed a hand over his phone. 'You're early.'

'Am I?'

'I'm on the phone.'

'I can see. And what followed was an extraordinary moment in which Kay stood in the open doorway waiting, until it became clear that her father was waiting too, for her to go. 'I'll leave you to it then,' she mouthed and didn't move.

He nodded. 'Close the door a bit.'

Stunned, she pulled the door closed and stood looking at it.

'You're early.' Craig glanced up. He was leaning against the counter, reading the cooking instructions on a ready meal.

'So, I hear,' Kay said and looked at the clock, narrowed her eyes and looked harder. It was five o'clock. She couldn't make sense of it. Five o'clock was a part of the day that hadn't really existed for the last thirty years, squashed as it had been between lesson-planning, marking, supermarket runs. It meant at least another two hours before she could sit down with *Real Housewives*. It meant that she'd reached the end of all the things she had to do today with time to spare. And although this adjustment always took some time at the beginning of the school holidays, the necessary slowing down of her days had been something she'd welcomed. A six-week respite from the hamster wheel. Only now it wasn't a respite. Now it was forever. She bit down on her lip. All this time. How on earth was she going to fill it?

'Five.' She nodded, her chin lifting as she breathed in a familiar rich smell. 'Who is Dad talking to?' But she didn't wait for an answer. 'Is that what he's having?' she said, staring at the packet Craig held. 'Chicken Tikka? Dad doesn't eat Indian.'

'He does now. He asked me to pick it up.'

'Right then.' She glanced at the bag she'd just dropped on the kitchen table. It was full of ready meals: fish pie, chicken pie, toad-in-the-hole. Her father's usual fare.

Craig put the packet down. 'I don't know who he's talking to, but it's every day now.'

'Every day?' Kay looked back along the hallway, but even with elephant ears she wouldn't have been able to hear. 'Who is she?'

'She?' Craig arched his eyebrows. 'You know more than me. Have you booked Cyprus?'

'Not yet.' And from along the hallway, she heard laugher. 'Whoever it is, he obviously finds her amusing.'

Ignoring her, Craig took a fork and set about stabbing the plastic covering of the ready meal. 'So, you haven't booked Cyprus, and you're probably bingeing on *Real Housewives*.'

Kay smiled. 'My retirement hasn't even started, Craig. Not officially. Not until September.'

'And I'm not going to let you become a recluse, Mrs B.'

'I'm not going to ––' But again she was interrupted by laughter. She turned to look. 'You've really no idea?'

'I've really no idea.' He waved the fork. 'Maybe your father has an admirer. One of the ladies I care for has a new boyfriend. She met him at her husband's funeral.'

'He's eighty-six.' Kay frowned. 'And there were no single ladies at my mother's funeral. Not that I remember anyway.'

'And my lady is eighty-nine!' He opened the microwave and threw the meal in. 'Maybe he put himself on Tinder.'

'He's eighty-six, Craig.'

Fork in hand, Craig turned. 'Is there an age limit?'

She opened her mouth, but nothing came out. Her father wouldn't be on Tinder! That was the most ridiculous thing she'd heard. Not least because he could barely work his phone as it was, constantly archiving messages from the doctor and the bank, and then ringing her in a panic when he couldn't find them. 'No,' she said and sat down. 'I don't suppose there is an age limit, considering I'm on it now.'

'Tinder!' Craig fell back against the counter, his hands covering his face. 'Mrs B is on Tinder?'

'Don't laugh.' Chin dipped, she ran her finger along the edge of the table. She felt exposed, as if he'd caught a glimpse of her in her underwear. 'I was persuaded,' she said. 'That's all.'

'I'm not laughing.' The smile dropped from Craig's face. 'I think it's great,' he said. 'I really do. Have you met anyone? Can I see? You can't give your number out, you know that ...'

'Stop!' Kay raised her hand. 'Just stop there. My friends set it up, and to be honest I haven't even looked at it. I'm ...' She paused.

'Scared?'

As she looked up, the smallest whisper of confirmation escaped her lips. *Yes.* Scared was exactly the right word for how she felt, and not for the first time she found herself amazed at the emotional intelligence of a young man who had gone through school failing almost every subject. 'Well ...' But she didn't know how to continue. To say she hadn't looked wasn't quite true. She had opened the app just once, done a tiny amount of scrolling before, very quickly, closing it again. The muscled angst of teenage memories had stopped her from doing anything as bold as sending someone a *like*. A like? When had she ever done that? She knew exactly when. Valentine's Day 1983. She had sent an anonymous card to Stephen Webber, the class heartthrob on whom she'd had a secret and intense crush. That was the only time girls were allowed to do the choosing. Valentine's Day and leap year. And it wasn't a joke. It really was that these were the only times it had felt acceptable for a girl to make the move, and only then under the protection of anonymity. The few relationships she'd had before marrying Martin had all been instigated by the man. Boyfriends she had acquired because it had been better to have a boyfriend, than not have a boyfriend. Because all her friends had boyfriends. Because it was expected that she have a boyfriend. And although there was no need to re-write history, and she had loved Martin, he had done the asking and she couldn't help but wonder now how things might have turned out *if* ... She took a deep breath in, her shoulders rising as she looked at Craig. If she hadn't been so scared.

'Maths used to scare me,' Craig said, and shrugged.

'I remember.' Kay smiled. She did remember him, right at the back of her class, a look of utter bewilderment on his face every time she said the word, *fraction*.

'But I can still remember what you said.'

'Really? What did I say?'

'You said that everyone finds everything hard, until they know what they're doing. And that it's difficult to like something, if you're not very good at it.'

'Did I?' Kay nodded. He'd hit the nail on the head, or she had. She had no clue what she was doing, she wasn't enjoying it, and she wasn't even sure she wanted to be doing it.

Popping the meal onto a plate, and the plate onto a tray, Craig turned. 'Let me get this to your dad and then I'll make a cuppa and we'll have a little Tinder lesson.' He winked. 'I'll be teacher this time.'

'THAT'S A NO. You never give your phone number out, and if they ask for it straight away it's a red flag.' As he spoke, Craig made a square shape with his hands. Her father had been served his dinner and now here she was, roles reversed as Craig started his lesson in Tinder etiquette. 'A big red flag,' he repeated.

'Good to know.' Kay nodded. 'Except flags tend to be rectangular.'

'They can be octonotical for all it matters.'

'Octagonal.'

'Whatever it is!' Craig frowned. 'You don't give your phone number out. This is serious Mrs B, there are some real looney-tunes out there. OK?'

'OK,' she repeated.

'What about this one?' Craig turned the phone. 'Adam. He's fifty-seven, he likes Netflix, sounds and football.'

'What are sounds?'

'A middle-aged way of saying music. Personally, I think he's trying to be too cool.'

'So, it's a, no?'

'It's a no.' Craig swiped left, and Adam disappeared. 'Richard? He likes football, cycling, running and hiking.'

Kay shook her head. 'I could never keep up. It's exhausting just looking at his photos.'

'John?'

'Why on earth has he chosen that photo?' She leaned forward to look closer at a profile picture that showed a heavy-set man striding out of the waves, a la Daniel Craig in James Bond.

Craig laughed. 'Oh, you have so much to learn, Mrs B. That is very tame.' And he swiped left. 'How about Tony? He's looking for that *special* someone.'

Again, she shook her head. She was just looking. *Special* was an adjective too far. Plus, Tony's profile picture showed him clutching a cat. 'Sorry,' she mouthed to the cat, as Craig swiped left.

Handing her phone back, Craig stood up. 'We'll have to carry on tomorrow.' he said. 'I'm going to be late. My five-thirty is grumpy enough as it is.'

Distracted, Kay nodded. 'This one is funny.' She was reading the profile of someone who had called himself Goose.

'Goose?' Craig wrinkled his nose. 'What kind of a name is that?'

'Goose was the sidekick in *Top Gun*. I think he's trying to ...' But before she could get any further Craig had leaned in.

'Oh no!' he said. 'A definite, massive no! Anyone who's anonymous is a big no. Swipe left.'

'Really?'

'You can't see his face! He's reading a book called ––'

'*How to be an Extrovert,*' Kay said. 'I thought that was funny.'

'Mrs B.' Craig straightened up. 'Why would anyone stay anonymous?'

She didn't answer, watching instead as Craig rinsed his cup and put it in the dishwasher. There were, she knew, a myriad reasons why people stayed anonymous. Her thirteen-year-old-self would attest to that.

AFTER SAYING goodbye to her father, she idled along the street toward her own house. Mid- July and the sun was high in the sky. She was reluctant to go home. What was there to go home to? Alex was out with his girlfriend again, and although the fact that he now had a social life, was, as Helen had said, brilliant, it was also a shock. One day it was her and Alex, trundling along together like a set of parallel lines, the next he'd taken a sudden detour. She'd looked up from her book one evening to find him gone. Or that's how it felt.

Stopping outside her neighbours, the Khans' house, she took her phone from her pocket and checked the time. What to do? The thought of going home to sit in an empty house on such a beautiful evening was intolerable. Forehead creased in thought, she sniffed the air. Someone was barbecuing and she knew it would be the Khans. They got their grill out on the first of April and didn't put it away again until mid-November, and if she had the kind of extended family they had, she would do the same. She'd long since lost track of who was living in the house now, but there was never a shortage of comings and goings. The children had grown, but judging by the car park that was the front garden, all of them were still living there and all of them had cars. Mrs Khan's mum had moved in a couple of years ago, and Mr Khan's brother, who she knew by sight, was a frequent visitor. He had grown children as well and one of them must have a baby, because this summer she'd seen a pram parked by the front door. Either way, there would never be a shortage of company in that house and as Kay put her phone back, she allowed herself to drift into a fantasy world. A world in which she hadn't got divorced and had instead gone on to have more children, who had also grown and settled nearby, who also came home frequently, off-loading tricycles on the front lawn and car-seats in the hallway. A world in which Martin's family had stayed her family too. Thinking this she pressed her lips together. Divorce. The very word meant a turning apart, a parting of the ways. Not just the couple, not just the estate, but the families which the marriage had joined. Reaching the junction halfway along her road, she stopped at the kerb and looked up. Martin's father had died last year. She'd sent flowers but she hadn't gone to the funeral. At the time it hadn't felt right, now it didn't make sense. A man who, half a lifetime ago had welcomed her into his house with a plate of jolly rice and an insistence that she watch the Arsenal game with him. What friends they might have been had they stayed in touch. Stayed family. She should have gone. She should have thrown convention to the wind and just gone, and as she stood blinking, she didn't know if it was the smoke from the Khans' barbecue or the breeze in her eyes or the idea of her lonely house waiting.

She did another walk around the block. If there was no company at home, there might be company to be had on the street: a wave, a passing greeting. But the tables outside The Carpenter's Arms, her local for so many years, were filled with people she didn't recognise. Men who wore cricket shirts, Summit Electronics emblazoned across the front. She didn't recognise the name of the sponsor either.

Head down she gave up and walked home, stopping only to look across at the darkened windows of Mrs Newall's bungalow. Mrs Newall, who had been her longest standing neighbour had also died last year, and Kay had gone to her funeral. Which is where she had met a daughter and son-in-law, she'd never seen before and why she recognised them a few weeks later carrying out box after box to a smart SUV. Including, she'd noticed, the leaf-blower Mrs Newall had bought, and which she'd used just once before she fell over, broke her hip and never really got up again. As the bungalow got cleared and put on the market, she'd seen the daughter and son-in-law more times than she ever had in all the years Mrs Newall had lived opposite. Then the *For Sale* sign went up and she never saw them again. A couple of weeks later a *For Rent* sign went up, and since then Kay had lost track of who did, or didn't live there. A young man who left early and came back late, a couple in their thirties who never seemed to go anywhere and didn't talk to anyone. Right now, it was empty and had been for a few weeks and it made her sad to see the garden so unkempt. She stood looking at the cluster of leaves under the Japanese maple tree, the limp gladioli Mrs Newall had been so assiduous with, supporting them with trellis and bamboo, talking and tending to them as if they were children.

Taking her keys out, she looked up at her own house. This was the house she had grown up in, the house she had moved back to after her divorce, when her parents had taken the bungalow at the end of the street, and she had needed to be close to them. Like, she had once thought, Alex would always need to be close to her. Unwilling to contemplate the idea that she might have been wrong, that her son was more than capable of the separation, that it might be something he was actively moving towards, she put the key in the door and turned the lock.

Inside on the kitchen table lay a package and a note from Alex.

THIS ARRIVED. *Out with ... Eme ...*

THE END WAS SUCH a scrawl she still couldn't make it out. Emmeline? Or EmmyLou?

Frowning, Kay turned the package over. The postmark was local, but it wasn't her birthday, and she couldn't think who would be sending her something. She tore it open and pulled out a white box, with stylish lettering.

Magic Wand.

Butterfly wings swirled; her knees went to water. *Use it or lose it,* Caro had said. But Caro had always had a gadget for everything: electric toothbrush, face massager. As if it were wired, Kay eased a hand into the envelope and pulled out another two small rectangular boxes, around which a piece of paper had been folded.

DEAR KAY, (she read)

Estrogen cream, (topical HRT) and lubricant. Start with the lubricant. The topical HRT will take a few days, especially as yours is vacuum-packed!

Lots of love,

Helen and Caro xxx

PS. There are three settings on the vibrator, we recommend you start slowly, with number one.

PPS. We charged it for you.

. . .

HER HAND WENT to her mouth, tears pricking at her eyes. What to do? What should she do?

THE FIRST THING she did was shut and lock the kitchen door. The second thing she did was take the vibrator out of its box, which proved difficult because her hands were shaking. Hands that had written out solutions to equations that had baffled her contemporaries at university, and impressed hundreds, probably thousands of teenagers, hands that had held and nursed another life, hands that had peeled and chopped a million carrots, that had combed the hair of a dying woman, that had comforted, nourished, educated, shook now at the sight of this small white torpedo? It was so ridiculous that she laughed, but still her hands shook and now her legs did too. She was all sorts of things, all at once. Terrified, excited, highly amused ... alive!

She checked the lock first on the kitchen door, then the front door and carrying the three boxes as carefully as if they were tiny people she went upstairs and laid them on her bed.

When was the last time, Helen had asked.

I don't remember, she had said.

But she did. Oh, she did. Two weeks before Martin had left. Maybe he hadn't known he was leaving, but she had. So yes, she remembered everything. The hard curve of his shoulder, the warmth of his skin, the familiar smell of him. Everything. Sixteen years then. That was how long, and she had meant what she had said to Caro and Helen. No one was coming into her home, while Alex had been so young. Celibacy had been a choice, that had grown into a lifestyle that she wasn't unhappy with. Then again, she wasn't sure she could say she was particularly happy either. She walked over to her bedroom window and looked out. The lawn was empty, cleared of all the scattered motorcycle pieces she had become accustomed to. Alex had moved on, losing interest in his latest hobby as quickly as he had become obsessed. It was a strength and a weakness, this ability of his to turn a corner and put out of mind what he had left behind. And now she was thinking of Mrs Newall's garden, last year's Maple leaves turning a slow black. It was time. She had to make a change. She had to try.

She pulled the curtains closed, took her clothes off, put her bathrobe on and picked up the torpedo. Pressing the button, the vibrator buzzed instantly into life. Kay jumped, her hands clumsy as paddles as she scrambled to switch it off. God it was noisy! There was no way she could ... If Alex was. ... Chewing on her lip, she hurried down the stairs and shut both the kitchen curtains and the living room curtains.

'OK,' she said, as back upstairs she looked at herself in the wardrobe mirror. 'You gave birth to a nine-pound baby Kay, you can do this.'

But *youch!* The lubricant was freezing, and sloppy and it was every awful smear examination she'd ever had. Sticky and naked, clutching her torpedo like an Olympic torch she wobbled across to the airing cupboard, found a towel and laid it across her sheet. And then she started.

Slowly, very, very slowly ... and carefully, because she was terrified and tentative and tense. And it hurt. God, it hurt! It scraped and it was sore, but the vibration was gentle. With a little more lubricant, which didn't feel so cold now, it began to feel something like OK. *'You can do this,'* she whispered and eased it in further, and as she did her hips began to move. She pressed again, and the vibrations increased and because the soreness had subsided, she pressed a third time and the vibrations increased again, becoming powerfully insistent, setting in motion the beginning of a physical reaction that she remembered as if from a dream. A response that she couldn't haven't controlled, if she'd tried. She didn't. She lay back, let her legs splay out and closed her eyes. It was pleasurable and it was easy and as the waves began, distant and small, her head tipped back, her arm splayed out and for the first time in sixteen years she surrendered herself to a pleasure she understood now was still a vital part of life.

—————

25

Monday came and went. Helen's day had been filled with the usual procession of fever and forms, sprains and sickness. And (not that she had been expecting anything), no word from Christian, or anyone at Stronger Together. The green cardigan had been taken out of the bin and hung back on the hook, and declining Tina's offer of a Bakewell tart, Helen had escaped on her coffee break to sit in the sun and brood over lost opportunities.

Back home, leaning against the kitchen counter, she ate a Quiche Lorraine straight from the packet, poured a glass of wine and took it out to the balcony. The park was full of families and Helen was full of regret. Thursday evening had been fun, but Friday had been lost to a hangover that had her eating everything in the flat. Including a Christmas pudding, found at the back of the cupboard which she steamed in the microwave and ate with the curtains closed watching *Pride and Prejudice* for the hundredth time.

And even though she had promised herself not to drink all week, here she was, Monday evening, starting again. But what else was there to do? The landscape of her evenings had changed dramatically. The peaks and troughs of family life, flattening out into this plateau, which she had to accept was probably going to be her home-screen for a long time now. Stronger Together, had obviously decided they were stronger without her (and who could blame them). So, what was she going to do?

'What Do People Do All Day?' she said out loud, and just hearing the words made her smile. When Jack was tiny, this had been his favourite book: *What Do People Do All Day?* It was a story populated by pigs with all the boy pigs wearing uniforms, and all the girl pigs baking pies, and although Helen had hated it, Jack had loved it. Sitting down, she stretched her legs out to the chair opposite and chuckled. She needed the sequel: *What Do People Do All Evening?* Because when the kids have grown and the pies have been baked and the uniforms put away, what *do* people do? Join a yoga class in a draughty hall? Join a gym in a windowless building? Light candles and write poetry? In another age, she was thinking, she would have been surrounded by company, generations staying under the same roof. And if that wasn't the case there would have been company to be had at the end of the street in a local tavern, or at least a chat over the garden fence with a neighbour. The only company she could expect for the next twelve hours was Netflix, or Instagram and the reality of her situation was suddenly so daunting, she put her glass down and leaned forward, chin in hands. This was not what she had envisaged divorce would be. The problem was, beyond vague dreams of a domestic space of her own, she hadn't envisaged anything. Then again, what would she be doing had she stayed? Drinking wine in the kitchen while she waited for Lawrence to return from his run, or his ride?

She took a sip of wine. It tasted bitter as grapefruit, and in a fit of decision she took the glass to the sink and poured it away, turned and stared at her empty flat. At least Lawrence did things.! He always had. Becoming a father had barely altered the course of his life, whereas motherhood had changed every aspect of hers. And although there was no doubt it had given her a purpose; it had also given her an excuse. All those years of sitting on the beach guarding the sandwiches? They hadn't been so much about sandwiches, as avoidance. The armchair-sized cushion Lawrence's wage had provided, had allowed her to let the seasons turn and the years pass. So, what on earth was she going to do with the rest of her life?

'You can start by unpacking, Helen,' she said out loud. 'And then you can stop talking to yourself.' So, she did. She opened Spotify, connected her speaker and set about unpacking. An hour later, with three boxes emptied and a shelving unit filled, she sat down for a break and an obligatory scroll through Instagram. When she reached an ad for *Seasons of Becoming* a coaching course for 'middle-aged women, seeking a new direction', she paused, reading through. *Are you restless in your career? Do you feel curious about what else is possible? Long for change?* It was disconcerting to understand how much her phone knew about her, but she was restless and she did long for change, and as she tapped the link and followed through, it was far more disconcerting for Helen to admit that the change she thought she had made, from being married to not being married, had changed the view from her kitchen sink and not much else.

But what had she expected? Backstage hands gliding new scenery into her life? A great package of an answer dropped from the sky? She took her reading glasses off, tapping the arm against her chin. It wasn't far from the truth to say that she had lived her life this passively, waiting for one scene to end, before another began. And now here she was, more alone than she had been at any stage of her life, centre stage of an empty stage. She opened her phone again and read on. Through guided reflection and honest conversation, *Seasons of Becoming,* promised to '*guide her towards who she was now, not ten years ago*'. It promised *realignment, reinvention, rhythm.* She got her bank card out and signed up. One hundred and fifty pounds lighter, but already that bit more, realigned, she followed the link and opened the first module, a video of a serene looking woman wearing neutral-coloured yoga clothing.

'Find a quiet room,' the woman said (serenely). 'And sit cross-legged on the floor, in a space where you won't be disturbed.'

Easy-peasy. Helen pressed pause, plumped up the cushion on her armchair, settled back and pressed play.

'It's important that you sit on the floor and not a chair so that you can feel grounded in the moment.'

Frowning, she slid to the floor, used the cushion to prop her phone, wrestled her limbs into some kind of crossed leg position, and pressed play.

'Close your eyes if it helps.'

It didn't. How could she see the pause/play button?

'Ask this one simple question.'

She took a deep breath.

'What am I truly longing for at this time in my life?'

Was that it?

'Listen without judgement.'

OK. She took another breath. *Don't judge, Helen. Don't judge.*

'Let whatever comes up rise without judgement. Don't censor yourself.'

And she tried, she really tried. But what came up was a screaming pain in her inner knee as the ligament stretched beyond memory and endurance. Twisting, her knee clicked and (it felt), fell apart. She grabbed the joint, manoeuvring herself out of hell, back to relief

'Return to the answer.'

Answer? Helen looked at her phone. She didn't have one to return to.

'Ask the same question again. Let more answers unfold. Don't rush it.'

Don't rush it? That was a bloody cheek. 'Can I sit in a chair?' she said, as she hefted herself back into the armchair.

'Reflect. What emotions came up during this exercise? How can you honour them? What's one action you can take next week to start exploring that longing?'

Falling back, Helen pressed pause again and held her phone at her chest. She could start yoga, that's what she could do. In some draughty hall somewhere, she could honour her knees by starting yoga. Or she could pour another glass of wine? Or, she could go to bed and start again tomorrow, because it didn't matter how grounded she was, or if her eyes were open or closed, she still would have no idea how to answer such a vague catch-all, 'what are you longing for' except with another vague catch -all, 'I have no idea'.

Frustrated, unrhythmic and not at all aligned, she closed the window, and opened her email, eyes widening in surprise as she read through the subject line of the newly arrived mail:

Admin Director. Stronger Together.

. . .

DEAR HELEN, (she read)

I hope you are well. Forgive this late mail, I had hoped to get round to this earlier, but we had a crisis in our Ecuador clinic that diverted me.

Anyway, I'm mailing to invite you back to meet our chief medical officer, Fiona Chambers. It's short notice, but could you make Wednesday this week?

26

Almost at the end of the second week of a holiday that had no end, and Kay was still waking at seven, as if her body clock had sensed the permanence of the re-wiring and was staging a fight-back. She closed her eyes against the sun, fingertips padding the lids as she lay listening to her empty house. What a conundrum middle-age was. There were no signposts to tell her which way. Not like childhood ... Step this way to grow up ... Turn right for university, left for a job. Not like young adulthood ... This junction to start looking for a mate, start pro-creating, start collecting twigs (well, Matalan cushions), building your nest. It was almost as if, once a woman reached a certain age, she was expected to just drop off the face of the earth. She sat up and propped herself against her pillow. What was she supposed to do with this almost empty, almost silent nest? What happened with birds? Didn't they just fly off? And then she was thinking about Helen, and her wall of boxes. Helen who had flown so far, only to come back to a nest she didn't want to be in. She hadn't said as much, but it was as clear to Kay as the nose on her face that

Helen didn't want to be back. And the irony of the situation was that Helen had the best reason in the world to stay, her grandson Ben, and she, Kay, had not much reason at all. And then she was thinking of her parents' house, the carriage clock on the mantel that had been her mother's retirement present, keeping time long after her mother's time had run out.

In a habit that already become worryingly established, she reached for her phone and opened Tinder. She had one new message. Phone propped on her knees, head propped on her pillow she swiped it open.

Hi, what are you up to? 😉

THE MESSAGE, she saw, had been sent at one am in the morning by James, who was fifty-two and liked, football (was there a man in England who didn't?), only 🍺 at the weekend and 🏆 often.

Shaking her head she unmatched and then blocked him. In her first Tinder- innocence days, she would have excused one am in the morning as a disrespectful mistake and given James another chance. But Craig had warned her. 'It's a booty-call', he'd said, the first time it had happened. 'Delete, then block.' Kay wasn't sure what had surprised her the most. The fact that here she was, a decade on from her last maths lesson with a young man who had possibly been her most hopeless student, and he was now the teacher and she the lost cause, *or* that middle-aged men who only 'drank at the weekend', were sending booty calls at one am to middle-aged women they had never met.

Tinder, she was quickly coming to realise was a tin of Quality Street, with a surplus of Toffee Pennys and very few Green Triangles. The app provided a masterclass in emotion and in just a few days she had run the gamut. Amazement as her very first 'like' had come in, astonishment and delight, quickly followed by excitement, as more had followed. Bewilderment, as she had read the messages, bemusement and now, already, scepticism. Because how quickly these would-be suitors gave themselves away, how unsavoury and disappointing they turned out to be.

Like Maurice, whose wife had recently died and who was new to Tinder, hoping to give love one last chance. Full of sympathy, Kay had exchanged several messages with him, until he had asked for her number and (remembering Craig's advice) she had declined. A response that had caused Maurice to vanish swifter than a magician's rabbit. She'd been left staring at the screen, disbelief turning to anger as she began to understand she had wasted time consoling a liar.

Or Graham. Fifty-five:

> A teacher? I love teachers! Do you use a cane? 😉

Or Florin. Fifty-one.

> You are being very beautiful.

Or Simon. Forty-nine.

> Just don't tell me you have a cat? You're too pretty for a cat. 😉

Or Nigel, Fifty-five (but my friends tell me I'm more like forty-five).

You don't run? Don't worry, I'll slow to a
walk for you! See if you can keep up 😅 😅

The only profile who hadn't disappointed, or leapt over
boundaries, who had responded in a polite timeframe,
consistently amused her, and hadn't asked for her number,
hadn't in fact typed a letter wrong was, Goose, whom,
despite Craig's insistence, she hadn't swiped left on.

Because although he was an expert in his chosen
subject, Craig was also young, born in a world where he'd
learned to take a selfie before he could write his name.
Offering himself into this human version of the pet-shop
window wasn't a giant step forward for him, not like it had
been for her. And not, she was thinking, like it obviously
was for Goose, who with his self-deprecating humour she
suspected was as scared of being the puppy left on the shelf
as she was.

Thinking this, she opened the chat window.

MORNING, she typed, now. *Hope you have good day today.*

UNIMAGINATIVE, but genuine. She did hope that he would
have a good day, she did enjoy 'talking' to him, and if that
was all it was, then compared to what else was on offer, it
was enough.

DOWNSTAIRS SHE FLIPPED the kettle on and read Alex's note.

Out tonight, don't make dinner for me.

SHE PUT the note down and opening the fridge for the milk, found herself staring at the macaroni cheese she'd taken out of the freezer last night. Along with half-completing one module of an on-line course in *The Psychology of Fitness,* and completing another season of *Real Housewives,* this was how she had spent her first full week of retirement: making dinners that no-one was around to eat. Her freezer was full of them. She'd even idled an hour away looking at smallholding properties in the North of Scotland, after which she had started digging a vegetable patch. She was meant to be flying to Cyprus. Every day Marianne texted for details of a flight Kay couldn't bring herself to book, and although the desire to make a change was real, she just couldn't work out how to take the first step. She was stuck; a fly caught in the web of a life years in the making. Superglued to her house and her garden, this tiny island that was beginning to feel as if it was all she had left.

She made tea, put the milk back and clutching her cup walked to the window. Once upon a time she had been a teacher, a wife, a daughter and a mother. Twenty-four years of full days, a child to care for and nurture, and then a mother to care for and comfort, students to educate, a husband to laugh and share with ... a life. What, really, did she have now? *Who,* really, was she now? An ex-wife? An ex-teacher? Just about an ex-mother? Even her father's social life was busier than her own. Last week he'd started a local-history course at the library. Which, after all the house-bound years of looking after her mother, was wonderful. But he hadn't told her. Craig had. And it seemed to Kay as she stood and watched the world go by, that if even her father didn't need her anymore, she might as well label herself an ex-daughter as well.

Outside, a well-dressed woman carrying a shiny handbag had stopped to let her dog pee against the corner post of Kay's driveway. She watched as the dog lifted its leg, and the woman got out her phone. Of course she did. Mobile phones, she thought as she sipped her tea, have destroyed the pause. Those moments in which nothing but a quiet patience is needed. She took another sip and frowned. The dog – in a change of toilet needs – was now squatting, the woman still scrolling. *Poop bag,* she thought as finally the woman looked down. But no poop bag appeared. The woman simply popped her phone away, did a double take along the street and, tugging at the lead began walking away.

Oh no! No No No No No! Kay slammed her cup down, flung the kitchen door open, and marched down her drive.

'Excuse me!' she shouted.

The woman turned.

'I think,' she said, pointing at the pile of steaming poo, 'that you've forgotten something.'

The woman froze, her dog looking up at her. 'It's not mine.'

It's not mine! Kay threw her head back and laughed. So, her son didn't need her anymore, and her father was busy every day talking to a secret admirer, and almost every conversation she had had on Tinder had led to a dead-end, but she would not stand by and let the world shit on her. Not today. Not tomorrow. Not ever. 'I know it's not yours,' she said, 'but it is your dog's, and if you don't come back and clear it up, I swear I will pick it up with my bare hands and stuff it in your handbag.'

The woman didn't move.

'Don't test me,' Kay seethed. 'I've tested me for the last twenty years and I haven't failed yet. Do. Not. Test Me!'

And she watched as, avoiding eye contact, the woman turned back, fished out a poop bag and set about cleaning up the mess.

Only when it had been cleared and they were on their way again, did Kay start back up the drive, slowly at first and then, as she heard her phone ringing, a little faster. Someone was calling. Someone still needed her.

27

Helen sat at the tiny table, in the tiny kitchen, in Libby's tiny flat, watching her daughter stir a pan of minced beef. The baggy jeans and sloppy t-shirt didn't disguise the extra weight Libby carried. And the way her hair had been scraped back into a thin, sad ponytail was a contradiction to the forced cheerfulness Helen had noticed her daughter had fallen into. The bossy confidence of Libby's teenage years had been replaced by this chippy, *I'm fine* attitude, which didn't fool Helen. It was, she understood, a riposte, Libby's defence against the world for having the temerity to think that she couldn't cope. For even considering that having a baby so young, with no resources, might not have been the smartest idea. And as Helen watched, she remembered the young men and women she'd met in the offices of Stronger Together just two days ago. They had been full of plans, full of ideas, shiny, confident, happy, and she had thoroughly enjoyed the hour long 'break-out' session she had spent with them, (the noodles were good too). Her heart ached. Almost the same age, Libby's stooped shoulders and tired eyes were the polar opposite, and thinking this Helen felt scared. She'd also met Dr Fiona Chambers, a smart, witty and formidably intelligent woman who had spoken to Helen as if she too were smart, witty and formidably intelligent. Her second interview had been interesting, thought-provoking and challenging. She'd kept her cool, answering questions that she'd prepped for and, knowing that this was her last chance, had tried hard to make sure that, if not exactly selling herself, she wasn't hiding under a bush either. Because wasn't that the best kept secret in life? Having the insight to understand when a never-to-be repeated opportunity has presented itself? And then possessing the courage to grab it? The interview had finished with Fiona standing up, shaking her hand and saying: 'Welcome to the team,' and Helen feeling supremely confident that she could do this job. More, she desperately wanted the opportunity to prove it.

Walking away, she had been walking on air, a feeling that had only inflated when the formal offer had come through. Terms and conditions. A list of vaccinations, visa requirements. Salary: for something she would have done for nothing. It had been an extraordinary couple of days in which she had struggled to keep the news to herself. With references still to clear she had held off from talking to either Caro, or Kay, wanting to present her achievement only when it was beyond doubt, a *fait accompli*. And maybe, like a child hiding a painting until completion, this was silly, but she couldn't help it. For years she had watched her friends' careers bloom, seen their professionalism, admired their achievements. Now that it might be her turn, she wanted to be sure. She picked up her cup and took a sip of lukewarm tea. It wasn't only the references that had stopped her calling Caro or Kay. It was Libby. She needed to tell Libby first. Ironic as it was, in a direct reversal of roles, she felt she needed her daughter's blessing before she could accept a job, halfway across the world.

'Won't be much longer,' Libby said turning from the pan.

'Don't worry.' Helen's stomach grumbled. She'd been here forty minutes, and she was hungry and hot. The windows were open, but it hadn't made a difference and with Libby so caught up in changing Ben and checking her schedule, she'd only just started on a dinner that Helen knew would take at least another half hour. Legs sticking to the back of the plastic chair she sat on, she watched her daughter move around the cramped kitchen, rinsing and stacking Ben's plastic cups, chopping carrots for him to snack on. 'Can I do anything?' she said. It must have been the third time she'd asked.

'All under control.' But Libby looked as if she'd lost something.

'Tomatoes?'

'Oh yes!' Libby grabbed a can of own-brand tomatoes. 'Ouch!' She yelped, pulling her finger back and dropping the tin in the sink.

'Are you OK?'

'Fine, mum.' Libby grimaced. 'I just cut myself. It's all under control.'

'OK.' Every minute she could feel herself deflating. How on earth was she going to start the conversation? She'd felt guilty enough accepting the job, which she hadn't. Not officially. Yes, she had shaken Dr Chamber's hand and beamed and said, *'thank you',* but she hadn't signed the contract. Not yet. She watched as Libby held her hand under the cold tap, a thin stream of blood escaping. How many times had she done that for Libby? Held a cut thumb or a cut finger under a cold tap, made it all better and safe again? They were, surely, in the wrong positions. It should be her making dinner and Libby sat, drinking tea at the table. Helen put her hand to her heart and held it there. It might as well have been yesterday that Libby *had* been the one at the table, still in her school uniform, while she peeled and chopped by the sink. Those afternoons, looking out of a kitchen window to a garden burnished by the last rays of a winter sun had been special, and she had felt the grace of them as she had lived them. Her nearly grown daughter munching on carrots, divulging gossip from school. Her boy, still a boy, safe upstairs. How did it go so fast? Where were those people?

'Ben!'

Like a nail through glass, the scream shattered her daydream. She felt a brush at her shoulder, a drip of water on her face as Libby flew past, crossed the living room in one stride and scooped Ben from the stool he'd climbed on. The stool he'd placed beneath an open window, forty feet above the ground.

Helen stood, her stomach cold, her legs like string. 'I'll hold him,' she stammered. She should have offered ... Libby shouldn't have opened the window ... 'I'll hold him.'

'I never open the windows.' Libby slammed it shut. 'It's just so hot.' She was crying, a look of wild bewilderment on her face, small as a child herself as she clutched her baby to her chest like a favourite teddy bear.

'It's OK.'

'I shouldn't have opened it ... what if —'

In the pan behind, the meat sizzled and spat.

'It's OK, it's OK.' She had her arms out, reaching for Ben.

'What if he had —'

'He didn't.'

'But if he had ... I ...'

'*Libby.*' And when Libby looked at her, Helen could have cried. Twenty-three years old and her daughter's face held the burden of a woman a decade older. 'This happens,' she said. 'It happens to all of us.' Whether Libby believed her or not, she didn't know, and it didn't matter. One day she would, but for now all that was needed was some forward motion, away from the window, away from the horror of *what if* ... 'You finish dinner.' She urged Libby back towards the kitchen. 'I'll watch Ben. They all needed to eat, sit down, calm down, and be thankful.

But Ben was heavy and sweaty, squirming his body and twisting his head. And although she was looking for somewhere to put him down, nowhere presented itself. The kitchen was too small. Two tottering steps and he'd be close enough to reach for the pan, if he tottered in the other direction, he'd fall down the steps to the living room.

'I'll sit with him.' She set about moving a pile of laundry, and a stack of paperwork from the small two-seater sofa. Libby was at the end of the first year of a two-year masters. Twenty-five hours a week, plus Ben, plus all the housekeeping that goes along with keeping a house, no matter how small. Helen piled the laundry to one end of the sofa, put the papers on the coffee table and sat down, wedging Ben between her knees. 'There,' she whispered. 'Get out of that one, Houdini.'

In response Ben picked up the top piece of paper and stuffed it in his mouth. Helen smiled. She didn't blame him really; he was probably as hungry as she was.

'*Ben!*' And now Libby was back again, manically tearing the paper from his hands. 'Those are my revision notes,' she cried. 'He can't eat them!'

Ben's face crumpled, he opened his mouth and let out an ear-splitting wail.

Nerves frazzled, Helen watched as orange sauce dripped from Libby's wooden spoon, onto the papers she was frantically sorting. 'I didn't realise,' she said then, 'we could go out to eat, Libby? If it's easier?' Breaking point was near. She could feel it. For Libby, for Ben, for herself.

'No!' Libby straightened up. 'I invited you to dinner, mum. We're not going out.'

'I just thought it might be easier ...' And watching her daughter blot tears away, Helen's voice trailed off.

'It's impossible, there just doesn't seem to be anywhere he can't reach now.'

'I know,' she said, and could have added, *I understand, Libby. I've been there too, Libby.* Something stopped her, and as Helen looked around her daughter's tiny flat, she understood what. She hadn't been there too. Not like this. Libby's flat was on the fifth floor of a block, where the lift didn't always work. There was no balcony, no dishwasher and only one tiny bedroom. To Helen, the space got smaller every time she visited. God knows what it was to live in it with a toddler. And she had tried. Before Libby had signed up for her degree, she had tried to explain the difference between a baby you can put down and find in the same place five minutes later, and a toddler that you can't. She'd tried suggesting that Libby put the studying on hold until Ben had started pre-school, but Libby hadn't listened, just as she hadn't listened to her own mother. And that was just the way of the world. 'You finish dinner,' she said, when what she really wanted to say, but didn't dare, was how on earth do you manage, Libby? How long can you keep this up for? At least she'd had Lawrence to pay the bills and share a bottle of wine with on a Saturday night. Libby was on her own, wholly naive to the toll of the workload she had heaped upon herself. This was going to be her reality for a while now, because the flat wasn't shrinking, and Ben was growing. And short of locking him in a padded cell, Libby was going to have to learn to manage, in the same way that every other mother before had learned.

Confident that she had her grandson contained, she put her hand on Ben's head and brushed his hair back, it was fine as spun silk, damp and warm and the urge to scoop him and his mother up, to take them back home with her, look after them and make everything alright again was a spark that lit a flame that grew into a bright light. She looked up. If she took the job, her flat would be empty, her lovely modern new-build, with its open-plan layout, and easy clean cabinets. The park opposite, the lift that worked. It was the perfect solution, so prefect that five minutes later when Libby presented her with an insipid looking plate of spaghetti bolognese, Helen barely noticed, eating quickly, impatient to get to her news, feeling herself inflate all over again.

28

'Red mite.'

Dazed, Caro turned to see Tomasz holding up a strip of sticky paper. She frowned; she wasn't sure what she was supposed to be looking at.

'I'm going to have to take them all out and disinfect.'

It was only as he put the paper on the garden table that she saw. Where there should have been white, the paper was black, covered in the carcasses of hundreds of tiny red mites.

'Does it have to be done now?' she said. The last twenty minutes, sitting in the garden listening to the hum of bees by the lavender had been such a respite, such an unexpected sanctuary from six days of self-inflicted torture, she did not want to leave the sunny spot she had found. She didn't want to break the spell.

On Friday evening she had arrived back at Hollybrook close to midnight showering for a full half hour before creeping into bed next to Thomas. Hoping he wouldn't wake, she had barely ruffled the bedcover. But he had woken, and his warm arm across her stomach had left her unable to move, stiff with regret, pinned down as surely as if she'd been felled by an oak. And although she had been sure she would never sleep again, within a few minutes she was snoring, her body capitulating to exhaustion.

That felt like the last sleep she had had. In the days and nights that had passed, her agitation and her distraction, had become obvious. In bed, she tossed and turned, at the table she picked and prodded. Tomasz had gone from concern to impatience, and now to this: a reserved detachment as he went about fixing and digging. It was a week in which she had lived so many different scenarios. The life in which she confessed all to Tomasz and he forgave her, and they carried on happily ever after. The life in which she said nothing, and they carried on, happily ever after. Or the life in which he didn't forgive her, ending it instead, so they didn't carry on. Or the life in which she ended it. The more she thought about it, the more the knot in her stomach tightened. How could she live happily ever after knowing what she had done? How could he?

He leaned across for his coffee. 'Isobella is preening herself to death in there, Caro. We can't leave it, not with Laura and Neil coming. You know what they said.'

Caro nodded. She did remember and if she didn't it was there anyway, under R, in the manual. A special chapter dedicated to Red Mite with specific instructions on how to clean the coup, how it affected the chickens, how, if it happened, they needed to act quickly. 'Of course.' Hands wrapped around her cup, she looked to the chicken village. The chickens had red mite, a couple she had nothing to say to were coming to dinner and six days ago she had slept with another man simply because she could.

'See you there?' Tomasz drained his coffee.

'See you there,' Caro said, but she didn't move. One

evening she would have decided. Watching him turn the pages of the instruction manual, her heart would contract with regret, her body shrink with self-hatred, and she would know that she could not say a word. The next morning, up early in the garden, with the dark peaks that filled her horizon watching her guilty footsteps, and she would feel with a cold certainty that she *had* to tell him. Confess not just the act, but the vanity that had led to it. Her load would be relieved completely then, and it would be up to Tomasz to decide. And then there were the times when, brushing her teeth, she would catch sight of herself in the mirror: Caro looking back at Caro, neither of them having any idea what to do.

She put her cup down and stood up. Two months ago, when they had visited Hollybrook for the first time, those hills had felt as exotically different as the sand dunes of the Sahara. Now, more and more, they felt like the walls of a prison. She was paralysed with guilt and weary with indecision, a darkness spreading inside her that she felt sure no amount of Cumbrian sunshine would ever reach again.

'ALL DONE.' Forty minutes later Tomasz emerged from the henhouse, with a bucket in one hand and a sponge in the other. 'All the perches need to be disinfected now,' he said, looking to the pile of wood they had, together, removed. 'Then fresh straw laid.'

Caro nodded. 'What do you want me to do?' She peeled off a pair of bright-blue gloves.

'Powder the hens?'

'I can do that.'

But she couldn't. And it wasn't that she was unaccustomed to grabbing hens by now, it was that the temperature was thirty degrees, and the hens resisted, and snows of grey powder settled in the crevice of her collarbone and along the fine hair of her nostrils. Frustrating her, distracting her, causing her guard to drop so images crashed through. The way she had leaned back to show her legs, his thickened waistline. Words echoed, words she would like to forget she had ever said or ever heard: *No train today. It's just that I have an appointment at six. Which you answered.* As if it was she that was infected, as if thousands of mites had nestled in her skin, infecting her, torturing her, she shook herself from head to foot, reached down and grabbed the next bird. But its squawk was shrill and as it twisted, her grip loosened and all she felt was a searing sting on her forearm! 'Shit!' Caro jumped back, a pool of blood forming at her wrist. 'Shit! Stupid, fucking ...' And nursing her arm she kicked the bench so hard it collapsed. The bird screeched, turning to her with a flap of wings and an angry stare of its strange orange eyes.

Tomasz looked up from the rafter he was disinfecting.

'It pecked me,' she said, nursing her arm.

He didn't speak. He looked, she thought, utterly exhausted.

'It pecked me.'

'Go in, Caro. I'll finish up.'

Caro pulled at her lip. 'I can't leave you with all this.'

'Just go,' he said and turned and carried on with the next rafter.

BY LATE AFTERNOON, the sting had faded to a small sullen bruise. She had showered and dressed and was standing now in a kitchen flooded with light. From the Aga came the delicious scent of rosemary and thyme, the herb crust on a roasting joint of lamb. Her neck ached a little and her fingernails still carried a trace of earth, but she had shelled a bowl of fresh peas and scraped the dirt from new potatoes, and the table looked as if it had walked straight out of the pages of *Country Life*. Laid with willow-pattern crockery, and dressed with a vase of lavender, linen napkins and rush placemats, it was the most beautiful table she had ever set. Looking at it, calmed her. 'You can do this', she said as she straightened a fork, 'you can do this'.

AND SHE MIGHT HAVE DONE. If Laura and Neil hadn't been as dull as she had remembered, she might have got through the evening, might have stood side by side with Tomasz as they washed glasses and re-lived the worst parts, the funny parts. Together, the two of them, making another deposit in the memory-bank of this life they were building together. And then, who knows where it might have led? A slow walk upstairs? A night where they held each other close, waking the next day to a fragile but tangible peace that would have allowed them to move past her prickly moods, forward to their happy ever after?

No-one would ever know, because Laura and Neil were just too dull, and with dessert served and eaten, they were showing no sign of leaving. Worse, they had only just reached K, in the manual, which Neil had insisted Tomasz bring to the table. As if they were schoolchildren, sitting an exam.

'R: Record-keeping,' Neil said, his thumb splodged across the page. 'Now this is important.'

Beside him, Laura nodded.

'You really do need to keep accurate records of just about everything.' Reaching across the table, Neil went to pour himself another glass of wine, but the bottle was empty. 'Planting schedules, equipment maintenance ––'

'Yields.' Laura interjected. 'It's really helpful to be able to look back at numbers when you're pickling and making sauces. You can see if you've got less jars of something.'

'Laura's right.' Neil flipped the pages of the manual. 'But you're getting ahead of yourself, sweetheart. We'll cover that on Y.'

Y? Caro glanced at the clock.

'I'll get another bottle.' Tomasz went to stand.

'I'll get it,' she said, and the scrape of her chair was loud. As she walked to the larder, she was thinking about the cabbages she'd thrown in the bin, the week every inch of bench space had been covered with jars of sauce she had zero appetite for. She reached up for another bottle and stood holding it to her chest. How long could she stand here, until M ... maybe even S ...

'We're still on R,' Laura whispered, as she came back to the table.

Caro sat down, her smile as thin as wire.

'Six am on a Saturday morning,' Neil was saying, 'and I didn't recognise any of them.' He turned to Caro. 'R for rural Network,' he said, 'and this is important, because you tell me, what three strangers were doing sitting in a van, outside the brickyard at that time in the morning?'

Caro pressed her lips together. 'Is that a rhetorical question?' Her irritation was obvious and rude.

'A what?'

'Well,' she said tightly, 'as we obviously have no idea what they were up to, I'm presuming you're not actually expecting an answer.' Her face ached, her nerves were razor thin and every cell throbbed with resentment. As she glanced up, she saw Tomasz watching her.

Oblivious, Neil re-filled his glass. 'I'm just saying you're going to need your rural network. Malcolm, from the stables, clocked them and called Jamie to let him know he better get down to the yard pronto. That's the beauty of a place like this. Everyone knows everyone. We look out for each other. You'll find they have your back up here.'

'I see.' Her lips barely moved. She was thinking about the day she'd walked back from the station. The men outside the pub. *Did some shopping in the big smoke?* In London, in her flat she could be gone for weeks, and often was, without anyone noticing. Like Spencer, who she supposed would be back in New York by now. The thought slipped in easy and light as a feather. She put her glass down.

'I'll miss that,' Laura said. Caro looked up. Laura wore a wraparound dress in a size too small and a fabric too thin to offer support. Her chest sagged, her arms were covered in freckles and the thin gold necklace she wore had irritated her skin, so patches of red bloomed along her throat. 'Have you met many people so far?'

'Not so many.' Tomasz smiled.

Probably, Caro thought to make up for her curtness just now, which only irritated her more.

'We've been to the pub a couple of times,' he added. 'But I don't drink, so...'

'You don't drink!' Neil guffawed. 'Not at all?'

Tomasz shook his head.

'Well, the rugby club in Alston does a fantastic 80s disco every other month.' Laura looked to Neil. 'I can't think of anywhere else, can you?'

Caro nodded. *I'll take you for cocktails at One World. Show you a view of my town.* She stood up, as much to silence the voice in her head as anything else. 'I'm sorry,' she started, and having started, had no desire to stop. 'I'm not feeling wonderful.' She looked to Tomasz, but his head was dipped. 'Maybe you could carry on without me.'

No-one spoke.

'Yes.' Caro picked up the bottle she had just placed on the table. 'Anyone for more?' she said, 'before I go?' But it had only been Neil and her drinking, and Neil had just filled his glass and ...

'Leave it, Caro.'

Slowly she put the bottle down again. She'd never heard such a tone in Tomasz's voice before.

'I think,' Laura started as she folded her napkin. 'I think we'd better be going. We can finish another time.'

But Caro didn't speak, she was looking at Tomasz, who was looking back at her as if he didn't even know her.

29

'That was lovely,' Helen lied, as she watched Libby rub a flannel over Ben's orange chin. The bolognese had been edible, and not much more. But that, she thought, was only to be expected. Libby had never shown any interest in cooking. She'd yet to learn that a Bolognese sauce was more than meat and a tin of budget tomatoes.

'Do you think so?'

'Yes.' Helen smiled.

'It's not as good as you make it.'

And there was such a plaintive tone to her daughter's voice, such a plea for reassurance, it had Helen frowning. Libby had always been straight as an arrow. Walking easy, talking in sentences with a confidence that Helen had known did not come from her. It was heart-breaking to see, in unguarded moments like these, how vulnerable she really was. To understand how difficult life was for her right now. 'Libby,' she started, pushing her plate aside. 'I've been thinking. This flat ...' And she raised her arm to wave at the tiny living room.

'What's wrong with it,' Libby said defensively.

'Nothing.' Helen shook her head. 'Nothing.' But she'd barely started and already she'd taken a wrong turn. 'Nothing's wrong with it. It's just small.'

Libby didn't speak.

'I mean to try and keep an eye on Ben ... I was thinking.' She leaned forward. 'My place is much larger and it's all on one level. I was thinking you and Ben might be more comfortable there?'

Libby's eyes widened.

Encouraged, Helen continued. 'You'll be able to watch him easily when you're in the kitchen. And with ––'

'Really, Mum?'

She paused. Something felt off track. 'You see,' she started, 'I wanted to talk to you. I've been offered this ––'

But Libby was on her feet, throwing her arms around Helen's neck. 'I'd love that!' she said. 'We won't be any trouble. Ben's little bed will fit easily into the spare bedroom with me.'

We won't be any trouble. Had there been a misunderstanding? Helen didn't speak. Pressed against her cheek, her daughter's skin felt smooth as silk, the press of it against her own opening up seams of memory, years and years of easy, warm cuddles.

'It will just be until I start working,' Libby said. 'I'll do my share, I promise. Dad said I could move back in at home, but if I did, I'd lose this place, and he's selling so I'd need somewhere anyway.'

Helen's hand moved as if it were not a part of her, patting Libby's arm to the rhythm of her mind as it replayed words. *We won't be any trouble, He's selling.* Slowly, she pulled out of the embrace. 'Dad is selling the house?'

Libby nodded. 'Didn't you know?'

'No.' And although she kept her voice light, the shock carried weight. She didn't live there anymore; she didn't own any part of it. Lawrence had bought her share, and she'd moved out over a year ago. Still, the news was visceral, a punch in the guts that bridged both her rational and irrational mind. *You're not the house. You're not the house.* No, she wasn't. But she'd invested deep. Time and energy. Maybe the best years and maybe the best energy, spent on fabric choices, garden plans, re-decorating, extending. What else had she talked about with as much consistency and frequency, other than *the house?* Which was still there. The lemon curtains she'd chosen for the front bedroom still fluttered in a March breeze, and the joke about grabbing the nose of the fox-head door knocker could still be made. All those little flags she'd planted, on all those little moons. *I was there, this was my family, I existed.* But Lawrence was selling. So, what would happen when the door was re-painted? When the curtains got replaced? When Libby and Jack's pencilled growth lines got slapped over in someone else's colours?

'You won't even hear us,' Libby said. 'He sleeps right through now.'

Slowly, Helen turned. 'The thing is,' she managed, mining the words from a place deeper than she knew existed. 'I wouldn't actually be there.'

'What do you mean, not there? You're not going hiking again, are you?' Libby laughed, and watching, Helen felt cold.

It was obvious that *not there,* for Libby meant something different to the *not there,* she was trying to say. *Not there* for Libby, meant that she would be in the next room, or the next town, or at the worst on another solo trip. She had no concept of the *not there* Helen had in mind, not even a glint of it. But Lawrence was selling the house, Jack was off living his life, and she hadn't asked her daughter to have a baby so young. She hadn't encouraged Libby to make a grandmother of her at fifty. Guilt crushed her as she watched Libby's face darken. Why would she understand? Why would she have seen it coming? Mothers didn't leave. Children did. It was children who packed rucksacks and applied for visas and had vaccinations. Parents stayed home, moving shoes that were no longer worn to the back of the cupboard, eventually taking down posters from a wall in a room busy only with the silent fall of dust mites. 'I've been offered a job,' she managed, the whisper so forced, she could hear it drag.

'A job?'

'In Bolivia.'

The colour drained from Libby's face. She sat down.

'So, I was thinking ...' She was laying a minefield, and she knew it. One wrong word and there would be casualties. Either of them could be blown apart. As she stopped talking, her mind started sprinting. Her limbs tingled, she felt weak. If she had known it was going to be this hard, if she'd been shown a picture of the distress on her daughter's face, would she have even started this conversation? All her beginnings, melted away, *It's the opportunity of a lifetime ... I really feel I can do this ... I always wanted to travel ...* Saying what she had come here to say, was going to take the kind of courage she wasn't sure she had. It meant turning her back on every idea of motherhood she had ever assimilated. It would make leaving her marriage feel like a walk in the park.

'Bolivia?' Libby said. 'What do you mean, Bolivia?'

Helen took a deep breath. 'I've been offered a job with a medical NGO. Initially it's a six-month contract.'

'So, you wouldn't be here?'

She shook her head.

'You'd be in Bolivia?'

She nodded.

'I...' Libby's voice dried. She turned to Ben, reached for his hand and held it. 'You won't see Ben,' she whispered.

Helen's throat was on fire. 'We have WhatsApp,' she said. 'I'll see him —'

'That's not the same!' Libby cried, her voice weak and strong, breaking like glass, sliding away like sand. 'It's not the same at all, Mum. I thought when you said ...' She put a hand on her chest and gasped for air. 'I thought you wanted us to come and live *with* you. I thought you wanted to see more of Ben, not less.'

'No.' Helen shook her head. 'That's not what I meant. I just –'

But Libby had dropped her head to the table, her shoulders shaking with grief. 'Don't go,' she sobbed. 'You've only just come back. Please, don't go, mum.'

And the only thing Helen could do was reach out and place her hand on her daughter's head, all the unimagined scenarios of how this scene might have gone, rising up before her. Like the one in which her daughter smiles, as she hears the word, NGO. The one in which she says, 'Work-flows? I didn't even know you knew what that meant. I'm proud of you mum. Go. You must go.'

30

The next morning, with Tomasz still sleeping, Caro woke early. In the kitchen she took a handful of tomatoes and sliced them open, the insides revealing glistening jewels of orange red fruit, golden seeded, intensely aromatic. She went out to the chicken village and collected eggs that she hard boiled and sliced open to see yolks more golden than sun. Even the cucumber she prepared, warped and ridged on the outside, had a taste and smell utterly unlike its supermarket cousin. She cut two chunks of sourdough bread and finished off with a chunk of crumbling white cheese, produced five miles away and bought from the local farmer's market. Then with a cafeteria of fresh coffee made, she woke Tomasz and told him to meet her in the garden.

After Laura and Neil had left, Tomasz had gone straight to bed and Caro had gone to sit in the garden, a blanket around her shoulders, recrimination blowing in from the peaks of the Lake District, whispering through the grass a rebuke she could not deny. She had never been beautiful, not at twenty-three, and certainly not now at fifty-three, and men like Spencer Cooper were seasoned pros, experts at sniffing out the plain woman's insecurity. Only the truly beautiful were immune to their callous efficiency, and if only for the pitifulness of her vanity she had deserved those bullets, those nine little words that a man like Tomasz would never, could never, have said: *It's just that I have an appointment at six.*

She poured a cup of coffee and waited in silence, the sun warm on her shoulders, a butterfly idling through air so still it might have been painted. She had made her decision. She would tell him and, one way or the other, they would have to find a way forward from there. She heard a footstep behind, a cough, and turned to see Tomasz. Reaching for his hand, she looked to the hills. 'I need to explain,' she said. 'About last night.'

But Tomasz didn't answer. He didn't sit down next to her and say, 'OK.' He didn't accept the coffee she offered him. He simply put his hand on her shoulder, and in a low voice said, 'I think you should go back to London.'

31

Her father, it seemed, still needed her. The phone call a couple of days ago, had been him wanting to arrange lunch; the call and the venue, coming as a surprise to Kay. They barely lived a hundred yards from each other. She could have popped in for lunch that day, or the next. But he had insisted. He wanted to take her somewhere special, he'd said. Besides he was busy, and today, Tuesday, was the only day he could do.

Busy? Kay hadn't asked. If that was the case, she was only glad. In the months following her mother's death, dropping in to see him had begun to be something she could not bring herself to look forward to. A fact that she was ashamed of. But conversation had become stilted and slow, and more and more it had begun to feel to Kay as if her father preferred the company of the TV to her. So, if the tide had turned and he was busy, it was good. A little strange, and obviously something to do with those phone calls, but good. And lunch out like this, was very good. Especially somewhere this special.

Finishing what had been a delicious ploughman's lunch,

she put her knife and fork down, wiped her mouth with a napkin and turned to look at the river, the floating tendrils of weeping willow, a pair of swans gliding across the dark surface. This had been her mother's favourite lunch spot. They hadn't been in years and as soon as Kay had walked out to the garden, she'd remembered why. The slope had become too steep for her mother to navigate with the walker. And the doorway had been too narrow for the wheelchair. 'Mum loved it here,' she said, and made a mental note. She must do the ringing next time. If her father was ready to face the world again, and it looked like he was, she could start by inviting him to places just like this. Scenes where they could both hear the whisper of memory. It would be a way to keep her mother close.

'That's why I chose it,' her father said, and he too put his knife and fork down, although Kay noticed, he hadn't eaten much. 'Have you booked Cyprus yet?'

'Not yet.' Always the same question. She smiled. 'I told you Dad, I'm waiting until after Caro's wedding.'

'I see.' He nodded. 'And that's all you're waiting for?'

'Yes.'

'Alex will be OK.'

She went to speak, but he got there first.

'And I will too, Kay.'

'OK.' As she picked up her glass, she turned away. The question, the directness of it, had thrown her. Marianne had stopped asking, Alex, she never saw. Caro was pre-occupied and, if she were to be honest, since school had finished, she had been floating along in a be-numbed stream of non-commitment. 'Dad,' she started. 'I —'

But he raised his hand, and, when he was sure she wasn't going to continue, lowered it again. 'I brought you here to today to tell you something.'

She nodded, watching as he took out his handkerchief and blew his nose. He was going to tell her about those phone calls, she was sure, which would of course be difficult for him. 'If,' she said, and smiled. 'If it's about the history course you've started, I already know.' The least she could do, was make it easy. Keep it light. Act like she had no idea.

But her father wasn't smiling. In fact, as he returned his handkerchief to his pocket, his face was as serious as she thought she had ever seen it. 'This feels like the right place,' he said, 'to tell you that I'm courting.'

At the sound of the word, so old-fashioned, so potent, all the clocks moving all the parts, stopped moving. Her head, her heart, her fingers, resting on her glass. Only now it had been said, did she realise how afraid she had been of hearing it. 'Courting?'

He nodded. 'Actually, Kay, it's a little more than courting. I've asked the lady in question to marry me.'

Marry? No sound came out, her lips shaping a word that made no sense.

'I expect you'll think it's too soon.'

She didn't speak. Like a cyclist pedalling in reverse, she was trying to loop it back, pin down the conversation to the point where it had spun out of control. Telephones calls were OK. Courting was hard, but manageable. *Marry.* That was the place. *I've asked the lady in question to marry me.*

'I don't want to see you upset, love.'

'I'm not upset,' she said, the shifting weather on her face making a mockery of her words. Her mother had only been gone twelve months.

Her father nodded. 'I understand it will come as a surprise.'

The quiet way in which he spoke, the gentle courtesy, masked a lethal blow. Like a bomb arriving in a silk case.

Slip it off, peek closer - which she had no intention of doing - and BANG! 'It's only a year,' she whispered.

'No.' He shook his head. 'You know yourself, Kay. Your mother was gone long before then. Long before.'

And how could she argue with that? Swallowing back a cruelly sudden grief, she pulled her sunglasses down and made a fist of her hand, balling it at her mouth as she leaned on her elbow. It was true that her mother had been gone longer than a year. So much longer, she couldn't place the last time she had been present: wholly present. Pieces had fallen away so quietly, no-one had noticed. If her mother had forgotten an appointment one week, she'd remembered the next. If she couldn't remember where she had met Kay for coffee one day, she would have no problem recalling both the place and even the table they had sat at, the next. It wasn't until the gaps started to overtake the whole that they knew. Her father was right; of course he was. Coming out to lunch like this, where her mother would spend half the time asking where she was, and the other half staring into space, no-one could say she had been present. Composing herself, she pushed her sunglasses back on her head. 'Can I ask who?' she said. It was still wrong. Who on earth would her father know well enough to ask them to marry him?

'Of course you can.' He didn't hesitate. 'Elizabeth Parsons.'

'Lizzie!' Kay's jaw dropped. 'Lizzie, dad? You hardly know each other.'

'Actually,' he said. 'I remember Elizabeth very well from when you first started at the school. I've always held her in the highest regard. And your mother and I always exchanged Christmas cards with her.'

Kay stared. She was remembering the way Lizzie and

her father had chatted for so long at her retirement party. The way Lizzie had handed her cup over, the way her father had taken it, the fluid synchronisation of the movement. 'This is ridiculous!' she said tightly. 'You've known her for a couple of weeks!'

'In which we have met frequently and spoken every day.'

'Met frequently? Where?' Slapping a hand on her chest, she stopped talking and took a deep breath.

'Elizabeth,' her father said simply, 'has made me smile again.'

There was nothing she could think of to say. Words that would be easy for him to hear ... words like, *I'm happy for you, dad* ... or, *If you're happy, dad* ... were simply too hard for her to form.

'I don't want to keep looking back, Kay.' His handkerchief was out again, a shaky hand dabbing a watery eye, and Kay could not look at him. 'I wouldn't change a single thing,' he said, 'but with what is left, I want to be able to look forward.'

'But why the rush?' she rasped, and when she swallowed it was like swallowing nails.

'Well.' He paused. 'Lizzie is ninety. And I am eighty-six. It's probably best we count in weeks, rather than years.'

'But you don't have to get married!' Her fist was at her mouth again. She could barely contain her anger. 'What about Mum? What would she think?'

And for the longest time her father didn't answer. He folded his hands together and dipped his head. 'Your mother and I,' he said, as he looked up, 'had a long and happy marriage, Kay.'

'Sixty years.'

'Sixty years,' he echoed. 'Where Elizabeth didn't even manage one day.'

Kay clamped her mouth shut. *That's not a reason,* she'd been going to say. *That's not a reason to marry someone!* It was only the stamp of family that stopped her. It didn't matter that he was eighty-six and she was fifty-two: the roles remained. She could no sooner tell him what he could and could not do, than Alex could tell her.

'I would like to be able to give Elizabeth that,' he said. 'So, I have asked her, and she has accepted. On the condition,' he added, 'that you have no objections. That was her only request.'

Her jaw was tight, her lips thin as wire as she picked up her glass and said, 'So that's what this is all about? To see if I have any objections?'

'Yes, I suppose it is.' He nodded. 'And of course, if you're not comfortable, we wouldn't expect you to attend the ceremony.'

She turned. 'Attend?'

'It would be very simple, Kay. Elizabeth has no relations, and we're not going to any expense. A registrar can perform the ceremony at the retirement home, and after that, I have decided to move there myself. I think it's time.'

Hand shaking, she lowered her glass. 'You're going to move, Dad?'

'It's what I want, Kay. We enjoy each other's company very much, and at my age that's all I can ask for.' He blinked. 'Actually, it's more than I can ask for.'

Kay didn't speak. She looked across to the swans, their tapered bodies, perfectly aligned as they glided across the water. The movement was so smooth, so coordinated, the river remained a mirror, not a ripple rising up to spoil the glassy surface.

'You asked me what your mother would think?'

Slowly, she turned.

'I can't answer that,' her father said. 'But I know that if it were the other way round, I would want to see your mother happy.'

It didn't matter that she was angry. It didn't matter that as she looked at her father now, she felt bewildered by the speed at which he was making decisions. It was of no consequence that she felt betrayed for herself, and her mother. It didn't even matter that it was Lizzie, a woman she had always admired. She had no choice. If she left her father today, withholding her approval, he would phone Lizzie and tell her and all that would have been achieved was a raising of the level of unhappiness in the world. Turning back to the river, she picked up her glass. 'If it's what you want,' she said. 'I have no objections.'

IT WAS HOURS LATER, cocooned within the floral sanctuary of her bedroom, lit by a mauve moonlight, that Kay opened her phone and began typing.

> If you're ready to meet. I am too.

GOOSE'S RESPONSE came through five minutes later.

> I would like that. Can you make tomorrow?
> Do you have anywhere in mind?

Tomorrow is fine. You choose.

SHE LET her phone drop and lay back on her pillow. Everyone was moving on, her son, her father, Caro, Helen, Marianne. If she didn't get started, if she didn't take a first step, she really would be left alone, stranded on a lonely hill, scanning the horizon for any sign of life.

32

Kay: Thanks for your gift, girls. It arrived a few days ago. 😶

Caro: You tried it?

Kay: 👍 And hidden it now in a safe place. Very safe.

Helen: Hidden?

Kay: What on earth would I say to Alex if he found it?!

· · ·

Helen : 😂 Does he usually go through your knicker drawer.

Kay: I'm not taking the risk.

Helen: So, how's everything going Caro? Are you ready?

Caro: 👍

Helen: How's Tinder going, @Kay

Kay: 👍 I'm meeting someone tomorrow actually. First time.

Helen : 😲 Really? Name? Age?

Caro: What does he do?

Helen: Has he still got hair? 😂

Kay: I don't know.

Helen: Let me guess? He's wearing a baseball cap in every photo? 🧢🧢🧢

Kay: There are no photos

Caro: WHAT?

Kay: It's just a silhouette. And his name is Goose.

Helen: Are you serious?

Caro: You're not really going to meet someone without knowing what they look like?

Kay: Why not? People get married at first sight. They made a TV show from it.

Helen: I knew you'd be watching too much Netflix. Caro's right. You shouldn't do this. If he's anonymous, there will be a reason, and it won't be good.

Kay: There was a reason I stayed anonymous when I sent my first Valentine's card, and it wasn't because I was a psychopath.

H*elen is typing ...*

CARO IS TYPING...

Kay : I'm an overweight fifty-two-year-old woman, meeting someone in daylight, in a public place. What do you think is going to happen?

Helen: Drink spiked?

Caro: Credit cards stolen?

Kay: 😊

Helen: I'll come as a chaperone.

Kay: NO

Caro: Me too.

Kay : NO. Caro don't even think about coming down. You're getting married on Friday for heaven's sake!

. . .

Caro: I'm already in London.

Helen: Why?

Caro: Change of plan.

Kay: Everything OK?

Caro: 👍

Helen: I can drive you, Kay.

KAY IS TYPING ...

Caro: Or I can.

Helen: How else are you going to get there?

Kay is still typing ...

Caro: And you're retired now. Taxis are expensive.

Kay: OK. Someone can drive. But no-one is coming in. You can go to one of the bars opposite. I'll text when I need a getaway car.

Helen: OK

Caro:

Helen: Why are you in London? I thought you weren't coming down until tomorrow evening.

Caro: Can't explain by text.

Helen: Are you OK?

Caro: I'm trying to be.

Helen: Do you want to call?

.   .   .

Caro: It can wait until tomorrow.

Walking into *The Crown & Thistle* felt to Kay, like walking into an old friend's house. Still the same display of black and white photos in the far corner, the same plush cushioning on the seats, the same swirly-patterned carpet under her feet. She hadn't been inside for years, but Goose had been right when he'd said it hadn't changed. It had always been, and obviously still was, a traditional pub, combining a public space with cosy private nooks: the perfect choice for shy middle-aged strangers meeting for the first time and the stylistic opposite of those cavernous modern bars where hard floors trebled the volume level, and harsh lighting reflected every frown. Instantly she felt less nervous. In a world that she felt she recognised less every day, this was familiar territory. Dressed in comfortable jeans and a loose fitting, floral blouse, (having resisted Helen's offer of a low-cut t-shirt), Kay felt a flutter of excitement akin to those Friday night feelings of her youth. Helen and Caro were going to a wine bar, directly opposite, and here she was! Out of her house after five in the afternoon. As if her phone could read her mind, it pinged.

. . .

> Helen: We're directly opposite. If you sit outside too, we'll be able to see you.

FROWNING, Kay did a swift scan of the bar. Behind the counter, a woman similar in age to herself, tapped a pencil against her lips as she read from an order list. Over by the window, three young men in yellow work shirts talked over pint glasses, arms folded, heads tipping back in laughter. There were two nooks either side of the fireplace, one occupied by a man who had spread a newspaper out, the other empty. Plenty of people to rescue her should Goose turn out to be a serial-killer, or more likely, a bore. She bent her head and typed out her response.

> Kay: I'm not sitting outside.

CARO'S REPLY was almost instant.

> Caro: We can't see you otherwise.

> Kay: Good!

'WHAT CAN I GET YOU?'

Surprised at the voice, Kay looked up. The woman behind the bar had moved across.

'Umm ...' Her phone pinged again. This time it was Helen.

> Helen: Sit outside. Please! (Caro is driving me mad.) 😡😡😡

'SORRY,' she said. 'My friends are ...'

> Caro: No-one does this, Kay! Sit outside.

'GOSH,' she stammered. 'I'm sorry about this. They're only across the square. I'm meeting someone and they're ....' And just in time, she found her handbrake. 'White wine,' she said. 'I'll have a white wine.'

As the woman turned away, she hammered out a response.

> Kay: Before smartphones, everyone did this! Blind Date. Remember?

> Helen: If you sit outside, we'll see when you want to leave.

.   .   .

Kay: No.

Caro: It's too risky, Kay.

TOO RISKY. Standing with her phone in her hands, the memory flooded back. Last year, in Vegas when she had had a statistically probable chance of winning five thousand dollars, she hadn't taken it. She had allowed herself to fall into the trap of *too risky,* bottled it and fled from the blackjack table like a hunted animal. It was a memory that came wrapped in layers of tender regret, and as she readied herself to respond, Kay paused. She'd never really spoken about that Vegas moment to either Helen, or Caro. She hadn't told them how it haunted her: the marrow-deep understanding of discovering that she really was the person she had always suspected herself to be, timid, contained, ordinary. Life is a risk, she murmured, shaping the words as she typed them.

Life is a risk. I'm fine. Stop messaging or I'll put my phone on silent!

SHE DROPPED her phone back in her bag, paid for her drink and settled herself in the empty fireside nook. She was done with *too risky,* done with *contained* and done with *ordinary.* Or if she wasn't, she really wanted to be. She wasn't the same woman of a year ago. She'd used a vibrator now! More than once. And she owned a leopard-print bikini, that just about fitted! And yes, it was scary, coming out like this to meet a stranger, but what was the worst that could happen? That he took one look at her and ran in the opposite direction? At least she wasn't at home, in her dressing gown, eating chocolate digestives, watching Netflix. She took a sip of wine, smoothed back her hair and waited, slightly nervous, slightly excited, emboldened from the inside out. Across at the window, the men in the work shirts were playing some sort of game that involved beer mats. It didn't make much sense to Kay, revolving as it did around the way the mat landed after it had been spun, but it was keeping them amused. Their laughter was contagious, and as she watched, she found herself more and more engaged as she too tried to guess the outcome.

'Hello, KB.'

The voice came from nowhere, and at the sound of it a jangle of emotion surged through Kay. It sounded in her ears as a loud buzz, showed on her arms as a rash of tingling goosebumps. She was both stunned and shocked, fleetingly annoyed and disproportionally amused, and for a long moment she sat soaked in the awareness of the universe suddenly making sense. *Of course it was ... It had to be ...* She'd only ever met one man who had been so effortlessly on her wavelength, so consistent in his ability to make her laugh. 'Martin,' she whispered and looked up to see her ex-husband.

35

C aro stood with her hand at her eyes, straining to see across a square crowded with people out to enjoy the warm evening. 'She's definitely not outside,' she said.

'I can't say I blame her,' Helen muttered, and closing her eyes she leaned back to lift her face to the sun. The patio they sat on was a mix of brightly painted tables and mismatched chairs. It had an outdoor bar and an unlit chimenea. Strings of fairy lights had been strung along the wrought-iron fencing and above each table a soft white lantern glowed. A distinctly youthful vibe, she was thinking, for the distinctly youthful crowd that surrounded them. Caro and her had to be the oldest customers by at least a decade. 'Did you see anyone likely going in?' she murmured, mostly to play along with Caro. Kay would be fine. It was Caro that she was concerned about. She was as jumpy as a frog.

'It's hard to see anything,' Caro said. 'Should we position ourselves a little nearer? We could sit on one of the benches in the square?'

'We've just ordered drinks.' Helen opened her eyes. 'Sit down, for heaven's sake. She'll text when she needs us.'

'It still doesn't feel right. Why would she choose to meet someone who calls themselves Goose?'

'It's a joke, Caro.' Helen nodded at the chair opposite.

'Well, I don't get it.' And reluctantly, Caro sat down.

'Goose,' she sighed as she leaned forward, 'was the side-kick in *Top Gun*. He wasn't the hero. I'm guessing that's what this guy sees himself as: a sidekick.'

'Oh.'

'You don't remember *Top Gun*?'

'Not much, no.'

'Never mind.' And leaning back to allow the waiter to place their drinks, Helen shrugged. She didn't think this was the best idea Kay had ever had either, but she could under-stand the reasoning behind it. 'He makes her laugh,' she said. 'And let's face it, Kay's had precious little to laugh about lately.'

'I see.' But Caro looked so lost in thought, Helen wasn't sure she saw anything.

Picking up her glass, she held the straw at her lips. 'Lawrence never really made me laugh.'

'Never?'

'Not that I recall.' Helen frowned. 'That's amazing, isn't it? That I married a man who took himself so seriously.' She took a long slurpy sip of her diet coke, put the glass down, stretched her arms and looked at Caro. 'I think,' she said, 'that when I met him, my life was so full of laughter I didn't notice it was missing in him. I was so young.' Helen smiled. 'Nothing awful had happened. My mother was still alive. Friday nights were still exciting and ...' Drifting off, she looked down at her hands. 'My guess is,' she said, 'that I thought there were more important things.'

'Looks?' Caro said quietly. 'Status.'

'Status,' Helen murmured, 'perhaps.' *Status,* she might have replied, was more your thing, Caro. She didn't have the heart. Not on this warm evening, not with the wedding just two days away and not with Caro so subdued. She looked away to the next table where a young couple sat, the man meticulously groomed, the girl, obviously entranced. 'I'll tell you something,' she said. 'Laughter would be right at the top of my list now. Whoever it was could look like Quasimodo, and I wouldn't care, as long as he made me laugh. If I'd known,' she added, and paused. 'If I'd only known how scarce laughter becomes, I would have placed so much more value on it.'

Caro didn't speak. And in the space where she might have, Helen dived in. 'Children laugh every day,' she said. 'And look at them!' She nodded at a group in the far corner of the patio. 'That crowd have been laughing non-stop for the last ten minutes. I mean what's so funny? When does life stop being funny, Caro? And why? Why does it stop?' The questions rattled across the table. 'Does Tomasz make you laugh?' she said, one final, fatal shot.

Caro looked up. 'Tomasz asked me to leave.'

Helen stared.

'That's what the change of plan is. That's why I came back early.

'What!' She put her glass down, leaned forward. 'What on earth has happened?'

But Caro had turned away, her eyes blinking rapidly. 'It's nothing,' she said waving a hand.

'It's obviously *not* nothing. What's happened? Are you still --'

'I slept with another man, Helen. That's what happened.'

Helen put her hand to her mouth and held her breath. Of all the things she had expected Caro to say about the 'change of plan' it had not been this. She didn't know what she'd been expecting. Nothing much. Last minute arrangements at the venue, perhaps? A change of booking at the hairdressers? No drama, nothing that, as Caro had texted, couldn't wait for an explanation. How contained then Caro had been on the journey over. How composed she had been, sitting on this bomb. Hands pressed together now, she held them at her chin, watching as Caro sat, twisting her engagement ring. She shouldn't have expected anything less. The girl she had met at university all those years ago, had kept her emotions as buttoned up as her cardigan, and so it had been all Caro's life. Thinking this, watching, Helen pressed her lips together. She was trying to remember a time she had seen Caro cry; she wasn't sure she could. The day Caro had come to tell her of Kay's diagnosis? Perhaps then? But when else? The revelation was a shock. The realisation that this was the only time she had ever seen her friend of thirty years lose her composure. 'When —'

'After I left your place the other week.' Caro's interruption was gentle as a tap, a paw without claws.

'Who —'

'It doesn't matter.' Caro shook her head. 'It really doesn't matter who it was, Helen. I met him through work. He was very charming and ... I was just going for a drink. That's what I told myself.' Head dipped, she pressed her hand to her nose.

Helen waited. Maybe she had never left enough space for tears. For Caro's tears.

'It's never happened to me before. No one has ever told me I was beautiful.'

'Caro, you —'

'Don't say it, Helen.' And pinching the bridge of her nose, Caro shook her head again. 'Please don't say that I am. We both know it's not true.'

'Caro.' But she didn't say it, because Caro was right. She didn't say anything, because this was no time for inauthentic consolation either. For pointing out everything else that Caro had been granted; it was beauty she had strived after, beauty, that had always remained out of reach. And Helen understood: the right comment, from the right person, at the right time.

'It's OK.' Hand on her chest, Caro shuddered. 'It's OK,' she said again.

'Did you tell him?'

'No.' Caro's smile was tiny. 'I was going to.'

Helen frowned. 'I don't understand,' she said. 'Does he know? Are you still ...?'

Caro nodded. 'This is only about the move,' she whispered. 'He said I needed space to decide if I really want to go through with the move. The wedding is still on.'

'And do you?'

'I think so.' Caro pinched her nose. 'But he's talking about the smallholding, Helen. And I don't know how to tell him about ...' Her voice drifted away.

'I see.' Helen looked across the patio. There was so much she wanted to say. She had doubts herself about the move Caro was making, but she hadn't voiced them. Cyprus had taught her that. The day she had found out that Caro had been planning to conceive a baby at the age of fifty, had been the day their friendship had almost crumbled. She hadn't held back then, telling Caro everything she thought about the folly of her decision, the selfishness of it. And it wasn't so much that she regretted what she had said, it was more that she understood now, in a way she didn't then, the limits of friendship. Caro wasn't family. She had no claims to stake on the way she chose to live her life. At a loss, she picked up her glass. So much she wanted to say, and so little that she could.

'You must think ... well, I don't know what you think.'

'I think,' she said as she reached across and squeezed Caro's hand, 'that everyone makes mistakes.' She squeezed harder, because the pain emanating through Caro's fingers was tangible and she wanted to take it away. Because she'd only added to it before, raging at Caro in Cyprus when she should have tried so much harder to understand, dismissing her in disgust the terrible night Caro had walked too far and too long, with Ben. Thirty years they had known each other, and she had only ever seen Caro cry once. And then the tears were for Kay, not for herself. Thirty years in which she had never given her friend the space to be vulnerable. 'What matters,' she said, her voice urgent. 'What matters, Caro, is if you think you can be happy with Tomasz. And if you think Tomasz can be happy with you. Life is very short ...' Choking up, Helen put her fist to her mouth. 'It's too bloody short to choose a path towards anything other than happiness.'

Eyes glassy as orbs, Caro sat, her hand in Helen's. 'So, you think I shouldn't tell him? You think I should let him believe it's the move?'

'Yes.' And as a tear finally broke free and fell down Caro's cheek, Helen took a napkin and reached across to blot it dry. 'If you truly believe,' she said, 'that you can put this behind you, if you think you can make him happy, then don't tell him. You have to grab your chance when it comes, Caro. It may not come again.'

36

'**G**oose?'

Martin nodded. He had a drink in each hand, a glass of Coke and a glass of wine. 'I got you a drink,' he said, 'but I see you already have one.'

Stunned, Kay looked at the drinks. She hadn't even seen him come in, let alone order drinks.

'You still prefer white to red?'

Now she looked at him. 'And you drink Coke?'

'I do now,' he said. 'Is it OK if I sit?'

She nodded. He'd lost weight and hair, and she was trying to think how long it had been since she had last seen him. It had to be at least two years. Certainly not since Alex had told her that Martin had separated from his partner, a move that had coincided with her becoming ill.

'You don't have to drink it,' he said as he put the wine on the table. 'I see you already have one.'

She snapped back into the moment. 'I may need it.'

He smiled. 'It wasn't too presumptuous then?'

'No. What was presumptuous,' she added, before he could speak, 'was staying anonymous, when you knew it was me? You obviously knew? Don't answer that. Of course you did!'

'Of course I did,' he said, and his smile faded.

'That's not fair, Martin.'

'I know.'

'It's not even nice.'

As he filled his lungs, his shoulders rose to his ears. Slowly, he let the air out again. 'Would you have come,' he said, 'if you'd known it was me?'

'No.' Kay picked up her glass. She couldn't look at him. Not because she was angry, but because she was confused. Of course she wouldn't have come. Of course she wouldn't have dressed up, washed her hair, got excited for and about, a man who had left her for an affair that had lasted all of three months. The only circumstances under which she would have agreed to meet, were exactly these. Those in which she didn't know. And yet she couldn't deny what she was feeling. She was happy she was here, and she wasn't unhappy to be here, with him. 'Well,' she said as she turned back, 'as you've already paid for it.' And she pulled the second glass of wine towards her.

Martin visibly relaxed. He nodded at her hair. 'I like it, he said quietly. 'It suits you shorter.'

'Thank you.' She felt her cheeks warm, which was ridiculous given the compliment was coming from a man who had seen her give birth. 'It grew back like this,' she said, 'after the radiotherapy.' Her hand was at the back of her neck, self-conscious.

'Well, at least you still have hair to grow back.' And now it was his turn to colour, to pat the bald spot on the top of his head, his mouth turning up in a wry smile.

'It's not too bad.' But this close, she could see how thin his hair really was. Another couple of years and he would be completely bald. She felt a pang of sympathy. No wonder he'd stayed in the shadows. The courage it took to put yourself out there. Older and greyer, fatter and balder. Not everyone who stayed anonymous did so for nefarious reasons. Some, she felt sure, were simply hiding. Not from wives or girlfriends either. They were hiding from themselves: from who they had become. All those photos of motorcycles and mountains? They were pleas. Petitions from men who knew time was no longer on their side to *please* look past their age, their grey hair, their no-hair, their jowls, their whiskers. See *me*. See who I am inside. Who I still feel like. And the irony of the fact that the one man in the world who should never have needed to stay in the shadows, had chosen to do so - the man she would always be able to see from the inside out - did not escape her. She could have laughed. She did. She took a sip of wine and shaking her head put the glass down.

'Something funny?'

Yes, it was funny, and sad that he couldn't see it. Together, they had the one thing that time could not distort or make ugly. They had a past. 'Just life,' she said, then nodding at his receding hairline. 'I think I prefer it to the style you had the first time we met.'

Martin laughed. 'You mean the perm? It was 1988, Kay. Everyone had a perm.'

'I didn't.'

'No.' He lowered his chin and wrapped his hands around his glass. 'You were never swayed by anything. Do you remember where we met?'

Kay smiled. 'Of course I do.'

'Rock Bottom Lounge,' he started.

'The Student Union bar,' she finished.

'We had some great times there.'

'We saw some great bands there.'

'OMD, Human League, Altered Images ...'

'The Jam, Spandau ...'

'Cider and Black for you.'

'A pint of Fosters for you.' Kay laughed. 'We made a good team. My Student Union vice-president, to your president.'

'We did.' Crossing his arms, Martin dipped his head as he smiled. He had a generous mouth, with lips that seemed to be perpetually shaped upward. It gave him the appearance of always being happy or at least pleased with life. Of course, she knew that wasn't the case but as Kay looked at him, she remembered how attractive she had found it. The way he took life easy, the way he shrugged it all off.

She picked up her glass. By the window, the men in the work shirts were still talking, shoulders rounded, and arms crossed as they leaned over the table, talking and talking and talking. 'We were like that once,' she murmured. 'We had so much to say, we were going to change the world.'

Following her eyeline, Martin shook his head. 'I was never going to change anything, Kay. I couldn't even get out of bed in time to catch the coach to London for the CND march.'

Kay laughed. 'It was a very early start. And remember, how cold your place used to be? Getting out of bed wasn't easy. The curtains used to stick to the window.'

'That's because it was next to a funeral parlour.' As he leaned towards her, Martin's voice dropped to a whisper. 'You do realise that every time you stayed over, you were sleeping three feet from a corpse.'

Her lips twitched. 'So romantic.'

'No.' He sat back. 'I was never romantic enough. And as for us changing the world? It was the other way round, wasn't it? The world changed us.'

'Did it?' Tears sprung. Uncomfortable, she looked away. Did Martin mean Alex? Was he talking about the way their world had bent and shaped itself to accommodate their son? How horizons had shrunk, and walls closed in, as they do, in a perfectly proportionate ratio: the greater the child's needs, the smaller the world.

'I failed to adapt,' he said. 'That's what happened. I failed.'

He did mean Alex. As she turned back to face him, she pressed her lips together. There was no point in denying what he had said, no point in offering words of comfort or mitigation. He had failed.

Neither of them spoke. She watched as the men by the window stood, scooping phones and keys, downing pints. Faces easy with laughter, all of them with full heads of hair.

'You made it,' Martin said.

'Made what?' She turned.

'The bus.' He smiled. 'You got up in time. You always did.'

Kay shrugged. 'Well as you said, it was cold ––'

'No.' He shook his head, his voice low. 'Don't make excuses for me, Kay. I don't do it for myself. Not anymore. That's why I stick to this.' And he picked up his Coke.

Kay didn't speak. The years following her divorce had been a quagmire of hurt and disappointment, and at times she had honestly believed she would never feel happy again. But she had. Oh, so slowly, she had begun to find herself on stable ground, woken up, gone about her day and, looking at the clock, realised that she hadn't thought about him once. It was a lonely and inhospitable place, the place she had dragged herself out of, and she had no desire to go back. What was there to discover anyway? That the man that she had loved had proved to be a disappointment? He was right. She shouldn't make excuses.

Holding her glass at her lips, she stared across the room. Was that really the whole truth? Or was it just the assessment she had made at the time, and nurtured ever since: a stand formed from the front-row seat of a marriage in crisis? Sixteen years further away and no matter how she tried to focus in, her perspective had changed, and the view of the stage on which they had moved around each other was different. Alex, she could see so clearly now, had filled her up. From the moment of his birth, he had filled her every sense. There hadn't been room for a husband. She hadn't – and this was something she'd had a long time to think about – always wanted one. 'Why did you match with me,' she said as she put her glass down. 'Why are you here, Martin?'

For a long moment he looked at her. 'I wanted to talk to you again,' he said quietly. 'It was always so easy.'

Her eyes filled with tears. 'You could have picked up the phone.'

'No.' He shook his head. 'We both know I couldn't have done that.'

Kay nodded. The extent of their communication for many years had been nothing more than an occasional text, and odd as it was this was probably the only way. How sad then. How sad in this lonely world, that two people who had once been so easy in each other's company, should become so estranged. 'Are you hungry?' It was a question that surprised her, as much as it obviously did him.

'I could eat,' he said slowly. 'There's a nice ––'

'How about my place?'

He blinked. 'Your place?'

Kay shrugged. 'Alex is out. He's always out these days.

And I have a fridge full of home-made macaroni cheese. Why not?'

37

Alone now, Helen checked her phone *again*. No new messages. She put it down and picked up her drink. Caro had left. She'd wanted to get back, call Tomasz, and get some sleep, something Helen suspected she hadn't had much of lately. So here she was, an hour later, agitated, bored and, as she was driving, sober. She'd sipped her way through another Diet Coke, tried reading another chapter of her book, (hopeless without her reading glasses), and scrolled aimlessly through every social media account she had. She was filled to the gills with artificial sweetener and increasingly sad. The young people around her made her feel nostalgic, the look on Caro's face earlier, left her worried and, now that she was on her own, the awful image of Libby dropping her head on the table and begging her not to go was more vivid, more real than the day it had happened. She was all out of options, unable to distract herself from a memory, she didn't want to remember. Not so much because she had been the cause of her daughter's tears, but because of the way in which she had stopped them.

'I won't go,' she'd said. 'I won't take the job.'

So easy to say to Libby, so impossible to repeat to anyone else, let alone Fiona Chambers, to whom she had written a long, overly apologetic and repetitive email.

Can I just ask for some time to think about this? she'd said in seven different ways. There are a few things I'd like to discuss with my family.

To which Fiona had – generously – responded: *Of course. Take some time, Helen. Christian and I totally understand. It's a big decision.*

She stretched her arms out, linking her fingers together as she flexed her wrists. Now that she had had that time, she was still no nearer to being able to send any kind of follow-up email. Either *I would love to accept/ I'm so excited ...* Or *I'm so sorry but/ Under the current circumstances I feel unable ...*

Current circumstances. Her smile was rueful. How long would they last, these circumstances that were not circumstances at all, but were responsibilities? The rest of her natural life? She would have liked to have talked to Caro, had been planning to talk to Caro, but Caro's news had been a torpedo, blowing every other topic of conversation out of the water, and thinking this Helen looked up and across the square. There was no doubt in her mind that in urging Caro to say nothing she had done the right thing. Her own adultery, the brief holiday fling she had had in Cyprus, had been the symptom of a marriage in terminal decline. It was something she hadn't felt guilty about at the time and didn't now. What had happened to Caro was ... Frowning, Helen picked up her straw and stirred the inch of Diet Coke left. What *had* happened to Caro? She had become accustomed to the air of confidence and authority in her friend, the polish and smoothness of a high-maintenance routine. But what she had never seen, and Kay had said as much, was the glow

Caro had acquired since meeting Tomasz. Caro had become a woman who, because she was desired, was desirable. That's what had happened to her. And a desirable woman, Helen thought as she finished her drink, is a powerful woman. And newly acquired power is always hard to control. On the table her phone buzzed.

> Hi. Goose is going to drive me home.

> NO!

HELEN BANGED OUT THE TEXT.

> You really don't need to worry. It turns out we know each other.

> Well enough for him to drive you home? Are you sure?

> Well enough to have married him.

38

Back at her flat, Caro threw her keys in the bowl on the hall table, slipped her shoes off and hurried into her living room. Standing by the window she could see the stream of red taillights heading out on the North circular, the flashing red sign of the Esso garage opposite. It was such a different view from Hollybrook Farm, all straight lines and angles, busy with cars, busy with people. Busy, busy, busy. She opened the window an inch and stood listening to the constant hum of traffic, an occasional distant shout.

It wasn't so long ago that, from the moment she came home of an evening, to the moment she left again, this muted London soundscape had been her only accompaniment. Now she had an abundance of voices to keep her company. The low bleating of the sheep on the hills, the twit-twoo of the owls, and of course, Tomasz, everywhere. His tuneless singing in the shower, his rambled conversation with the chickens, even his whistling while he cooked. His arm around her shoulder while he slept: her bulwark against the world.

Turning away from the window she took her phone and settled herself on the sofa. The talk with Helen had left her feeling as if she had opened the curtains to see a ray of tentative sunshine, after a week of heavy rain. Helen was right. Helen had driven a nail through her little box of torture and prised it open to reveal that yes, what mattered in all of this, was if she thought she could be happy. And she did. She really did. More than that, she could put it behind her. She was certain of that now in a way she had not been before.

The few days and nights she had been away had given her space to fill her lungs and breathe again. But it was Helen who had brought the epiphany. Helen who had drawn back the veil she had been living under from the moment she had left Spencer Cooper's hotel room. Tomasz never need know and together, they could be happy.

She'd done it before. Who hasn't? No-one gets to middle-age not having put things behind them, things that in the moment of living them felt as if they would always be horribly close-up and forever real. Things like the loud sniggering when, in a crowded boardroom, a month after cosmetic surgery on her nose, a junior male colleague had called out *That's not Caro. Bring back Caroline Hooter Hardcastle.* Things like the black, black eye of her unborn embryo. Things like Kay's voice, as she'd struggled to explain her diagnosis, like Helen's face emerging from the shadows the night she took Libby's baby and walked too long and too far. All these things she had survived and moved forward from. As Helen had too. Because if Helen could put that night behind her, then she too could put this version of herself in the past: the shallow, needy woman of yesterday. It was the privilege and achievement of maturity. The understanding that when you are surrounded by white water, all that is necessary is to hold your chin high until it passes. Because it always passes. She took her phone and pressed Tomasz's number, the warmth of a new beginning flooding her veins.

'I WAS IN THE CHICKEN VILLAGE,' Tomasz said, slightly breathless as he answered.

Caro smiled. She could picture it now. Him, standing in the kitchen, straw on his boots, the door open, a mauve twilight framing the hills behind. 'This is what I want,' she said. 'I'm absolutely sure.'

'OK.' And although the pause Tomasz left was loud, Caro didn't hear.

'I've been thinking,' she continued. 'After the wedding we should make an appointment with the solicitor. As soon as possible. Next week if we can. Definitely before we buy.'

'Before we buy?'

'Yes!' Caro, shifted her weight, tucking her legs under her. 'It will give us a much better bargaining position with Laura and Neil, if we know what we can do with the land. I'm really sure now, Tomasz. I know this is what I want.'

If she had expected an equally gushing response from him, she didn't get it. 'OK,' he said again.

'It might even be possible to be up and running for the autumn. People camp all year round now. If we can get the camping licence I mean.'

'I know what you mean, Caro.'

'I miss it,' she said

He didn't speak.

And into the silence she laughed. 'I'm sat here with the flashing neon of the garage opposite, and I really miss it. I wanted to say that. I wanted you to hear me say that.'

'I can hear you,' he said, and that was all.

39

'And your dad is still in the bungalow?' Hands in pockets, Martin leaned forward to look out of Kay's kitchen window.

'For now. He's getting married.' Kay dumped her handbag on the bench and opened her phone.

'Married? That's um ...'

'Quick? I know.' And to avoid any more questions, she went to the fridge and flung the door open. 'I did a load of batch-cooking last week,' she said, 'but Alex is never here so ...' If she didn't say any more, Martin would get the hint and not ask. Yesterday, her father had rung to tell her that he and Lizzie had set a date. He'd asked if she would like to come with him to visit Lizzie at her retirement home, a home that would soon enough be his home. She'd declined, using the excuse of having to shop for an outfit for Caro's wedding, which, judging by his response, she wasn't sure he'd believed. But wasn't it enough to have given her blessing?

Notice had been given. The process had even been expediated because of the advanced age of both bride and groom, and there wasn't a damn thing she could do about it.

But no, she didn't want to visit Lizzie, and she didn't want to discuss it with Martin. She couldn't bring herself to get excited or participate in the planning of something that upset her just to think about. She wasn't even sure she would attend, although if she didn't, the only witnesses would be Alex, who had accepted the news with his usual equanimity, and whoever happened to be on duty at the time.

'Is he happy?'

She turned, her face blank. It wasn't a question she had expected him to ask. 'I suppose so,' she said and paused. What she'd been expecting was, *How do you feel about it? Are you comfortable with it?*

Martin nodded. 'I was sorry to hear about your mum.' His voice was quiet, as if having read her thoughts, he was tip-toeing in.

Her mum. Yes. Who was thinking about her mum in all this! Her ex-husband of all people. 'And I was sorry to hear about your dad,' she said. 'I wish I had come to the funeral.'

'Me too. I mean, I wish I had come to your mother's.'

Kay smiled. 'She always liked you. Well, not so much after, you know.'

'Of course.' And now Martin smiled. 'I didn't like myself as much after.'

Neither of them spoke. The hum of the fridge behind her was low, the light bright, and now that he was here, exactly where she had invited him to be, she didn't know what she was feeling. She had, long ago, spent time and mental effort constructing scenarios exactly like this. Scenes in which they were alone again, in which he would apologise, beg her forgiveness, declare his love, and everything would go back to what it once had been. It all seemed so childish now. As far-fetched as a fairy-tale. They could never go back. *What it was,* was scorched earth. She turned away from him and stood staring at her fridge. 'It's sad, isn't it?' she said. 'It was only us that got divorced, but I don't think I ever saw your dad again.'

Martin nodded. 'It is sad, yes.'

'I hope you're hungry,' she said, her voice bright as she pulled out a macaroni cheese.

'I'm hungry.'

Kay nodded. 'Get some plates then,' she said, because what else was there to say?

'So.' Martin scraped together a last forkful of food. 'Tell me about this girlfriend then. Emmylou?'

'It's either Emmylou or Emmeline. I'm honestly not sure.' Kay put her knife and fork down. 'I've met her for five minutes and that was by accident. Alex is avoiding introducing her to me. I think he's embarrassed about the whole girlfriend thing.'

Martin laughed. 'You think it's the girlfriend?'

'You don't?'

'Well ...' He paused. 'Don't take this the wrong way.'

'But?'

'But ...' And again, he hesitated. 'You have always been very protective of him.'

'Have I?' Under the table Kay's hands curled to fists. His words felt like a rebuke. A rebuke from a man who had walked away. 'Someone,' she said, tightly, 'had to stay.'

'Kay ––'

No. She raised her hand, shook her head. *No, no, no.* She was thinking about the difficult months before she had made the decision to change Alex's school; how his face had crumpled, when she had told him. Where was Martin then?

If she remembered correctly, he would have been in North London, with woman he had left them for. And if he hadn't used such a tentative tone of voice, if he hadn't paused for so long beforehand ... But how the hell was she supposed to take it? She stood up, her chair scraping.

Martin stood too. 'Where are you going?'

Where was she going? She didn't know. Out the door? Up the street? This was her kitchen, and he'd said he just wanted to talk and already it had come to this. She shouldn't have invited him back. She should have just finished her drink and left him at the pub. She crossed to the bench by the back door and got no further. It didn't matter where she went. The sting of truth in his words would follow wherever she went. She had always been protective of Alex. Very protective. Maybe too protective. But no-one had had told her. No-one had sat her down and had a quiet word: *he's twenty-four now, he's going to be all right, you can let go a little, Kay, breathe again.* Martin was right, and she knew it. The boy who wouldn't go to sleep without calling out a last 'I love you', the child who would plead with her to sit with him while he took an hour to eat two fishfingers was embarrassed - but not about having a girlfriend. He was embarrassed about having a mother. A mother like her.

'Do you want some more,' she said, one hand on the bench, nodding grimly at Martin's empty plate.

'Kay.'

Without speaking, she took his plate and dolloped on another slice of macaroni.

'You have every right ...'

'Just eat,' she said and put the plate in front of him.

'OK.' And slowly Martin sat down again, picked up his knife and fork, and began eating.

Now Kay sat. She did have every right, of course she did,

and she could spend the rest of the evening listing those rights. *I stayed; you left. I was true, you cheated. I hung on, you gave up.* But what was the point in waving all those angry placards now? They sounded archaic; they belonged to another time and another place. She put her hands together under her chin and turned to look out of the window. The evening was warm and sunny, and as she looked it felt to Kay that she was living a moment she had always been destined to live. Martin, here in her kitchen, saying things that needed to be said, and that perhaps only he could say. Things so very different from all those imagined scenarios of yesterday. 'I don't want to keep looking back,' she said, and her words sounded like the echo of something.

'In anger?' Martin's smile was small.

That's why the phrase was familiar. Lyrics to a song from their youth. Kay smiled.

'I don't want to either,' he said.

'Well then.'

'Well.' He put his fork down. 'That was lovely,' he said and for a long moment Kay sat, looking back at him. They had so much history, they had a son, they had the pulse of a connection still between them and they always would. But beyond that ... Upstairs, a door creaked open. Her eyes went wide as plates.

'I thought you said he was out,' Martin whispered.

'That's what he told me,' she whispered back.

She sat, not daring to move as she listened to the voices that had started up: the deep tones of her son, followed by lighter female tones.

Opposite, Martin did the same. 'Emmylou?'

Nodding, Kay pressed her lips together. In her house? With her son? But before she could get any further in processing the situation, heavy footsteps came pounding down the stairs and Alex tumbled into the kitchen.

'Dad?' He was dressed only in boxer shorts, his face and hair putting on a united front of shock.

'Son.' Martin's mouth twitched.

'I thought you said you were out!' Alex said accusingly as he turned to Kay.

'And I thought you said you were out!'

'I came to make toast.' He went bright red.

She didn't dare speak. She wanted to help him, every nerve and sinew strained to stand up, throw her arms around him and steer him out of his discomfort. How could she, when she was the cause of it? How could she go anywhere near him, when all he would be wanting was for her to disappear.

Smiling, pushing his chair back and waving his hand, making both noise and movement, Martin chopped the moment into harmless chunks. 'I think we can do better than toast. Pop some clothes on,' he said, 'and I'll put some of your mum's macaroni in the microwave. And bring Emmylou down as well. It is Emmylou, isn't it?'

Frozen in the doorway, Alex nodded.

'Great!' Martin rubbed his hands together. 'There's plenty to go around isn't there?' he said, turning back to Kay.

And frozen at the table she too managed a small, bewildered nod.

WITH ANOTHER TWO PLACES SET, another two macaroni banged in the microwave and served, Kay was still only partially defrosted. Alex too. Fully dressed, but still a deep shade of crimson, he had introduced an equally mortified Emmylou and kept his eyes on his plate ever since. So now, there really was nothing anyone could do but wait until the tide of embarrassment in the room had receded to wading level. Thank goodness for macaroni cheese, Kay thought as she watched them both tucking in. And thank goodness for Martin. Looking across at him, she smiled. Would she have dealt with the situation so well? It was doubtful.

'This is delicious, thank you.' Emmylou's voice was tiny.

'Would you like some more?' she said.

'Yes please.'

As she stood to refill plates, her heart swelled. Four of them, in her kitchen. Almost a family again. Keeping her back to the table, watching the seconds tick down on the microwave, she listened to the conversation. Alex was talking now. *I could help, dad. You could bring it here.* He wouldn't, she knew, ever question her as to why his father was here. There would be no judgement. He wouldn't even ask and now the embarrassment was manageable, he was behaving as if finding Martin in the kitchen like this, was an everyday occurrence. She tapped her fingertips on the counter and squeezed her eyes shut. This was her son's most beautiful quality, the non-judgemental acceptance he brought to every situation. It was also his most dangerous. Anyone could say anything, and he would accept it. As the microwave pinged, she opened her eyes, a silent prayer on her lips. *Don't let this girl break his heart. Please don't let her hurt him.* 'What could Dad bring here?' she said, as she came back to the table.

'He needs somewhere to keep the VW he's renovating,' Alex said. 'And we've got loads of room. Remember my motorbike? Shook helped me build it.'

Remember? How could she forget the season Alex had been obsessed with *Rags to Riches,* buying himself a DIY motorcycle kit, littering her lawn with spark plugs and fuel hoses, for months on end. Eventually it had all come together, all those unfathomable bits. Alex had even taken part in a couple of races, something else she had never imagined him doing. As she handed Emmylou her plate, Kay smiled. If she'd been over-protective towards her son, she'd also been unimaginative.

'Shook?' Martin frowned.

'It's a long story.' Kay sat down. 'His real name is Tomasz, the guy Caro is marrying on Friday?'

'I see.' Martin turned to Alex. 'Your mum doesn't want —'

'Actually,' Kay interrupted. 'I think it would be lovely.' She meant it. Alex had proved himself to be a good mechanic and this was exactly the kind of project he would enjoy. But it was more than that, and as she glanced up at Martin, she saw that he felt it too. *I wanted to talk to you again.* That's what he'd said. Well, she did too. She wanted to talk to him too.

AND SO IT was that the next evening Martin drove a battered VW van around to her house and Kay made tea, carried it out to the garden and watched as heads close, her son and her ex-husband inspected the van together. They didn't have long, twenty minutes or so before Alex's phone pinged, and he was gone.

'Emmylou,' Kay said wryly. 'I won't see him now until tomorrow.'

Martin smiled. 'Let him go.'

'Of course.' She nodded. Of course, she would let the most precious thing in the world go, and of course she wouldn't have to hide how much it hurt, not in front of the only other person in the world, for whom Alex was equally precious.

'Would you like to see inside?' Martin said, as together they watched their son walk down the drive and disappear along the street.

IT WAS EXACTLY as she might have imagined it. Cosy and tiny. Wood-panelling and blue plaid, a sink, a two-burner grill and mini-fridge. 'And you're really planning to drive this across Europe?' Kay stood in the doorway.

'Once it's finished,' he said.

'How long will that take you?'

'Well, I'm retiring next year, so ...'

'You too?' She smiled.

'Me too.'

'Where are you going to sleep?'

'The table folds out. Here I'll show you.' He moved across to the table and unfolded it, laying the cushions from the bench as a mattress.

Still in the doorway, Kay stiffened.

'I just like to lie here sometimes.' And he stretched himself out on what was now a double sized bed. 'Come over,' he said, patting the empty cushion. 'You can't see it from there.'

'See what?' Her voice was terse. Alex had barely been gone five minutes. And this? This didn't look like *talking*.

Martin sat up. 'I'm not going to try anything, Kay. Just come and lie down and then look up. I think you'll like it.'

Cautious and tense, she inched over and sat down on the edge of the cushion.

'Lie down,' he said. 'And then look up.'

So, she did, straight through the open sun-roof and up

into a heaven of mauve twilight, where pinpricks of starlight shone, millions of years still in the vault. Where planets turned and turned. It made her think of another time, in Vegas, when she had sat and looked at the desert trying to imagine what life for her son would look like without her. Fine. It would look just fine.

'Kay?' Martin rolled onto his side.

'I'm all right,' she said, but she could feel the cold wetness of tears on her cheek. 'Come here.'

Kay stiffened. She put a hand on his chest and held him away.

'It's just a cuddle,' he said. 'If you want one.'

She did. She really did, and because that was all she wanted, and it was all that was offered, she let her hand drop and allowed herself to relax into his arms.

PART III

40

The sun was strong, Helen's neck pickled with heat, and her bra strap slipped under the flimsy chiffon of her dress. Straightening up, she blew the feather fascinator from her eyes and pushed the bike forward only for the wheel to jump as if it had hit brick. Ouch! The vibration of the impact stung her hands. She pushed again, but the bike didn't move and suddenly, despite the heat, despite her itchy neck and damp back, she felt the coolness of Deja vu, that overwhelming oddity of living a moment she knew she had lived before.

Of course! She looked up. This rut in the road was *always* where the bike had stuck. And never mind just once, she would have lived this moment hundreds of times. Months and years in which her belly would have been swollen with first Libby, and then Jack. When her front basket would have been loaded with nappies waiting to be filled, and vegetables waiting to be pureed. How strange then, she was thinking as she put the back of her hand to her brow, how odd to stumble across this younger version of herself, at a junction that never changed. A turning in the road where, at this time of the year blackberry brambles would always show pimples of reddish-green, and the green canopy of the horse chestnut would always spread above her head. A place where the milestone stood, silently marking every version of Helen that had ever passed: *London: seventeen miles.*

Reading it, Helen smiled. If only she had access to a similar marker to measure her own life. How straightforward, for example, if she knew how many more Helens, she ran the risk of stumbling into? Or how many were left? Helen, the child, the teenager, the young woman, the new mother, the wife, the divorcee ... Helen the grandmother? She was already there. Helen the adventurer? Was that over before it had even begun? Helen: mark seven... mark eight ...

Tensing her arms, she gave a tremendous push forward and the front wheel jumped free. As it did, she swung one leg over the frame, pushed down on the pedal, flicked the battery power to maximum and breezed up the hill towards her old home, swift as Mary Poppins and her umbrella. How easy, she was thinking, as the wheels turned and her neck cooled in the breeze, how easy an electric bike would have made her life in those days of babies and vegetables.

As she reached the top, the ground flattened out. She slowed the bike down, brought it to a halt and dismounted. Who was she fooling? An electric bike wouldn't have made a difference. The Helen who had schlepped home with a kilo of unwashed carrots, instead of buying a pureed jar, had also been the Helen who had insisted on using washable nappies. Insisted on packing a school lunch, insisted on organising, hosting, catering every birthday and every Christmas of a picture-perfect life, in a picture-perfect house. All to keep busy. So, so busy. And standing for a long moment to look back down the hill, Helen's eyes narrowed, focusing on a point by the chestnut tree. As if she was still there, as if she could still be seen: the burdened young woman she had passed along the way.

FIVE MINUTES LATER, and the first thing she saw as she wheeled the bike into the driveway was the blue and white *For Sale* sign stuck amongst the roses. So, it was true then? Although she'd had no reason to doubt Libby, she hadn't contacted Lawrence to confirm the news that he was selling. Why should she? It wasn't, strictly speaking, anything to do with her. And yet here she was, evident in every flowerbed and every window. Those lemon curtains, the magnolia tree she had planted when Libby and Ben were still in primary school. These colours, these living things, framed her as well as any photograph could.

She parked the bike and walked to the door, the gravel (as it always had been), painful through the thin soles of her sandals. As she raised her hand to knock, the door swung back.

'Helly!' Lawrence was in his running gear (unspeakably tight Lycra shorts over pale hairy legs and a neon green vest), hands on hips, panting like a Labrador. Grinning, he leaned in to plant a sweaty kiss on her cheek. 'You look marvellous,' he said. 'Big day today!'

Helen nodded. There was a wet patch on her cheek now, messing up her make-up.

'What's this?' He pointed at the bike.

'An electric bike,' she said tightly. 'I bought it before I went to the states.'

'An electric bike!' Lawrence guffawed. 'That's not cycling, Helly! You should have asked me. How much did it set you back?' He didn't wait for an answer. 'Come in! Come in!' And as he raised a sweaty arm to let her in, Helen felt wobbly, stepping over the threshold, back in the scenery of what had been her life.

'LOOK AT YOU!' Lawrence exclaimed, as they entered the kitchen. 'All that walking has done you good, Helly. You look wonderful.'

Walking? A three-day hike across Yellowstone: *walking?*

'Libby's upstairs changing Ben.'

'OK.' Helen nodded. She hadn't seen her daughter since the evening at Libby's flat, and she felt a sense of dread at their imminent meeting. At some point, Libby would be expecting a conversation, a dialogue between them that would include Helen confirming the fact that she wasn't going anywhere. Something she hadn't managed to say to either Fiona Chambers, or herself. 'And you're sure you're going to be OK with him?' she said, more to distract herself than anything else. The arrangement couldn't be changed now anyway, Lawrence was taking Ben for the day, while Libby accompanied her to Caro's wedding.

'Of course.' Lawrence smiled. 'Me and babies, Helly. You know me and babies.'

Did she? Helen frowned. The baby years she remembered were the years Lawrence had left the house at seven and come back at seven. They were the years of extended trips every summer when he went off to climb a mountain or cycle the length of a country. 'Well.' She smiled and left it at that. It was all water under a distant bridge now and there was no point in trying to scoop even the smallest bucket back. If he was proactive in his grandson's life, that was only good. Besides, she was increasingly distracted by the smell of something cooking, something delicious. She turned to look at the Aga where Lawrence now stood, pulling on a floral oven glove she recognised as hers. An everyday item she had used on an everyday basis, for years. Something she hadn't taken with her and hadn't missed! In fact, it was possible to go further. Until this moment, she had forgotten the glove even existed. 'You made a casserole?' she said, staring at the glove.

Lawrence grinned. 'It's pretty easy, Helly. You just throw it all in. I thought Ben and I would have it later with these.' He held up a clear plastic bag of green beans. 'I found them at the bottom of the freezer.'

'Right.' Helen nodded. She'd grown those beans herself, in this garden. Seeded, harvested and frozen them. Turning away, she grabbed a tissue from her handbag and held it to her nose. She should have taken a taxi directly to the town hall, she should never have accepted Lawrence's offer of a lift, never have come back into a house that was no longer hers. A house she had brought her children home to as new-born babies. The house where she had sat with a three- day-old, Jack, that long sunny afternoon Libby and Lawrence had made the biggest mess over a ham salad dinner. The afternoon, she'd been painting the French windows and turned to see Libby crawling towards the road. The winter of heavy snow when they had pretended to be snowed in. The Saturday, Libby had sulked up the drive having failed her driving test. The watermelons she had tried and failed to grow. And those darkest times when her first born hadn't come home, when her mother had died. Days and weeks in which she had closed her door on the world and this house had been her sanctuary. As she pressed the tissue harder, her eyes stung. She didn't want to cry, she didn't want to spoil her make-up, but leaving was a river in flow. It was not an action that could be completed in one step. Things got left behind, things she hadn't even known she'd left. Like that stupid oven glove, those beans, the pieces of her heart she had painted and nailed and dug into this house. 'So ...' she said as she pretended to blow her nose. 'You're selling the house?'

'I am.' And reaching to a cupboard, Lawrence pulled out a tin of protein powder. 'Excuse me a minute. I need to get this down quick while the muscles are still warm.'

Numb, Helen watched him scoop powder into a glass of water. She used to do this for him. His power drink, or recovery drink, or whatever it was. 'You could have told me,' she said. 'I had to hear it from Libby.'

'Oh.' The slackness of surprise on his face was genuine. It hadn't, she realised, even occurred to him. 'Should I have?'

Helen shrugged. No. Legitimately speaking he had been under no obligation to inform her about the sale of a property she had no interest in, the sale of a property where the roses and clematis that she had planted still bloomed, where the bones of two cats, and at least one gerbil whose burials she had overseen, now decomposed. Unable to stop herself, she shrugged again.

'I thought it was time,' Lawrence said. 'Lib has her own place now.'

'And Jack?'

'Jack's due back three days before university starts.' Lawrence took a spoon and stirred his drink. 'And then he's talking about a gap year.' He dropped the spoon in the sink, raised the glass and swallowed the contents in almost one gulp. Job done, muscles still warm, recovery in progress.

'I was surprised,' she said as she watched him. 'That's all.'

'Well to be fair, Helly,' he said as he put the glass on the counter, 'we haven't been in touch much, have we?'

'I suppose not,' she said. She used to do that do as well. Move the glass from the counter to the dishwasher, move it back from the dishwasher to the cupboard. 'No,' she said, looking at the glass, wondering how long it would sit there. 'No, we haven't.' Since she had left, Lawrence had periodically sent her an email with news about the kids (of which she was already aware, and to which she had responded, because it was polite). But over time even this communication had tailed off; something Helen had taken as a good sign. A signal perhaps, that he was beginning to accept his new reality. It had after all been nearly a year since their divorce was finalised, and, as the hardest part of leaving had been knowing how much she was hurting him, she had remained alert to any signs that might begin to relieve the guilt. Snowdrops of hope that he was recovering, maybe even meeting new people? So how ironic. How strange that far from a snowdrop, this oak tree of a sign that he was moving on, should feel less like a blessing and more like a wound.

Lawrence raised his hands, a genial gesture. 'The thing is,' he said, 'I'm rattling around like a spare part in this place. And it's not as if anyone will ever be homeless. The kids will always have a bed at yours or mine.'

'I suppose so,' she conceded.

'Besides,' he said, rubbing his hands together. 'I'm thinking of doing the same as you. It's one of the reasons behind all this.' And he turned and waved an airy hand at the kitchen, the hall beyond, the house in general.

'The same what?'

'A gap year, Helly!' He grinned. 'I'm thinking of taking a gap year. Like you.'

Helen couldn't speak. Her jaw dropped and her mouth gaped. 'Like me?' she gasped. 'I took six weeks, Lawrence! That's not even a quarter of a year. And now I'm back at work.'

'I know.' He nodded. 'How is the job?'

'The job?' she echoed. Had he even heard her? Dazed, she pulled off her wrap and fell into a chair. 'It's shit if you must know. It's boring and unfulfilling and ...' Pausing, Helen took a deep breath, watching for any sign that he had heard, that he understood. There was nothing. 'I was only meant to be there a year,' she said quietly. 'I've been there ten.'

'Ten?' Lawrence pushed his lips together. 'That long?'

'Yes,' Lawrence. *That* long.'

'Why?'

'Why?' She stared at him. '*Why?*' And before he could answer, she put her hands to her face and dropped forward on her elbows. 'Let me see?' she said, through her hands. 'How about the fact that the hours worked with school? Or that it was close to school, in case one of the kids fell down a well and we were needed, and you weren't around because you were climbing a mountain. Is that *why* enough for you?'

'Helly ...'

'Or' she seethed as she turned to look at him. 'How about the fact that it worked for you, because it meant I was around to make dinner and make sure homework was done and hair was washed and be a parent to our children. *Our* children, Lawrence.' Folding her wrap into an angry square, Helen stood up. 'And by the way I want them.'

'Helly!' Lawrence raised his hands. 'Want what?'

'The curtains,' she snapped. 'Those lemon curtains in the front bedroom.'

'You can have them.'

'Good.'

'Anything else?'

'No!' She turned to stuff the wrap into her handbag. It wouldn't fit. 'Yes,' she cried, as she yanked it out again. 'You can't go on a gap year, Lawrence. You can't!'

'Why ever not?' he said, a look of genuine confusion on his face.

'Because ...' Helen threw her hands up. 'Because,' she started. 'Because it's not fair, Lawrence!' And collapsing back into the chair, she slumped forward again, the feather of her fascinator, bowing in sympathy. 'I've been offered a job in Bolivia.'

'Bolivia?' Lawrence drew his own chair out.

As he did, Helen looked up. 'It's a six-month contract.'

'Helly!' Lawrence smiled.

'Very similar to what I do here,' she said, sounding thoroughly miserable.

'That's marvellous.'

'Is it?'

'Isn't it?'

'No.' Helen shook her head. 'No, it isn't, Lawrence. How can I go?'

Leaning back, Lawrence stretched his arms. 'I'm not sure I see the problem,' he said drumming his fingers on the table.

'Libby is the problem,' she said flatly.

Lawrence didn't speak. Frowning, he pushed his chair back, went to the fridge and took out a bottle of champagne. 'I had planned,' he said as he poured two small glasses, 'that we could have a tiny, tiny toast to Caro. But it sounds like we should have one for you as well.'

Numb, Helen looked at the glasses. 'Did you even hear me?' she said.

'I did.' He handed her a glass. 'But you're over-thinking this, Helly. You really are. Libby is fine. She has her own home now. She's a young woman. A very capable one. She doesn't need us. Cheers.' He raised his glass.

And in return Helen raised hers, silent as she watched the champagne bubbles popping in a hundred harmless explosions. She could take a mouthful – she did – and they could go on exploding and it wouldn't harm her one little bit. But the image of Libby did. The picture she held in her mind of her daughter, head on the table, crying and begging her not to go, was a knife that sliced to the marrow. It was not the image of a capable young woman. It wasn't a picture of a daughter who didn't need her parent.

'I think this is a great opportunity,' Lawrence said. 'It's time for all of us to move on. Like, Caro's doing today. Time for all of us to spread our wings, don't you think?'

Slowly, Helen turned to him. From the day she had met him, Lawrence had done nothing but spread his wings. Thirty years of flying he'd have the wingspan of an albatross by now, and still it wasn't enough? Still, he wanted more? 'It's so easy for you, isn't it?' she said, her voice thick with resentment.

'Easy?' Lawrence smiled. 'I'm not sure what you mean by that, Helly.'

'No.' She nodded. He couldn't see the problem, because in his world there was no problem. He would, she knew, sell the house without a second thought, buy himself a one-way ticket to Tasmania and leave. It's what men did. Women stayed; men left. And if he left, she couldn't. She took off her fascinator and held it in her lap. The feather, so jaunty when she had set off, had folded in on itself as if it had accepted its fate, and given up. Which was, she was beginning to think, what she should do to.

41

S tanding in front of a full-length mirror, Caro heard the sound of her intercom buzzer like a diver hears voices from the surface, it was soft and warped, and she was so deep in her dream, so lost in the spell, it simply didn't register. She turned sideways, to look back over her shoulder. There were many words she might have used to describe herself, elegant, chic, sophisticated, but the rose-tinted glasses were off now and beautiful was not among them and she was at peace with that. The dress, however? Well, the dress remained gorgeous. Across her back she could feel the pull of the zipper, a tension that hadn't been there on her last fitting. She bought her hands to her chin and turned back. *Is that you?* she whispered, *Is that really you?* And suddenly her hand was at her mouth and her eyes were full of tears and she was unsteady in the flow of a sudden and warm yearning. A desire strong enough to raise the dead, to haul her mother up and out of her grave, have her standing alongside, finally proud.

Dipping her head, Caro put her hands on her hips and took a short shuddery breath. Her mother had been buried twenty months ago, in a cemetery less than a mile from the terraced house she had spent all her life in. A small funeral, for a small life and exactly why today, she had wanted as much family around her as possible. Her brother, of course, and Helen and Kay, naturally. But her godchildren as well, Alex and Libby. And Kay's father, whom she'd known since she was eighteen years old. The constants in her life: these were the faces waiting for her. The thought made her smile. 'I'm getting married,' she whispered. 'What would you say about that, mum?'

The answer came from the intercom, a louder, more urgent buzz than that of a moment ago. Frowning, Caro picked up her phone and checked the time. Her car wasn't due for twenty minutes. She slipped off her shoes and padded to the front door. They would have to wait. She wasn't ready, and they would just have to wait.

But it wasn't the driver, it was Tomasz, and as she pressed the buzzer to let him in, the reality of the words they had just exchanged, versus the implications of them was such a juxtaposition, her brain couldn't keep up.

'It's me, can you let me up?'

'What are you doing here?'

'We need to talk.'

So, the moment was long; the moment in which she stood with her hand on the door handle, looking at him. He was in his wedding suit, a fact that as she put her hand on her heart and exhaled, gave relief. Panic receding, she stepped aside to let him in.

'What's going on? We're not supposed ——'

'Let's go and sit down,' he said quietly.

'Tomasz?' She followed him along the hallway. Something must have happened. They were doing it traditionally, and he'd stayed with a friend last night. The same friend, who was going to be his best man, with whom he should be at the registry office right now. Maybe the friend had let him down?

'Sit down, Caro.'

She did, watching as he took the chair opposite. Although he didn't sit. He perched, half on, half off, elbows on his knees as he clasped his hands together and looked at the floor.

'What's going on?'

But he didn't look up, and with every second that ticked past, a numbness spread. From her toes to her shins, to her gut, seeping upward like a stain, until it was at her fingertips and her hands lay, useless on her lap. It wasn't the friend.

'Caro.' Now he lifted his head. 'This is the hardest thing.'

Caro nodded, the stiff double-stitched edge of her sweetheart neckline cutting into her skin. It wasn't a dress made for sitting. 'What?' she managed.

'I don't think you're being honest with me. And until I'm sure ...' Tomasz paused. He looked up at the ceiling, took a deep breath and finished, 'Until I'm sure, I can't do this.'

The words were physical, like hands around her neck. She squeezed her knees together, an instinctive response to a dreadful fear. He knew then. Somehow – and she was already somersaulting backward, trying to join the dots – he had found out about Spencer Cooper. Had discovered how easily she had climbed into another man's bed, the thinness of flattery that had been needed. Her hands went clammy; her heart rolled into her throat.

'If there's something you want to tell me,' he said, 'then I need to hear it. Now.'

And because she couldn't look him in the eye, because she wanted to rewind her life, go back to that moment at The Langmere, and re-write the scene, she kept her eyes fixed on her lap, on the beautiful pearls, of her beautiful dress.

'It's only fair, Caro.' He slid off the chair onto his knees, taking her hands in his, as if it were the other way around, as if this were the beginning and he was asking her to marry him; not telling her that he couldn't. 'I need to hear it now,' he said. 'Not a year later, when it's too late.'

'What do you want me to say?' she whispered. Such a coward. Even now with her back against the wall.

'That this is what you want. That you are completely sure, about what we're doing. And this is really what you want.'

Poof! Everything vanished. The clamminess of her hands, the weight of her heart in her mouth. All gone. The remembrance of how she had leaned back to show her legs off, the *I would have loved to* ... All gone because ... 'The smallholding?' she said, sun in her world and her face again. 'You mean the smallholding?'

Slowly, Tomasz let go of her hands and edged back to his seat. 'Of course,' he said, not taking his eyes off her. 'Of course, the smallholding.'

'Yes!' Caro smiled, almost delirious with relief as she pressed her hands together. 'I told you! I'm a hundred percent sure. And when we get back, we need —'

'What did you think I was talking about?'

She blinked.

'What else, Caro?'

She looked at him, and he looked back at her, and above them, the sky closed over. There was no point in trying to fudge a denial of what they had both so clearly seen. That moment of blue, when she had thought all her storms were over. And if it had been deniable before, a nebulous cloud that she might have dispersed, it had solidified now, this heavy third presence in the room: her dishonesty. She had two choices. She could tell him and lose him. Or not tell him and lose him.

Tomasz shook his head. 'I can't do this.'

'Please.' But the genie was out of the bottle, and they both knew it.

'This is not what you want,' he said, as he stood up. 'I don't know what it is that you're not telling me. I don't know if you're having doubts about me, or the move, but something doesn't add up. You say you're certain?' He shrugged. 'I'm sorry, Caro but I don't believe you. No,' he added, raising his palm as if to stop her speaking, as if she'd tried to speak.

Had she? She didn't know, she sat, hands still clasped, ears ringing.

'I can't marry you, when I know you're not being honest.'

And in the pause that followed, all she had to do was stand up and say, *I am being honest. I am.* She stayed silent and she stayed sitting.

Hands in his pockets, Tomasz nodded. 'If we go ahead, one of us - or both of us - is going to end up unhappy. I don't want that,' he added. 'I don't think either of us have time left for that.'

Still, she didn't speak.

'Caro.' Tomasz sat down again. 'I know you've been trying, but it's not you. This life we're trying to make, it's not you.'

'It can be,' she whispered. 'It really can be.'

'No.' He shook his head. 'I don't think you even know yourself, what you want.'

Lips pressed together, she listened to the echo of his words. They sounded as if they were coming from a place that was light and spacious, a place that, amidst this sudden darkness, was tantalisingly reachable. 'OK.' Slowly, she looked up. 'You're right. The smallholding is a lot more work than I had imagined.' Hearing herself say the words out loud, felt like forcing open a door that had been wedged stuck.

'It is,' he agreed. 'It's a lot of work.'

'So.' Her face brightening, Caro inched forward to the edge of her seat. 'If we're not sure, let's have a re-think? After the wedding, we can move back here and ...'

'No.'

One softly enunciated syllable. *No.*

'No?' she said

'No,' he repeated.

'Why not?' She'd flung a rope out to him, and he'd walked the other way.

'Because I am sure,' he said. 'This is what I want, Caro. And that leaves us wanting different things.'

'But we can ...' Her voice died. There was nothing left to say, and as they sat looking at each other they both knew it. If they came back to London, Tomasz at her flat, never going barefoot, doing a job he hated, he would be as unsettled as she had been. It was exactly as he had just said, they wanted different things. 'What will you do,' she whispered, as if it was all decided.

'I'm going back to Poland. I'll see the contract out first, we made a commitment, and I'll fulfil it.'

She bit down on her lip. It was decided then.

'You don't have to come back. In fact, it's probably for the best that you don't.'

As a tang of blood washed through her mouth, the sound of the intercom buzzer filled her ears. They both turned to look. 'That will be the car,' she said.

'I'll tell him ——'

'No.' Already, she was on her feet, moving to the doorway. 'I'll do it.'

'Are you sure?'

Jaw tight, Caro nodded. Whatever needed to be done, she would do. This was her wedding, and she would do it.

'I'm sorry.' Tomasz leaned in and kissed her cheek. 'You look beautiful,' he choked, and then he was gone.

42

Despite the tall, sashed windows either side of the entrance, the reception room of Brackenford Town Hall was a dark room. The floor was tiled chequerboard and the chairs positioned along each side were covered in a sombre, muted material. The brightest light came from a digital TV that had been mounted against the wood-panelled wall. Sweeping images of parkland and busy markets played on loop, conspicuously modern against the Edwardian setting. On the far side stood a desk with a perplex screen and a signing-in book. Aside from a young couple with a new-born baby, Kay, Alex and her father were the only ones there.

'Why don't you take a seat?' she whispered, as she turned to him now. He'd stumbled on the steps up and supporting him she had been startled by his frailness. 'It's very warm and we still have a few minutes.' The ceremony was due to start in a quarter of an hour, but with no one else here, it looked like they were the first to arrive.

He didn't protest, and after she had settled him into a chair, Kay looked across at Alex who was watching the TV.

'Pop outside,' she said, 'and see if there is any sign of Helen and Libby? I'm going to find out where we need to go.'

Alex left, and Kay approached the desk. There was, she saw immediately, no need to ask. A list of names already signed in the book, answered her question. Her finger traced the lines. Caro's brother and his wife were here, their names listed underneath two Polish sounding names. Against every entry, in the far-right column were the words, *Heritage Room*. So, they weren't the first, they were almost the last. She frowned. Caro wouldn't arrive until just before, but she was surprised not to see Tomasz's name, he was leaving it a little fine.

The only other things on the desk were a small brass bell and a stand full of leaflets. She inched her foot out of her shoe and reached down to press at the red bulb appearing on her toe. A blister. Already. That had to be a record. Winching with pain, she pushed her foot back in, pressed the bell and turned to read through the leaflets, top to bottom: *Registering your baby's birth. How to give notice of a marriage. What to do when someone dies.*

'We had to press it twice,' the woman with the baby called across.

'Oh.' Kay turned. 'Thank you,' she said. She was about to ring a second time when the front door swung open, throwing a rectangle of bright light into the room. It was Helen. Or it looked like Helen, the figure was mostly a silhouette, an outline topped by a dancing feather.

'Lovely dress,' Kay said as Helen stepped out of her shadow. 'I was worried you wouldn't make it out of the t-shirt.'

Helen smiled. 'Well, I still haven't finished unpacking, so obviously I had to buy something new.'

'Obviously.' Kay laughed. 'I'm beginning to wish I hadn't bothered.'

'Why?' Helen put her head to one side. 'The dress is lovely.'

'Not the dress. It's my shoes. They're killing me.'

They both looked down at Kay's feet.

'Don't you have liner socks on?'

'What,' Kay said, 'are liner socks?'

'These.' And lifting her leg, Helen pointed down to a neat little flesh coloured sock, peeping out of her sandal. 'Honestly, Kay. Before you go to Cyprus, I'm going to have to take you shopping. You'll need these, they make life that little bit more comfortable. Have you ––'

'No Libby?' Kay blurted. Nothing was booked; nothing was happening ... those were the only honest answers to questions she didn't want asked.

'SHE'S WITH ALEX,' Helen said, oblivious. 'I left them catching up. They haven't seen each other in ages.' Glancing at the couple with the baby, she frowned. 'Are we first?'

'I think we're just about last,' Kay said. 'Everyone must have gone through already. We need to sign in.' And as if she had only to have given the right cue, a security guard appeared.

'Sorry to keep you waiting,' he said, wiping crumbs from his shirt. 'You're here for?'

'The Hardcastle-Nowak wedding,' Helen said.

'Great.' The guard nodded, trying and failing to hide his hand as he wiped it on his trousers. 'If I can just ask you to sign in and we need to do a light bag search.'

'Bag search?' Helen dipped her head as she handed her

bag over. 'It's a bit different from St Marys, where I got married.'

'Me too.' Kay nodded.

'Mind, Caro's dress is a bit different as well.' Helen chuckled. 'When I think back. I was like a giant meringue!'

Kay smiled. 'I had an enormous bow on my backside.'

'To be fair,' Helen whispered, 'everyone who got married back then had a bow.'

'But not everyone's bow fell off,' Kay whispered back. 'You had one job, Helen. One job.'

'I was scared of pushing the pins in too far! Thanks.' Helen took her bag back. 'I've been telling you that for thirty years,' she said as she turned to Kay. 'One day you'll believe me.'

'You were tipsy before we left my parent's house!' Kay said, as she handed her own bag over. 'And one day *you'll* believe *me*!'

'Maybe.' Helen picked up the pen, as she did Kay waved to her father.

'I'll sign in for you, Dad.'

'Oh!' Helen looked up. 'I didn't see your dad there.' She waved across, and turning back to Kay said, 'He looks well.'

'He's getting married.'

'He's what?' Helen blinked.

'Next week.' Kay nodded. 'Don't ask me how I feel, OK? I know the lady and she's lovely but ...'

'Next week?' Pen in hand, Helen didn't move.

'At the retirement home where Lizzie, lives. That's her name.'

'Oh.'

'And then he's moving there.'

Helen nodded, slowly she turned back to the book, but she didn't write anything. 'Is he happy?' she said.

Is he happy? This was the second time in just a few days that Kay had been asked a question she hadn't been expecting to hear. Holding her jaw stiff, she moved her eyes to look across at where her father sat, small, suited and still. He was dressed in the suit he had worn for her mother's funeral, the suit he was wearing the day he met Lizzie, smiling as he watched the baby across the room. The baby, she supposed, who was here to have its birth registered. That first leaflet in life. The broad end of a funnel that would inevitably lead to the last leaflet, *What to do when someone dies.*

She took a deep breath, her eyes moist with tears. And what should you do when someone dies? Move on? Forget them? Ask someone you barely know, to marry you? There would be nothing in a three-page leaflet to explain this third option.

The baby burped, a loud and uninhibited sound that slapped off the walls like a wet flannel.

'Babies don't care.' Smiling, Helen bent to sign her name.

Kay watched. Her father was also smiling, and the baby? Nestled against its mother's breast, the baby sucked a finger, oblivious to any unspoken etiquette it might have broken.

'Here.'

She turned to take the pen Helen had offered, but before she could make a single stroke, a buzzing sound stopped her. A low constant vibration, that sounded like ... Heart thumping, she looked up to see the security guard holding her vibrator. 'It's a ...' But her voice died, crept back down her throat and gave up.

Helen put her hand to her mouth.

Limp with mortification, she watched the guard turn a

pillar-box red as he fumbled to turn it off. 'Shall I ...?' she managed. 'I can ...'

He almost threw it at her and switching it off she stuffed it back in her bag, deep out of sight. As she did, she felt a firm arm linking through her own, leading her away.

'Why,' Helen hissed as soon as they were out of earshot of the guard, 'would you keep it in your handbag?'

'I needed somewhere safe,' she babbled. 'I didn't want anyone to find it.'

Helen's lips twitched. 'Who was going to find it, Kay?'

Kay shook her head, but the words she was going to say wouldn't come. Words like, *don't laugh. It isn't funny.* But it was funny, and why shouldn't Helen laugh? A woman of fifty-two hiding a vibrator because she had been terrified of anyone finding out she owned one? Not just hiding it. No, that wasn't good enough. She'd had to carry it with her everywhere. As if it were a gun. Or a signed confession to murder. Adding weight where there wasn't the slightest need. As if life wasn't heavy enough. It was simply an instrument of pleasure, her pleasure, and wasn't she allowed to seek and find pleasure in life? In the same way an infant is allowed to burp in public, she was surely permitted to find a way towards pleasure, towards happiness. She looked back at her father. He was watching a point across the room, a square of sunlight reflected on the wood panelling, one small space of light amongst the dark. And now she remembered what he had said, and why, when she had repeated it, so soon after, it had sounded so familiar. 'I don't want to keep looking back.'

There was only one way, and it was forward, and what should be done when someone dies, was not a leaflet. There wasn't a prescriptive or a commandment to be followed, there was only life. Messy, embarrassing, imperfect, and most of all, continuous

43

Leaving Kay to regain her composure, Helen pushed the heavy oak door open and stepped outside into a flare of daylight. Libby and Alex should be seated before Caro arrived; she needed to call them in. She raised her hand to her face, shielding her eyes as they recalibrated to accommodate the sunshine, the piercing glint from passing cars, the shimmer of sandstone steps. It was a busy scene, with people coming and going through a side door, hands full of paperwork in pastel colours. This front entrance of the town hall she had just used was obviously reserved for the more important milestones of life, those infrequent occasions when the stroke of a pen recorded a name that might otherwise have gone forever unspoken. The side door, she realised as she watched, was for all the stuff in-between: finding a place to live, registering a vote, gaining a driving licence.

Letting her hand fall, she turned back to the stairs and was immediately drawn to a young couple standing on the top step. The man was tall with a mop of dark hair. He had his hands in his pockets as he listened to the woman talking.

They looked so comfortable in each other's company, heads tipping back as they laughed, it took Helen a long moment to understand that she was looking at Libby and Alex. When she did, when the realisation had seeped through, the tears that pricked her eyes were sharp as needles.

Libby and Alex, her baby girl and Kay's baby boy, all grown up.

Of course, they would be comfortable with each other. Libby was closer in age to Alex than she was to her brother. Born six months apart, for the first five years of their lives they had been the best of best friends, sharing birthday parties and beds, paddling naked in the splash pool, falling asleep, heads touching, in their toddler car seats. She still remembered how they always held hands, no matter how short the walk. From the car to the house, the car to the supermarket, the car to nursery school, they would seek each other out and hold hands. So, it should have been a joyous sight, but the feeling she had as she watched was tinged with sadness. It was a merciless proof of how swift it all was, how a decade could pass easy as water through hands. A breeze came gusting up the steps, cold enough for her to pull her wrap tight over her shoulders. She tipped her chin to the sky. The clear blue of earlier had gone, and all she could see now was slate grey. She shivered. The morning had turned colder.

'I SUPPOSE you're too big now for a hug!' she said, as she put her arms around Alex. (It wouldn't have mattered what he answered, there was no way she was missing out on hugging him). 'My goodness!' She took a step back. 'You just get taller all the time.'

As Alex mumbled an embarrassed response, Libby said,

'We were just trying to remember the last time we saw each other.'

Smiling, Helen tucked the edge of her wrap in place. She knew exactly when the last time had been, and although she wasn't entirely surprised that Libby didn't seem to remember, it was still disappointing. 'Your eighteenth birthday party, wasn't it?' she said, the light stress making it a question, when she wasn't looking for an answer.

'I think it must have been,' Libby looked away, her cheeks colouring.

So, she did remember. Not having wanted Alex there in the first place, Libby had spent the whole evening avoiding him, and Helen had spent a large part of the evening looking out for him. Making sure he had a drink, attempting to engage him in conversation. His buttoned-up silhouette, lonely at the edge of the dance floor was a memory she would never forget. Neither was the comment she had overheard Libby make to a group of her girlfriends. 'He's someone my mum knows. She made me invite him.' It had been one of those moments when she hadn't liked her daughter. When she had found the hubris of a single-minded eighteen-year-old, with skin as unblemished as her grades, a repellent thing.

'That was a great night,' Alex said now.

Helen nodded. This was why Kay carried her son's heart in her hands. If she left it with him, he'd bring it home every day torn to shreds, and he wouldn't even notice. Not until it was completely broken, not until it was dying. One step lower, she watched Libby lift her face to Alex, saw how she bit down on her lip, how her eyes were glassy with tears. Libby knew; she had her own child now. Finally, she knew.

'I might have a party,' Alex said brightly.

Helen laughed. 'Am I invited?'

'Of course you are.'

'Thank you,' she said, matching his sincerity. Of course, he would invite his mother's fifty-two-year-old friend. And suddenly she was thinking of the time, Kay had told her how, the day after they had watched *Lady and the Tramp,* Alex had gone into school and told his whole class that he could speak French, 'Oh la la Pussycat,' he'd repeated proudly. A story that was as funny as it was terrifying. Because as Kay had explained, if he thinks he can do it, it's enough: her greatest fear was Alex's greatest strength.

'You're invited too, Libby,' Alex said. 'And you can bring your baby.'

'Oh.' A spot of pink appeared on each of Libby's cheeks. 'I'd love to,' she said.

Beaming, Alex turned back to Helen. 'I'm only going to have it, if Mum's in Cyprus. She hasn't booked her flight yet. Dad will get there quicker than her at this rate.'

'Really? Why's that?' Helen kept her voice light as a feather. Talk about blood out of a stone! The only thing Kay had given up about the fact that her anonymous admirer, had turned out to be her ex-husband, (Helen's worst nightmare), was that it had been a lovely evening and she might see him again. If she hadn't had so much else on her mind, not least keeping tabs on Caro, she'd have taken a trip across, and armed with a bottle of Prosecco, bubbled it out of Kay. She'd always liked Martin, had always thought Kay and him were a perfect match. Their divorce had been such a shock, it had just about ended Helen's faith in marriage as an institution. If Kay and Martin couldn't make it, who could? Nobody, it turned out, and thinking this her mind went back to Caro, who had so nearly messed it up before she'd even started. Who had been positive and cheerful every time Helen had phoned.

Too positive and too cheerful for Helen's liking. She took out her phone and glanced at the time. Neither Tomasz nor Caro had arrived.

'Are you OK, Mum?'

'Sorry?'

'You're shivering,' Libby said.

'Am I?' Helen laughed. 'It's just the wind.'

'What wind?' Alex said.

Helen laughed again. But as swiftly as it had risen, the breeze had dropped. She hadn't been shivering because she was cold, she'd shivered in the foresight of something she couldn't see or hear. Something she could only feel.

'Is your dad going to Cyprus as well?' Libby said, dragging her back into the moment.

'He's bought a camper van,' Alex said. 'It's at Mum's house and I'm helping him fix it up. He's going to drive around Europe in it.'

So that was what *might see him again,* meant. Helen smiled. A to B to C. You could always rely on Alex to take a direct route.

'I think she's worried about me,' Alex said. 'She doesn't think I can look after myself. But I can. I have a girlfriend now.'

'Oh, Alex.' Helen put her hand on his arm. Alex had always been more capable than Kay had ever dared allow him to be. Except for the heart bit. His pure, pure heart. 'What's her name?' she said, welling up again.

'Emmylou. She works in the gift shop at the garden centre.'

'That's great, Alex.' And Libby too smiled, and for a moment the three of them stood, held in the arms of a pure and gentle emotion.

'I want Mum to go,' Alex said. 'She really enjoyed herself

last time. I don't want her to think that she has to stay and look after me all the time.'

'No,' Helen murmured.

'That's not fair,' Alex said.

She shook her head.

'So, I think she should go.'

Helen dipped her chin. She understood what Kay would be thinking, how impossible the decision to leave was. What she couldn't begin to understand, not here, not now in the blistering truth of Alex's words, was what Libby would be thinking. The situation was too complicated, too fraught with emotion to be broached five minutes before a wedding. 'I think,' she said cheerily, 'that we really should be going in.' She turned to Alex. 'Your mum is getting your granddad seated and then she's coming back out to wait with me. Libby why don't you ––'

But she didn't get any further because the door swung open and a tall woman with startlingly orange lipstick, big teeth and bigger hair called out.

'Anyone here for the Hardcastle – Nowak wedding?'

Helen gathered her wrap together. 'We are,' she said.

'Excellent!' The woman stretched out a hand. 'My name is Chloe. I'm your celebrant today.'

'Excellent!' Helen mirrored. She'd never met a celebrant before, but if she'd been expecting anything it would have been a suit, somewhat authoritative, somewhat smart. Chloe was dressed in what looked like a cross between a robe and a poncho. Purple-satin, neatly fringed with gold. Suppressing a smile, Helen stepped aside, allowing Alex to go ahead.

'Mum.' Libby's hand was on her arm. 'Wait, please.'

Aware of Alex and Chloe going through, of the door beginning to close, Helen stretched her arm out to hold it.

'You should take the job,' Libby said quietly. 'I want you to take the job.'

'Libby.' The door was heavy, she had to take a step back to hold the weight. 'We can talk about this after ––'

But Libby was shaking her head, her chin set. 'I was so mean to Alex at my eighteenth and he doesn't even remember. Or if he does,' she added, 'he's forgiven me.'

'Libby ...'

'He is a better person than me.'

'He's different,' Helen said. 'You're just different.'

Libby looked up. 'Do you know how many of my friends have been to visit since I had Ben?'

One hand on her chest, the other still holding the door, Helen took a deep breath. She couldn't answer the question, but it wouldn't be many. No, she couldn't imagine that many of those shiny bright girls at Libby's eighteenth birthday party would have been back to sit amongst Ben's nappies, in her tiny flat.

'None,' Libby said. 'Joanna came once and stayed about ten minutes. She had a party to get back for.'

Helen nodded.

'I can manage, mum.'

'I know that.'

'I have to. For Ben's sake, I have to.'

And what could she say? Libby did have to manage. There was no choice now. No parties to get back to.

'Everyone,' Libby whispered, 'thinks I've messed up my life.'

'Libby,' Helen sighed. 'You had a baby early on. That's all.'

'I won't get anything else wrong.' And as Libby stood, one step lower, her hands clenched to fists and her chin wobbled.

Helen let the door go, her arms reaching for her child. 'You will always get things wrong,' she whispered. 'And that's OK. And maybe I should have let you see this before.' She could feel Libby's back move up and down as she cried, the knuckled bones of her shoulders, where there should have been wings. Because this was girl who was going to fly. Everyone had said it. The child who had insisted on pairing her own socks since she was eight. That was the family joke. On the straight and narrow, striving toward the best grades in every exam she ever took, with Helen always one step behind. When maybe she should have stayed back. Lingered out of sight a while and allowed Libby to wander off the track now and then. 'It's OK,' she whispered, as she always had. 'Everything will be OK.'

'I'll miss you, Mum,' Libby sobbed. 'But you need to go.'

And because it was too hard to say what she was thinking, to echo Libby's words and say, *Yes, I need to do this, Libby. I need to go*, she didn't say anything. She kept her arms around her child and held her as close as the day she had been born.

44

‘Nearly there, love.’

‘Thank you.’ As Caro glanced out of the window, she was just in time to see the classical façade of Brackenford station pass by. Another two minutes then. She looked down at her bouquet. It was a tall and striking arrangement, to suit a tall and striking bride. Red and fuchsia pink gladioli, those last sentinels of summer, filled out with silver-green eucalyptus. Not once had she considered the softer blousy heads of a hydrangea, or the traditionally safe lily. The bouquet she'd had in mind, and seen through to completion, was bold and modern; they would see her coming a mile off: this middle-aged, jilted, bride.

Chin tilted, head pushed back against the seat, she watched as the car passed a park where a man and a woman played tennis, and dogs strained on leads. Where children ran in and out of a playground, spilling apart like the beads of a broken necklace, shrieking and calling. She kept watching until the last moment, until the car turned left and the park disappeared and the wide steps leading up to the town hall came into view.

It had been a quiet journey. 'No-one riding with you?' had been the driver's first and last question. No jovial banter. Perhaps, she thought as she looked up at him, he had sensed nerves? Although she didn't feel nervous. The taint of tragedy then? She didn't feel tragic either. It didn't matter, she had been glad of the space, twenty minutes with the camphor scent of eucalyptus slowly drawing her back to the surface. Because although the car had only travelled only a few kilometres, Caro had dived deep. Without forethought, without planning, without courage or cowardice, she had trawled in the depths for answers to this oddest of mornings, and these oddest of feelings.

'I don't think you even know yourself, what you want.'

When the needle hits true north, it doesn't wobble and so it was with Tomasz's words. He was right. One day she'd been entranced with the serenity of Hollybrook, another day she'd been Queen of London. The only constant, the love that had never wavered, was her love of the idea of love. Romantic love. Ideal love. Tomasz had ridden into her life at her lowest ebb, scooping her into his arms and rescuing her from a place and time that had felt un-survivable. What he offered, just hadn't been enough. Or it had been too late. Or it had never been needed in the first place. She looked down at her engagement ring, the diamond daisy, still waiting for its promise to be fulfilled. She was thinking about the day Tomasz had first shown her the ring, how happy she had been to finally feel she belonged to someone. And then she was thinking about something Helen had said, just a few months ago, at a pavement café in Cyprus. *You never waited for a hero to turn up.* The irony! She almost laughed. On this oddest of mornings, she almost laughed. The irony was as inescapable as the archetype itself, because when her hero had finally turned up, she had allowed herself to be rescued when she had never needed saving.

Oh, it had been lovely. He had been lovely. The warmth of his body at night, his companionship in the evenings, his care of her, running a bath, massaging her feet, mixing a drink. No wonder so many desired and needed it, settled for it. But Helen had been right, and now she felt as if she was waking from what had been a long and comfortable dream. She tipped her head back and closed her eyes. This had been the closest she would ever come, and as the car glided to a halt, all she was wishing for, all she hoped, was that it wasn't the same for him.

'Here we are.'

She looked up to see a wide, red-bricked building with rows of symmetrical sash windows. An imposing façade, a design that spoke of important decisions and memorable moments, which was exactly why they had chosen the venue and thinking this, Caro released the breath she hadn't known she was holding. Tomasz hadn't chosen the venue. He would have married her in a field, had she wanted. It was her that had chosen, as if at some level she had understood that her belief in what she was doing, needed underpinning with Portland stone and Doric columns, when all he had ever needed were daises. He was right. It would never have worked. What had started out in such happiness, would have ended in misery. She leaned forward. At the top of the steps, she could see two figures. Helen and Kay, waiting where they had said they would.

'It's going to rain,' the driver said as he opened the door. 'You want to get inside quickly.'

.   .   .

'IT'S GOING TO RAIN.' Helen was waving her arm, urging Caro in. 'We need to get inside.'

But she didn't rush. She couldn't have rushed if she'd tried. Her feet were heavy, the air she walked through, dense. She reached the top step and looked up and as she did, Helen's arm dropped. She knew. One glance and Caro saw that Helen knew. She turned to Kay.

'We need to get inside,' Kay said, she had her palm up, ready to catch the first fat raindrop.

'It's not happening, Kay.'

Another raindrop fell, equally as fat. And then another and another and another ...

'Your flowers,' Kay said.

Caro looked down. Even the robust stems of the gladioli were no match against the weighty punches of this rain, already the top petals were folding in, giving up. 'Kay,' she said. 'It's not happening.'

'What's not happening?' Kay turned to Helen, who shook her head. 'What's going on?'

'We ... I ...' But it felt to Caro as if suddenly, without any warning, she had turned a corner only to discover that she had reached the end of a very long journey. Her knees buckled. 'I'm so sorry,' she whispered, ready to fall to the floor, to sleep a thousand years. And she would have, if Helen, and then Kay hadn't stepped in and put their arms around her and held her upright. The three of them together, rain bouncing off shoulders and arms, running down the back of necks, staining dark the toes of Helen's neat liner sock.

45

'Well then.' Standing at the far end of the Heritage room, Chloe held a black binder, with a gold crest, her face frozen in cheerful panic. 'This has never happened to me before,' she said.

Kay managed a weak smile. It felt like the polite thing to do. There were only four of them left in the room now, herself, her father, Alex and Helen. Caro was outside, talking to her brother and his wife. Tomasz's two friends had left. Libby had gone to call her father and arrange a lift home.

'Anyone have any suggestions?' Chloe grinned.

This time Kay didn't smile. The woman was relentless, like a stand-up comedian continuing with an act that was obviously failing. Besides, she didn't have any suggestions. The situation hadn't happened to her before either, or anyone else in the room. And certainly not to Caro, who had been dignity personified. Who had come in and made her announcement, no drama, no crying, just a simple explanation, which didn't go into particulars, but did contain sincere apologies. It had been a superb display of calm under pressure, and she was proud of her friend. Very proud.

Smoothing down her poncho/cloak, Chloe turned to look at the clock. 'It's OK for everyone to sit as long as they want,' she said. 'The room is free all morning. Unless,' she laughed, her head jerking awkwardly, 'anyone else wants to get married!'

Stunned, Kay looked up.

'Sorry!' Chloe waved a hand. 'Forget I said that.' Her eyes were wide with astonishment as if she too, couldn't believe what had come out of her mouth. 'I'll um ...I'll just go see ...' And she was gone, through a side door, exiting stage right.

Kay leaned back, her hands in her lap as she looked up at the elegance of the oak panelling and the decorative scrolls of the cornice plasterwork, the ceiling rose, from which hung a tiered crystal chandelier. It was a nice room to sit in, to wait, as they were doing, while Caro had some space to explain further to her brother. Explain what, Kay couldn't guess, and as she thought this, she frowned. Helen, she was thinking, hadn't even seemed surprised.

'Mum.' Alex nudged her.

Kay turned.

'What about Grandad?'

'What about him?' Instantly her eyes flickered past Alex, to the next seat where her father sat. 'Is he OK?' He'd been so breathless after that stumble.

'He can get married. He's given notice.'

She blinked. 'I know,' she whispered, which should have been the beginning and the end of the conversation.

Unperturbed, Alex leaned in. 'The registrar just asked if anyone else wants to get married.'

'It was a joke, Alex.' Kay kept her chin down and her

eyes focused straight ahead as she spoke. This wasn't a fair-ground. Taking turns. Who's next? Your turn, my turn. But how to explain that? How to explain to a boy who had always experienced the world in straight lines, that there was an infinity of shapes in-between? Wobbly lines of inappropriateness, wavy lines of doubt, great circles of assumptions and huge squares of prejudice, influencing decisions, sculpting lives, manipulating behaviour. How to tease out the nuances, make it clear, again, that most of the time what people said, wasn't what they meant. That you couldn't trust the world enough to take it at face value. This was the boy who had once asked her if miniature daffodils grew in a minute. How to pollute such a beautiful mind?

'We're all here,' Alex persisted. 'Except, Lizzie, but we can call her.'

Kay turned.

'I even have my suit on.'

Her lips pursed, the corners of her mouth curling as she gave up and laughed. He did have his suit on, which didn't mean anything in her world, but made perfect sense in his. And whose world trumped? Whose world got to make the rules? Caro was going home. Once she had finished taking to her brother, she was going home. Which left Alex in his suit, and her father in his suit, and herself in a dress that had cost the best part of two-hundred pounds, and shoes that would leave her limping for weeks. All here to witness a marriage when there was no longer a marriage to witness, when, in such a short time from now, her father would marry in a room with an aertex ceiling and fluorescent lighting, where the only witnesses would be those who were paid to be there. And more, he would be marrying a woman she admired, a woman who had once ordered a wedding bouquet that she never got to hold. Slowly, she looked across at her father. He sat fingers entwined as he rubbed his thumbs together. She leaned back, thought for a moment and turned the other way, to Helen

'Ask him?' Helen said.

Kay startled. 'You heard?'

'I heard.' Helen nodded. 'And sometimes I think Alex has more sense than any of us.'

The words were little pillows of air, they filled Kay's chest, they made her heart swell with pride. Sometimes, she had thought the same herself, that her boy did have more sense. The easiest way, the path of least resistance in keeping himself and everyone else happy, that had been his one and only life-plan. 'What about Caro?' Her whisper dragged, hoarse with emotion.

Helen dipped her head. 'I'll talk to her, but she said she wants to be alone.'

'OK.' And although the situation – in her world – felt absurdly inappropriate, she leaned across Alex, into his world, and tapping her father on his arm said quietly. 'I'm just thinking.' She paused. 'Actually, Alex was thinking, if we could possibly arrange it, do you think Lizzie would prefer to get married here? Today?'

For the longest moment her father didn't speak, and Kay watched as he raised his chin and looked around. 'It is a nice room,' he said eventually, nodding at the chandelier.

'Oh, Dad.' She reached for his hand and squeezed it. 'Should we ring her? See what she says?'

'I'LL WAIT,' Caro had said, after Helen had floated the idea, launching it as tentatively as a paper boat. 'I think it's a lovely idea. Lizzie can have my bouquet.'

With a taxi already booked to take her home, it hadn't been a response either Helen or Kay had anticipated. And, as she sat next to Helen in the gloomy reception room, waiting for Lizzie to arrive, Kay glanced across once more to where Caro sat, her bouquet taking the adjacent empty chair. Exactly as she did, Caro looked up and smiled, a faint but definite message, *It's OK. I'm alright*, that Kay felt sure she was reading correctly. She smiled back. It still felt wrong. A wedding called off at the last moment was a dramatic event, that called for dramatic emotion. Caro was acting as if nothing about the morning was particularly surprising or unexpected, as if she'd known the ending all along. And again, she remembered Helen's reaction. She lowered her chin, and without moving her mouth, said, 'Did something happen?'

Helen rubbed at her nose. 'Sort of.'

'Sort of?'

'I can't go into it now, but ...' Helen paused. 'I'm not sure this is a bad thing.'

'OK.' Kay nodded. As far as she had known Tomasz was a good thing for Caro, but if there were to all take their cue from the leading lady (and what else was there to do), she had to agree with Helen: this was not a tragedy. Shifting her weight, she looked down at her feet. The bright red bulge of the blister already showing. She glanced at Helen's feet, encased in their liner socks and comparing them with her own made a silent promise. *I will spend time seeking and finding all the pleasurable and comfortable things in life. Liner socks to start, because I'm going to need a jumbo pack of them in Cyprus, because I am going.*

It felt like the day for such promises. It felt like the place. Here, where in so many vaulted rooms aldermen and women had debated, voted, decided, it was time that she,

Kay Burrell made good and decided too. Courage. That was all that was needed to change a life. The courage to choose. And now she was thinking about the afternoon her father had told her. The way in which he had fiddled on with his handkerchief. So loud had her hurt and anger been, she hadn't considered his feelings. It must have been excruciating for him. He would have wrestled for days, with the dilemma of how to break it to her. Filling her lungs, her eyes smarted as she looked through the open front door and out to the August morning beyond. Even Martin, with his VW, had tangible plans. And all this was courage. Everyone around her displaying the quality she had been so praised for during the worst days of her treatment. *So brave, Kay. How brave you are.* But that had been a time of a vast and empty plain when there had been nothing to fall back on except courage, and she wasn't fooled. When it's the only choice, it's easy. When your usual armchair isn't waiting, standing is the only option. And when she got home, she would book that flight.

Helen's phone pinged. 'Lawrence is here,' she said. She leaned forward. 'And I can see a taxi. I think the bride has arrived.'

'Yes,' Kay said, because she too could see the yellow markings of the taxi that had just pulled up outside.

IMMEDIATELY LIZZIE WAS WHEELED IN, dressed in the prettiest lemon blouse and matching skirt, Kay went over to her. It was imperative she got there first and she got there quickly, that she let Lizzie know. Blister rubbing, knees creaking, she crouched by the chair.

'Kay.'
'Lizzie.'

They spoke over each other.

'I'm so sorry,' she said. 'I should have come to see you. As soon as I knew, I should have come.'

Lizzie shook her head. 'Your father said you needed time.'

'I don't.' She took Lizzie's hand. It was light as lace, intricately patterned with the lines of a long life, frail as tissue paper. 'Dad said you wanted my blessing. You have it, Lizzie. I have no objections to anything that will bring happiness into my father's life, or yours. None at all.'

Smiling, Lizzie placed her free hand on her chest. 'I had no idea, Kay. No idea at all that he was going to propose, but when he did ...' Her eyes, pink-rimmed, filled with tears. 'I'm not sure what to say to you. It was the most wonderful thing.'

'You don't have to say anything.'

'I couldn't think of a reason to say no.'

Kay didn't speak.

'And that seemed reason enough to say yes.'

'I understand.' She did. At ninety, why would you say no to anything? It was a lesson she could do with learning herself. Why say no, when you can say yes.

'Your father makes me laugh.'

She smiled. 'He says the same about you.'

'Does he?' Lizzie nodded. 'Well, there has been a lot of laughter these last few weeks.'

'And a lot more to come I hope.'

'Hello.'

Standing up, knees wrenching, she turned to see Caro standing just behind. 'This,' she said to Lizzie, 'is Caro.' And stepping back, she conceded the moment. There wasn't anything more to say. Lizzie had been told about the situation, she knew who Caro was, what had happened. She watched, as bending low, Caro placed her bouquet on Lizzie's lap, as Lizzie reached a pale arm around Caro's neck and drew her into a shaky embrace. She meant what she had said, because why would she hold any objection to anything that would bring happiness to the people she loved most in the world.

46

Outside, standing on the top step, Helen and Libby watched as a tall man, standing on the bottom step, struggled to persuade a toddler up the stairs.

'Shall we help?' Libby whispered, leaning in.

Helen shook her head. 'I'm enjoying it.'

The man was Lawrence, and the child, Ben, and their battle had been going on a few minutes now. Up the stairs Ben had sprinted, then back down again. Up, and then down again. With no obvious gain on either side, things had reached a stalemate and right now, Ben was lying flat on his back, all four of his limbs stretched to sky like an upturned insect. Chin dipped, Helen chuckled as first Ben threw the banana Lawrence had been trying to bribe him with, over his shoulder, second as Lawrence then threw Ben over his shoulder and hefted him up the stairs.

'Have you two had a good morning?' she said, when they reached the top step.

'Fine,' Lawrence muttered, and turning to Libby he thrust a still squirming Ben towards her. 'Time for Mummy.'

'Ugh! He stinks!' Libby screwed her face up. 'When did you last change him? And what is ...' She stopped talking, prising Ben's fingers open to reveal a handful of crushed fries. 'McDonalds?' she cried. 'Did you give him McDonalds, Dad?'

'I had to,' Lawrence said helplessly. 'I had bananas with me, but they're the wrong shape apparently. And he wouldn't eat the casserole.'

Oh, Helen could have laughed! She could have fallen back on a big fat pillow embroidered all over with, *Told You so*. She didn't. She simply stepped aside as Libby, unburdened Lawrence of the changing bag, and with an exasperated, 'I'll sort him out', disappeared inside

'So,' Helen said.

Lawrence tucked his shirt in and ran his hands through his hair. He had a haggard look about him, not so dissimilar, she was thinking, from the look he'd had after he'd climbed Everest.

'What happened?' He nodded toward the door.

Helen also turned to look at the closed door. 'I'm not entirely sure,' she said. Which wasn't quite true. She had a good idea. Caro would have told Tomasz.

'Was it Caro?'

'I think so.'

Lawrence nodded. 'Well,' he started. 'She ––'

'Don't.' It was a command, and to back it up she raised her hand. She didn't want to hear his opinion. She knew what he thought anyway. He thought that Tomasz and Caro were a pair of odd socks. And although she couldn't help but agree, she did not want to hear that echoed. For a while Caro had been happy, and for now, that was where she wanted to stay.

'I was going to say ...'

Helen lowered her hand.

'I was just going to say that Caro deserves to be happy. If this wasn't ––'

'It wasn't.' Helen shook her head. 'I don't think it was right. I don't think she would have been happy.'

'Helen.'

'Lawrence.'

They spoke together, and then neither of them spoke and in the pause that followed, Helen lifted her chin and looked away. This was why people cried at weddings. Promising yourself to another, doing that publicly, took courage. And it didn't matter if those promises got broken because the memory could not be defiled: the truth that, in one time and at one place, two people had been so sure, so selfless in their commitment to one another, they were able to stand up and say, *I do.* Like she had, with Lawrence, and Lawrence had with her.

'We were happy, weren't we?' he said, as if he had read her thoughts. 'When we first started, I mean?' His hands were in his pockets, his head tilted as if he couldn't be confident of the answer.

Helen smiled. 'I was very happy.'

'Until you weren't?'

'Until I wasn't. Yes.'

He nodded, his back straight, his jaw set as he stood looking across the stairs.

'I think,' Helen started, 'that we ––'

'You should take this job.' Lawrence turned. 'You stayed home long enough, Helen. You should take the job.'

Helen didn't speak. She looked down at her hands, folded over the thin strap of her purse, her throat hard.

'I'm not going anywhere.' Lawrence coughed. 'Libby

can... well, he's a handful, Ben, but I think I can be of some help, while you're away.'

'I'm sure,' she said quietly, 'that you can be of a lot of help.' As she looked up, she smiled. 'If you get the right-shaped bananas, that is.'

And although he returned the smile, his eyes were glassy. 'Well.' He paused, his jaw grinding side to side. 'If it's OK with you, I'll still be selling the house.'

'Lawrence ...'

'It's you who made it a home, Helen.' His voice sounded like metal scraping on metal. 'Without you, it's gone back to bricks and mortar.'

'Lawrence.' It seemed to be all she could say. As she gripped her purse, her mouth turned down. She didn't want to cry, but she had made that house, a home. A warm and inviting home. A sanctuary for her children, a haven for the family. Her greatest achievement.

'So.' Lawrence took a great breath, his shoulders rising and falling again. 'There's still a wedding, I hear? And you're sure it's OK to come in?'

'There is.' Helen smiled. 'And I'm sure. It was the bride and groom's express wish. The more the merrier.'

47

Caught in a shaft of sunlight, the embroidered pearl on Caro's dress shimmied like a mirage. Deep in thought, she sat towards the back of the room, because who would want a jilted bride in the front row?

Lizzie, that's who.

It had been Lizzie who had asked if she wanted to stay. Lizzie who had pressed Caro's hand between her own and whispered the story of a wedding bouquet she had once ordered. And, as Caro sat gazing up at the dripping tiers of the chandelier, she was trying to understand why she had agreed. Why, instead of escaping to the solitude of her flat, she was still in a designer wedding dress, about to watch another bride take their vows. Maybe it was Lizzie herself? A woman who had taken the word the world had forced upon her – spinster - and re-spun it, threading it through with seams of achievement and adventure. A woman, who as Kay had explained, had lived life on her own terms, in a time when women didn't do that. Who had taught thousands of children, travelled extensively. A woman who was an example and a reassurance, reminding Caro as she did, of herself. Who wouldn't want to stay and witness this? Who wouldn't want to enjoy such a last-minute bloom?

Behind her, the creak of a hinge pulled her out of her daydream. She turned just in time to see Lizzie wheeled in, the bouquet in her hands almost taller than her. Caro smiled. How perfect. Lizzie would not have suited the blousy heads of a hydrangea, either.

'You, OK?' The whisper came from Kay.

'Fine.'

'Sure?' This time it came from the other side. Helen.

'I'm sure.'

And as everyone settled back in their seats and waited for the service to begin, Caro put a hand to her chair to steady herself. Across London, when it was all over, the silence of empty rooms beckoned. She could see it clearly, her sofa with its plumped-up cushions, that only she would sit on, the empty space in the toothbrush holder. This was where she would land, right back where she had started. The thought wasn't anything more frightening than a wide-open door she wasn't quite ready to walk through. Not right now. Not just yet. Still gripping the seat, she glanced first to Kay, then back at Helen, and then she knew. Nestled between them like this soothed like a rocking chair, held her like a safety net that soon enough she knew she would be able to get up and walk away from, but right now she really needed. And that was why she had stayed. To be with her friends.

48

C loak/poncho on, lipstick reapplied, Chloe opened her black binder. 'We are here today,' she read, 'to witness the union of two people in the autumn of their lives. Two people who have experienced much and whose decision today shows us that there is always room for a new chapter, a new adventure, a new journey.'

Always room for a new chapter. Helen's eyes smarted. Never had words carried more meaning and listening to the echo of them in this elegant room she didn't know what she was feeling more surprised at. That Chloe, with her fringed cape had read them, or that she was listening to them alongside her ex-husband, as he cuddled their grandson.

'This,' Chloe continued, 'is a joining together of two people who have come to know the value of companionship. Because marriage is not just for the young. It is for the ever-wise, the ever-hopeful. Those who know the quiet strength that comes from sharing a life.'

She moved her eyes sideways to look at Lawrence. Ben lay against his shoulder, a saliva-sodden thumb in his mouth, cherubic cheeks filling and falling as he slumbered on. He looked like his mother. Or his uncle. Or both of them. And as she watched him, all her babies seemed to morph into one. She reached out and stroked his tiny hand. When she was very young, her heart had been whole and uncompromised, and life had been easy. But she had broken it up and given it away. First to Lawrence, then to her children. Now to her grandchild. It was time, to take back a piece for herself. Not all of it. Never all of it. Just enough to be able to kickstart herself into the rest of her life. Enough to be able to mail, *Stronger Together* and accept the job. Enough to get her jabs done, her suitcase packed, her new email set up. Enough to provide the sustenance needed to board a plane and fly six thousand miles away. No one else could do it for her, and she was only just beginning to know, only just beginning to feel, all the tiny recalibrations needed for a woman to live life on her own terms. Each turn of the screw as impossible as it was necessary. She took Ben's thumb and pressed it between her fingers. Each tiny turn of the screw.

WITH THE CEREMONY OVER, the bride and groom had gone ahead in a taxi, accompanied by Alex. 'I've got so much food at my house, it's coming out of my ears,' Kay had insisted as a hasty wedding breakfast was arranged. 'And I'll drop into Tesco for a sponge cake.' Lawrence had also gone ahead with Libby and Ben, to collect the car. Kay and Caro were outside and only Helen lingered, alone in the sombre reception room. She'd wanted to say a personal thank you to Chloe. The words had been perfect, and Chloe had conducted the affair faultlessly, bending low to accommodate Lizzie, annunciating clearly and loudly, for Kay's father. It had been a beautiful ceremony, and against all the odds the morning had provided joy. From behind the desk a door opened, the squeaking of hinges loud in the silent space.

'I'm glad I caught you,' she said, as Chloe approached. 'I wanted to say thank you. You really rescued the morning.'

'Oh, it was nothing.' Chloe beamed. 'I'm quite accustomed to thinking on my feet. I used to be a weather girl. Live TV prepares you for all kinds of storms!' She laughed. 'Excuse the pun!'

Helen's lips twitched. 'Yes,' she said. 'I suppose it does.'

'Have to rush.' Chloe waved a hand. 'I'm off to officiate at a funeral now.'

A funeral? The cloak and the lipstick were still in place.

'It shouldn't be too sad an affair,' Chloe said thoughtfully. 'He was fifteen.'

Helen's mouth fell open, the moment was so surreal she couldn't be sure it was happening.

'It's a good age for a Labrador.' Chloe nodded, and with a final swish of her cloak/poncho she was gone.

Outside Caro and Kay were sitting on the top step. They had taken their shoes off and turned their faces to the sun, like schoolgirls do in summer. They looked so peaceful, she didn't want to disturb, so Helen stood a moment, watching. High above, thick white clouds floated past windows of blue that were stretching wider with every moment. The rain had passed, it was going to be a fine afternoon, a lovely evening.

She scooped her dress together and sat down alongside Caro, tilting her head to the same angle. She wasn't going to start the conversation. It wasn't her conversation to start, and besides, none was needed. Together, the three of them had lived through enough of these moments to know them from the inside out. To understand that there was no point in bracketing them with anything as ineffective as words. Just living them together was enough to ensure that, in years to come, when one or the other of them took the memory down from a dark and dusty shelf, the comfort of friendship would be apparent in every frame. The sun was buttercup warm on her chin, a gauzy wash of orange seeped through her eyelids, and the scratch of pigeons squabbling a step below, filled her ears. A layer beyond came the hum of traffic, someone laughing. She took a deep breath in, filled her lungs, let the air out again. A silent cue, that Caro picked up as she said,

'I'm so glad I was able to give Lizzie my bouquet.'

'I'm glad Alex made the suggestion.' Kay opened her eyes. 'I wouldn't have.'

Caro nodded. 'She said my time would come.'

'Do you want to tell us what happened?' As she spoke, Helen looked straight ahead.

'Not what you think.'

'I see.' She nodded, feeling, rather than seeing, the shift as Kay lowered her chin.

Caro must have felt it too, because she turned to Kay and said, 'Something happened, Kay. Helen knows. I'm not proud of it and I will tell you, but to be honest right now, it doesn't even matter.'

'It's OK.' Kay smiled. 'You'll tell me in your own time.'

'I will. Yes.'

'And maybe Lizzie's right,' Kay said. 'Maybe your time will come.'

'No.' Caro lifted her chin. 'No, I think that was as close as I will ever get.'

'Caro —' Helen started.

'I was chasing a dream.' Caro smiled. 'And it wasn't even my dream to chase.'

There was nothing to say. Helen drew her knees up and wrapped her arms around them. Hadn't she thought the same herself? Hadn't she, privately, wondered about the shape-shifting Caro had undergone? Hadn't she noted the brittleness of her enthusiasm? 'There are,' she murmured, 'so many other dreams to chase.' She wasn't worried for her friend. The last couple of years had been difficult for Caro, but this ending felt like the right one. No-one could call it happy, then again no one could call it unhappy. And anyway, she had long since stopped believing in happy endings herself. She had even stopped believing in endings. Leaving her marriage had felt like the biggest ending of all, but here she was, standing on the edge of what could be the biggest beginning of her life. She turned and squeezed Caro's hand.

'What will you ––' But she didn't even get to the end of the sentence.

'I'm going back to work,' Caro said, stretching her legs out and pointing her toes. 'I love my work. I might even relocate. Have a whole new start.'

'That makes two of us then,' said Kay. 'Dad's moving, Alex is fine. And I'm definitely going to Cyprus.'

'In a VW van?' Helen smiled.

Kay laughed. 'No. I might, every now and then, take an overnight trip in a VW van, but not a long voyage. Not again. I'm striking out on my own. I want to see what's out there and, in the meantime, I have this.' And winking at Helen, Kay lifted her handbag.

Caro looked from one to the other. 'Am I missing something?'

Kay nodded. 'You and I have some stuff to catch up on.'

'Well ...' Helen smiled. 'It would actually make three of us. Relocating.' And she waited a moment to let her words sink in, to watch with a shy sense of pride long years in the making, as both Caro and Kay turned to look at her. 'You remember that thing I had?' she said, 'in London? I sent you a photo remember, Caro?'

Caro frowned.

'The Bolivia thing?' Kay said. 'I thought you had messed that up?'

'So did I.' And again, Helen smiled, a huge beam that despite the events of the morning did not feel out of place and wouldn't, she knew, be unwelcome. 'It turns out, I didn't.'

'And you're going to take it?' Kay gasped.

Caro's eyes went wide as buttons. You're going to Bolivia?'

'I am,' Helen said simply. 'Yes, I am.'

The end

A LAST WORD FROM ME

Thank you for reading. And yes ... before you ask I truly hope to continue the series. The best way to keep updated is probably by following me on Amazon, or social media.

Without the backing of a publishing house, gaining exposure as an independent author relies upon word-of-mouth, so if you have enjoyed the book please do tell your friends. Or gift them a copy! And please leave a review or rating at the site you purchased from. I know, everyone from the bus company to the dentist, asks for a review nowadays! But again for independents like me, with nothing else to rely on, it's about the most helpful thing you can do.

And finally, if you're interested in having me participate in your reading group, drop me a line through social media. (Instagram)

Or at info@caryjhansson.com

You can find out more about me and Writing for Wellness on my website:

www.caryjhansson.com. Or by following me on Instagram or Facebook

PAPERBACK INFORMATION/ WHERE TO ORDER

Looking for a gift? Or just prefer a paperback? (I know I do.)

As well paperbacks on Amazon, all my books are available to order as paperbacks, through any good bookshop. This will be easier in some countries, than others - and that I'm afraid is out of my control.

A Midlife Holiday Use ISBN. 978 91 987587 3 3

   A Midlife Baby Use ISBN: 978 91 9875 8795

   A Midlife Gamble Use ISBN: 978 91 9875 8771

   A Midlife Marriage Use ISBN: 978-91-5278 6048

Back to her future Use ISBN: 978 91 5278 6017

Close to You Use ISBN: 978-91-527-8603-1

ALSO BY CARY J HANSSON

The award-winning, best-selling Midlife Trilogy. Start with book one: A Midlife holiday

⭐⭐⭐⭐⭐ *'Totally addictive reading.'*

⭐⭐⭐⭐⭐ *'Bridget Jones meets Shirley Valentine.'*

⭐⭐⭐⭐⭐ *'It's sad, it's funny, it's every woman's life.'*

⭐⭐⭐⭐⭐ *'Heart-warming, heart-breaking and hilarious.'*

⭐⭐⭐⭐⭐ *'I feel as though I am part of their friendship group now.'*

ALSO BY CARY J HANSSON

⭐⭐⭐⭐⭐ 'Achingly sad, but beautiful.'

⭐⭐⭐⭐⭐ 'Wow! There is no other word that will do.'

⭐⭐⭐⭐⭐ 'Beautifully and boldly crafted.'

⭐⭐⭐⭐⭐ ' Few people write female friendship as well as Hansson.'

Back to Her Future is the compelling first novel in *The Gen X* Series of women's contemporary fiction. If you like scarred but resilient heroines, nostalgic interludes, and transformative epiphanies, then you'll love *The Gen X Series.*

ALSO BY CARY J HANSSON

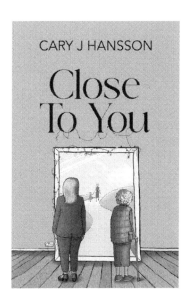

'Years ago, watching a late night movie in which a mother had turned to her son and said, I have never loved you, Toby had yawned, declared the film unbelievable and taken himself off to bed. But Jo had watched to the end, a morbid curiosity carrying her through, because she'd known. It wasn't unbelievable. Sometimes, parents didn't love their children.'

Close To You, is the second novel in *The Gen X* Series of women's contemporary fiction.

Made in the USA
Columbia, SC
05 June 2025

59000208R00188